IMPROBABLE SOLUTION

By

Judith B. Glad

GCT, Inc.   Aloha, Oregon

2014

Published by GCT, Inc.
eBook published by Uncial Press
978-1-60174-190-5
http://www.uncialpress.com

For Neil, Charles and Tony

I'm really, really glad you were there that night I walked into the observatory. Not everyone can point to the day when her whole life changed for the better.

PRELUDE

Awareness...

Memory...?

Movement at interface with emptiness...

Mobile. Animate. Ephemeral...

Vital/inert/mobile/immobile/like/unlike...

Sensation/smell/touch/taste...taste...taste...?

Vibration/smell/taste/hear...hear...HEAR...?

"Good land...homestead...settle...good land...crops...cattle...good land..."

"Build...house...town...settle...land...church...build...build...

"BUILD!"

Whiterock...town...Carruthers...name...house...store...

Carruthers...church...name...Whiterock...name...Carruthers... Whiterock...Carruthers...name...?

More...more...more...unit...integer...augment...increase... reproduce...?

I/we/us/you/they/them///who...who...who...who...name... name...NAME...?

WHITEROCK?

I/we/us/you/we/me/I/us/WHITEROCK!!!

Identity. Gratification.

Energy. Strengthen. Strengthen WHITEROCK. Strengthen fortify empower WHITEROCK.

Sensation? Not taste/smell/hear/touch.

Word...name...designation...nomenclature?

Emotion? Excitement? Sentiment? Wrong...weak...feeble...need word!

Passion?

More. Something more...love?

Strength. Passion.

Power. Passion.

Endurance. Love!

Love. Energy.

Love energy.

Good.

ONE

WHITEROCK (E-12) pop. 639 elev. 3,151 ft.

Whiterock, established 1888, was originally a farm community, but in 1894 the vast beds of diatomaceous earth underlying and surrounding the town (locally called chalk beds) were discovered to be of marketable quality. An early pioneer, Abner Carruthers, already a cattle baron of considerable wealth and regional influence, established the first mine and mill in 1896. The town grew to a maximum size of 5,321 in 1930, but when the market for diatomaceous earth declined during and after WW II, the population slowly dwindled to its present level. Consolidation of county school districts in the 1970s led to the closure of the local high school, although Whiterock Grade School still serves the surrounding agricultural areas. Gas and food are available, but there are no other tourist facilities. *Whiterock Chamber of Commerce, P.O. Box 12, Whiterock, OR 97947.*

G US LORING TOPPED THE HILL AND LOOKED DOWN INTO THE valley. Whiterock, Oregon. As gray and colorless as the surrounding desert, as dismal as the dreary rain that streaked his windshield. A sorrier excuse for a town he'd never seen, and he'd seen some real losers these past three years.

He drove down the main street and counted the boarded-up stores. More than half. Those with OPEN signs on their windows or doors didn't look much livelier, except for the Bite-A-Wee Café.

He pulled into a diagonal parking slot about half a block from the café. He hadn't eaten breakfast before he left Ontario.

All three booths were occupied and only two seats were open at the U-shaped counter. He took the one closest to the door, out of an irrational need to know escape would be easy.

"Mornin'," the stocky fellow next to him grunted.

Gus acknowledged it was, indeed, morning.

"Paper?" The old duffer on the other side shoved the front page of the *Idaho Statesman* at him.

Gus took it, planning to hide within its folds. A reddened hand pushed it aside and plopped a coffee cup before him without spilling a drop.

"Cream?" The hoarse voice of the waitress fit her appearance. Big, raw-boned, out-of-a-bottle blonde, she looked more ready for the stage than a family café in a dreary little town in Oregon. Her eyeshadow was blue and gold, her rouge bright pink and her lipstick a violent fuchsia.

"Please," he said, and a brown pottery pitcher appeared before him, its fat sides beaded with moisture, the cream within it thick and golden.

"What'll it be?"

The smells contained within the small, warm room awoke an appetite he hadn't had for months. Years? He gave his order.

It was a good thing he had the cream. The coffee would have taken paint off a battleship. Sipping cautiously as he worked his way through the paper, he gradually became aware that a desultory conversation was going on around him. That was all right. He'd gotten pretty good at being the invisible man.

His breakfast arrived before he finished the first section of the paper, on a platter almost big enough to hold a turkey. Two eggs, four slices of bacon, an enormous mound of real hash browns and two thick chunks of golden-toasted homemade bread. As he gaped, a ketchup bottle, one of hot sauce, and a pottery crock of jam materialized with the same abruptness as had the rest of his breakfast.

"More coffee?" the waitress said, as she refilled his cup.

"No. I don't think my stomach will stand it." But he said it softly, to his eggs.

"Better get used to it, bub," his stocky neighbor said. "Georgina, she don't think coffee's fit to drink unless it dissolves the spoon you stir it with."

Gus couldn't resist grinning, but he didn't answer. The fellow seemed friendly. Gus wasn't into friendly these days.

He finished his breakfast, marginally aware it was one of the best he'd ever eaten. That jam must have been as homemade as the bread. The bills he tossed on the counter covered his meal and a generous tip. As he pulled the door closed behind him, he heard the waitress call, "Come on back, now."

Back in the truck, he checked his route book. A torn, almost illegible photocopied map was taped inside the front cover. Four of the six stops here in Whiterock were within a block of the main street, which apparently comprised the entire business district. He looked at the tiny print more closely. Yes, it was even called Main Street.

He delivered a package of prescription and patent medicines to the drugstore, paper products to the small grocery store and the grade school, shop rags to the implement dealership and roller towels to a tavern that reminded him of something out of a John Wayne western. The last drop was at a big old house, larger by far than its neighbors and set right in the middle of a spacious lot that showed signs of having been nicely landscaped once. Now it was overgrown and weedy, with a lawn that should have been mowed last fall and a hedge that had grown into an undisciplined wall.

The house itself reminded him of the one he'd lived in as a child with its white siding, black shutters and uncompromising squareness. Whoever built this house, he decided, had come from New England.

A small, discreet sign just above the doorbell read *Mending and Alterations*. He rang.

The door opened within seconds. "Yes?"

He peered through the screen. "Dry cleaning."

The screen opened and a slim white hand motioned him inside. It was like walking into a cave. The only light in the house was the white flicker of a TV from the room on the left.

He handed her the paper-wrapped package.

"You're early. Wait here." She disappeared into the gloom. Her voice sounded young, but her body, clothed in shapeless sweats, spoke of middle age. A lank ponytail hung down her back, vaguely blond. Yet, her scent was sweet, floral with just a hint of something indefinably feminine.

His eyes gradually adjusted. The hall was wide, with a flight of stairs about fifteen feet from the front door. The hall continued past the stairs to a partially open door through which Gus could see the pale gleam of kitchen appliances. More doors opened off the hall, but he couldn't see what they opened into, for all the rooms were darkened by drawn shades.

He stepped to the left and peered into the room with the television. A man sat slumped in a big, overstuffed chair before it, his face slack, his eyes fixed on the rolling picture.

The woman returned, carrying several hangers holding plastic-protected garments. "Where's Ed?"

"He quit last Friday." Gus had been hired Monday morning, put to work with a minimum of instructions and even fewer questions. All Frank Tsugawa had checked was that his commercial driver's license was current and his last employer had been whom he said. This was his third day on the job.

"I can carry these out," she said as he reached for the hangers.

"No problem," he said, just before his fingers touched hers.

Touched...and jerked back from the shock.

She snatched her hand away just as quickly. The garments dropped into a soft mound at their feet while they stared at each other.

"Static electricity." she said after a moment, as she bent to pick them up.

Gus looked at the floor. Some kind of wood. And he was wearing sneakers. Nothing in his engineering curriculum had ever led him to believe static electricity could result from a combination like that.

Again he reached for the hangers.

This time Sally was careful not to touch him. She wasn't sure what had happened, but she did know she hadn't felt a shock like that since she'd stuck a bobby pin into a wall plug at the age of five.

He left without another word.

Curious about the man who'd replaced Ed, the would-be ladies' man, she watched through the screen door as he trotted down the walk to his truck.

Wide. That had been her first impression. His shoulders were wider than a man's had any business being. His hair was a blazing, true red, without a hint of orange. The rest of him wasn't anything special. There seemed to be just the hint of a belly under the white shirt with the Tsugawa Linen Supply logo on its back. His forearms, revealed by sleeves rolled to just above his elbows, were sinewy and tanned, his hands broad and capable, with long fingers.

He must be just over six foot, she decided, even though the shoulders made him seem shorter. His mouth was wide, too, and looked as if it would smile easily; and his eyes were the deepest, most wonderful green she could remember.

That rear view should be on a calendar.

Startled, Sally bit her lip. *Where did that thought come from?*

AFTER WHITEROCK, GUS HAD STOPS IN HARPER, WESTFALL AND Juntura, all wide spots in a road that wound through sagebrush-covered hills where the only living creatures he saw were a couple of watchful pronghorns and a suicidal jackrabbit. A long day. He didn't get back to Ontario until almost six, not because he'd had so much to do but because he had so many miles to cover.

Frank Tsugawa came into the drivers' room and perched on the edge of the table while he was checking in.

"Have any trouble finding your stops?"

"Huh-uh." Gus barely paused in his counting. "Fifty-five, sixty, sixty-five." He set the short stack of nickels aside and slid the three dimes over beside them "Ninety-five." He balanced with his sales slips. "Sure is a lot of nothing between here and there." He put the few bills and the loose change into the zippered bag. "I'm surprised you make any money."

"I don't, not on that route." Frank straightened the stack of receipts. "But I don't lose too much, either, since I get a commission on the dry cleaning and prescription deliveries." He looked at Gus, speculation in his eyes. "I talked to Roger Franklin this morning."

Crap! He shouldn't have put Roger's name down as a past employer. His former partner wasn't above using underhanded methods to get Gus back.

"He told me you're a hell of an engineer." Frank said. "Seems to me you're wasted on a job like this."

"Well, I happen to want a job like this," Gus snapped. Damn it! Next time he'd simply say he'd been self-employed for ten years and forget to mention he'd had a partner.

Frank sat silent for a moment, the quintessential inscrutable Oriental. Finally, he slid off the table and stood in the doorway, not looking at Gus. "He wouldn't tell me what you're running from, but he said you'd been doing it for three years."

Gus made a formless sound of agreement, not trusting his voice.

"Just give me some notice, will you? I can't depend on drifters showing up at the right moment like you did." With a casual wave, Frank walked away.

"I'll be damned," Gus said. A couple of times before, his employers had discovered what he really was. They'd both let him go, insisting he was overqualified and likely to walk at the first opportunity.

He finished up his check-in and dropped his route sheet and moneybag into the lockbox on the office wall. With its hours of mindless driving, its lack of pressure, this job was as close to perfect as he was going to find. No one was depending on him for anything but regular linen deliveries. The last thing he wanted, the last thing he needed, was another job that demanded his total dedication.

He'd never walked off a job until the nightmares grew so bad he stayed awake all night to escape them. That meant he wasn't likely to kill anyone else, didn't it?

SALLY CARRUTHERS PAUSED AT THE EDGE OF THE FRONT PORCH AND wondered if winter was going to last all year. There hadn't been any snow on the ground for a month, but the soil still harbored rock-hard pockets of frost.

Perhaps springtime would pass by without pausing in Whiterock. Bleak, cold winter would turn to bleak, hot summer, as it had done every year since she came back. Even the grass barely became green before it turned brown.

Her life matched the weather. Bleak. By her own choice. No one had forced her to come back to Whiterock. No one had demanded she stay with her father.

When she thought of returning to Seattle or Portland, of once again creating magical worlds out of cloth and glitter and imagination, she had to tell herself she was here because she wanted to be. Still, sometimes, in the middle of the night, she prayed for Pop to die and set her free. Free to leave Whiterock and find a life again. In the morning, she always hated herself. Pop had given her life, love, security. She owed him the contentment and dignity of spending his last years in his own home.

As she did each morning, once she had Pop settled before the TV, Sally went to the Post Office, the liveliest place in town. It sat at the corner of Main and Second, two blocks down and four blocks over. She was never gone long—thirty minutes maybe—but she always felt as if she had been set free.

"Good morning, Grip," she said to Mrs. Alpin's bulldog at the first corner. "How are your roses this morning?"

"Getting ready to leaf out, Ms. Carruthers," she answered for the asthmatic dog as he wagged his stump of a tail. She waved at his owner, sitting frail but alert behind white lace curtains. One of these days she should stop and visit. Too bad the old woman was so perceptive. If anyone could discern the wicked, selfish thoughts Sally harbored in the middle of the night, Elizabeth Alpin could.

"Slim pickings this morning," Sally commented to starlings and crows that scattered before her along the cracked sidewalk on Fifth Street. They scavenged people-leavings, replacing them with sticky white droppings that clung to soles. She picked her way carefully past the library.

"Mornin', Miz Sally," old Ernie Green called out as she passed his bench at the front of the brick building. "How's your pa?"

She mentally spoke the words along with him, for they never varied.

"About the same," she answered, as she did every morning, "and how are you?"

"Gettin' older." He cackled. "And meaner."

"Aren't we all," Sally agreed. Older? Yes, she was getting older. When she came home to nurse her mother through her last illness she'd planned to go back to her career after the funeral. Instead, she had stayed with her father for a while. He'd been irritable and absentminded, conditions she assumed were a result of the terrible strain he'd been under during her mother's long illness.

But he hadn't gotten better, and finally she'd taken him into Ontario to the doctor.

"What'd you think of the hunk?"

Sally broke from her brown study to see Georgina sweeping the sidewalk in front of the Bite-A-Wee Cafe.

"Sorry, Georgina, I was wool-gathering. Did you say something?"

"Yeah, I asked you what you thought of the hunk yesterday." Georgina patted her bright blond hair and whistled. "Best lookin' piece of man to come to town in a long time."

"I must have missed him," Sally said.

The café owner's long-standing affair with her cook was an accepted fact in Whiterock, as was her total fidelity to the relationship. It didn't keep Georgina from looking.

"You couldn'ta missed him, not if you got your regular delivery."

"Oh, you mean the new man on the linen truck?" Sally shrugged. "He was just a man."

Sure, and she was so hungry for a man that a single touch of his fingers had galvanized her.

"Yeah, right. A tiger is just a pussy cat, too." Georgina leered. "He's a little loose around the edges, but I'll bet he cleans up real good."

"If you say so."

"I do. I do, and so would you, if you ever did anything but take care of your pa. Are you gonna waste away in that big old house, or are you gonna have a life?"

"At this point, I don't think I have much of a choice." Sally stepped around Georgina and walked briskly in the direction of the Post Office.

There was no one else to take care of Pop, no one at all. While there was money enough to put him into a nursing home, she couldn't do that. He'd been born in the big house on Fifth Avenue and he would die in it, if she had any say in the matter. When she was small she'd loved listening to him tell the stories he'd heard from his grandmother, how her great-great grandfather Abner Carruthers had come to Whiterock in 1878. He'd lived in his wagon while he built first a barn, and then a house. He'd opened a feed store a few years later, and the town had been born. His son, Sam, had built the big house she'd grown up in.

No, she had no choice. That she was gradually losing herself, little bit by little bit, didn't—couldn't—matter. Sally knew her duty to her ancestors, her responsibility to her father. Once he was gone he would never know how quickly she shook the chalky dust of Whiterock, Oregon, from her feet.

The postmistress, thankfully, was not at the counter when Sally entered. She pulled the *National Geographic* and two bills from the box and slammed it shut, jerking her key free.

"That you, Sally Carruthers?"

"Yes, Wilma, it's me." She made herself smile at the short, square woman whose shoulders scarcely showed above the counter. "How are you this morning?"

"So-so, just like always, till the weather warms up." Reaching under the counter, she brought forth a fancy tin and pushed it towards Sally. "Have a mint."

"No, thanks. I've really got to go—"

"Land sakes, child, you look like you haven't slept in a week!" Again, Wilma pushed the mints toward Sally. "Take one. You could use the sugar."

Obediently, Sally accepted one of the cellophane-wrapped, green-striped mints.

"Pop had a bad night," she admitted. "I didn't get much sleep."

"Oh, my. What'd he do this time?" Since Wilma had been through the same thing with her mother a few years back, Sally never felt shy about sharing her troubles. She had to talk to someone, and at least Wilma simply listened and never, never showed pity.

Sally couldn't handle pity. It ate at her already fragile emotional defenses.

"He got it into his head that the taxes were delinquent—you know he was never late paying his taxes in his life! If he didn't get over to the assessor's office in Vale right then, they'd take the ranch. He practically tore his room apart, looking for his car keys."

Wilma simply shook her head in understanding.

"So, I gave him an old set of keys, thinking that would satisfy him. It seemed to, because he quieted down."

"That's a blessing."

"Not really. As soon as I went back to my sewing machine, he snuck outside and tried to get into my car."

Not that a few more scratches in its paint mattered, she supposed. Not beside the dents where he'd taken a hammer to the trunk lid last month.

"I got him back inside and into bed, but I couldn't get to sleep for worrying he'd wake and start in again."

"Did he?"

"No, and this morning he's in one of his melancholy moods. I don't know which is worse."

The sight of tears running down her father's sunken cheeks almost broke her heart. In some ways, she preferred his manic periods.

She reached across the counter and squeezed Wilma's hand. "Thanks," she said, knowing Wilma understood why she was grateful. "I've got to go." She'd stayed longer than she should.

Pop hadn't ever gotten into trouble when she'd left him, but she knew how easy it would be for him to do so. He still had his strength. What he was lacking was common sense and judgment. Like that time she'd caught him laying bacon slices on a red-hot stove burner. Or when he'd let the bathtub run over, or when...

Never mind. She hated to remember all the potentially disastrous things he'd done. What she had to do was think about the Pop she loved. The hearty man with a ready smile and broad shoulders, the generous man who shared his time and his energy with his neighbors. Not the shambling, testy, almost mindless hulk who hung onto a life without hope, without future.

Stop it! How do you know he's not in there somewhere, trying to get out? Isn't that why you chose to stay with him, instead of putting him into a nursing home?

Despite her worry, she never walked as fast, going home. It was too much like going back to prison.

INTERVAL

Unforeseen intrusion?
Reaction indicating potential.
Enhance?

TWO

THE NEXT TIME GUS TOPPED THE HILL OUTSIDE OF WHITEROCK, he was surprised to see that the town didn't look quite so bleak as he remembered. A few days of warmer weather had brought out a little green in winter-brown lawns. The lack of paint on most of the buildings in town wasn't so obvious with the sun shining.

"Mornin'." The same stocky man was seated at the counter in the Bite-A-Wee.

Gus sat beside him, accepted the sports page from the old duffer on the other side. He grinned his thanks when a cup of coffee and the pottery cream pitcher appeared before him.

"Y' want the same thing?"

The waitress was just as extraordinary as he remembered, but her smile reached her eyes and told him he was welcome.

"Yeah, please."

"Comin' right up. Hey, Jack, fix me up a special," she called through the window to the kitchen.

Gus should have ordered oatmeal, or unbuttered whole-wheat toast and OJ. Only this morning he'd noticed he was developing the beginnings of a paunch. But he hadn't been able to forget the delicious honey-cured bacon, the perfectly cooked eggs and the fat, yeasty slices of toast slathered with strawberry jam tasting of sunlight and spring rains. Tomorrow, he resolved, tomorrow he would rise earlier and run. Then he'd eat yogurt and fruit to make up for his sins this morning.

He hadn't run in three years.

The waitress slapped his platter before him.

"You new to these parts?" She set ketchup, hot sauce and the crock of jam beside the platter.

"Yeah." He forked his eggs on top of the hashbrowns. "First time in Oregon." He took a bite of bacon—as good as he remembered.

"You married?"

"Nope." *Go away, lady and let me eat my breakfast.* He tilted the sports page up in front of his face, hoping she'd take the hint.

"Good." She topped off his coffee before walking away, filling cups as she went.

"Don't pay Georgina no never mind," his stocky neighbor said. "She's just bein' friendly."

Damn snoopy, that's what she was being. Next week Gus would drop off her roller towels and go his way. Another dose of this coffee and his stomach would be rotted through anyway. He poured in an extra dollop of cream.

Replete and satisfied, he returned to his truck. Today would be a short day, since he only went all the way to Juntura every other week. Perhaps he'd take time on the way back in to detour into the badlands area over towards Westfall. He'd heard it was worth seeing.

Frank didn't care what time he got in, or how much time he wasted, as long as he got his work done. The longer he delayed getting back to Ontario, the less time he'd spend in his room, staring at four stained walls and remembering.

This time he took a minute to appreciate the Carruthers house when he got to his last stop. Instead of the gingerbread so common on houses of its era, this house stood foursquare and solid, without decoration, without whimsy. It was a house built for the future, a house meant to impress and to protect.

It should be cared for, instead of neglected. It needed paint, its chimney repointed, a missing shutter replaced on a second-story window and the weeds cleared from around its stone foundation. If it were his...

He wasn't man enough anymore to own a house like this.

The door opened.

Her hair was down this morning. As she opened the screen and motioned him inside, he noticed a faint pink to her lips and cheeks, a better definition to her dark eyebrows. He hesitated, uncomfortable with his body's sudden warming, awakening.

"Are you in a hurry this morning?" Her hands were clasped at her waist, but not still. They twisted together, rubbing against one another.

"No, I... Why?" He didn't mind waiting if she didn't have the pick-up ready. Frank had explained that she did mending and alterations for most of the laundries and dry cleaners in Ontario and Vale.

"I bought some cookies." Her voice faltered on the last word. "Oreos. I thought, if you wouldn't mind waiting while I finish one last seam... There's fresh-made coffee, too."

He'd eaten a big breakfast less than an hour ago, so he shouldn't be interested in food. But somehow, nothing sounded better to Gus than Oreo cookies and coffee.

INTERVAL

Ephemeral humans. Inconvenient...

Variable as energy sources secondly. Undependable...

Susceptibility differs. Not all effortlessly influenced. Carruthers best...

Good source of energy. Love strong. Passion mighty...

Humans receptive to auspicious environment. Enhance. Beautify. Embellish...

Keep Carruthers. Encourage reproduction. Steady, dependable source of energy...

Provide favorable milieu, inhibit departure...

Mutual advantage...

THREE

SALLY COULDN'T BELIEVE SHE'D JUST OFFERED HIM COOKIES. ALL she knew about this man was his name—Gus—embroidered on his shirt, just above the pocket.

Why had she bought the cookies anyway? She didn't need the calories, and Pop certainly didn't. And hadn't she learned anything from her experience with Ed? He'd been certain he was God's gift to womankind and hadn't been shy about showing it. Sally had only invited him inside once, and then it had taken her half an hour to convince him she wasn't interested in a weekly tryst.

"I wouldn't mind a decent cup of coffee." His voice grated slightly on her ears. It sounded rusty from lack of use, and reassuringly impersonal.

She glanced up at him, uncertain. There was nothing in his eyes. No threat, no desire. Nothing at all.

Could it be that she'd found a kindred soul? Someone who had nothing more to live for than she did? *And if you have, do you want to have anything to do with such a loser?* a small voice way in the back of her mind wondered.

Go away, she told it.

"It's...they're in here." She gestured vaguely toward the kitchen. She led him along the dim hallway, hoping Pop would be content a while longer with the rolling TV screen. It often seemed to soothe him, as if there was something there his failing mind could latch on to.

For the first time in months—years?—she noticed how dim and sinister the long hall seemed. As a child, she'd feared its shadowy corners and high, unseen ceiling. Today it seemed to trap her within its murk, just as it had threatened her younger self. She pushed the library door open as she went by. It didn't help—the blinds in there were pulled tight against the morning light.

"Your coffee sure smells good." His voice startled her as it sounded from just behind her shoulder.

"I...ah, I had some fancy beans." Would he get the wrong idea from knowing she'd gone to extra effort for him. "Sumatra." *I don't know anything about him. Nothing! He could be—No! Frank wouldn't have hired anyone dangerous.*

"I had breakfast at the café," he said, as he followed her into the dark kitchen.

She pushed the old fashioned two-button light switch. "Oh, dear. Have your taste buds recovered yet?"

In the fluorescent light from the ceiling fixture, she saw shadows under his eyes, as if he slept poorly and too little.

"I was careful to use plenty of cream." It was only a hint of a smile but there, nonetheless.

"I wish I dared do that." She set the plate of cookies before him and gestured for him to be seated. "Georgina's cream is as rich and thick as it comes." Her mouth watered at the very thought.

"So's everything else I've eaten there. Rich, I mean." He hesitated before sitting in the chair she indicated. "It's a shame the coffee isn't as good as the rest of the food."

"Actually, that's a good thing. If it was, I'd be tempted to stop in every morning. In a month, I'd be as big as a house." *You're babbling, Sally Carruthers.* She felt about as sure of herself as a girl on her first date.

She poured his coffee, waited for him to taste it. When he didn't she said, "Is something wrong? Oh, you want cream." She started toward the refrigerator.

"I was waiting for you to join me." His voice, for all its harsh overtones, held a gentle invitation like a cool breeze on a summer's day.

"Oh!" Sally turned and looked at him, waiting politely, as Pop no longer did. When she set food before her father, he either stared at it stupidly or delved into it with both hands, shoving it into his mouth like an undisciplined child. Or a starving man. "Of course. Just let me get the cream."

He raised a staying hand. "I don't need cream, Ms. Carruthers. I only use it at the Bite-A-Wee."

The hint of a smile came again with his naming of the café. If he ever quit stifling his urge to smile she probably wouldn't be able to resist him.

She perched on the edge of her chair, wondering again how she could have been so foolish as to invite a total stranger in for coffee. If he were to attack her no one would even know. Pop was long past being her protector.

She set her cup down with a clatter and stood up. "I'll finish that seam. It won't take me a minute."

This was not one of his better ideas, Gus acknowledged as the fragrant steam tickled his nostrils. He still wasn't sure why he'd accepted her invitation. He finished the coffee, wondered if good manners would allow him to help himself to a second cup.

"All done," she said, as she came back into the kitchen. "I put everything on the bench by the front door, so you won't be delayed any longer."

"I'm in no hurry." He looked around the big, high-ceilinged room. "This reminds me of the kitchen I grew up with."

"It's the only one I've ever known." She pushed the plate of cookies closer to him. A shy and tentative smile lit her face.

Shy? Sure, she's shy. That's why she invited a perfect stranger in for a snack.

Curious, he looked straight at her. She lowered her eyes. *No. She's more frightened than shy. Probably having second thoughts. As well she should.*

Gus forced unaccustomed facial muscles to widen his lips in a smile. It felt strange to do more than raise the corners of his mouth in a perfunctory gesture.

Her eyes still avoided his, but her lips widened in answer.

She reached for a cookie.

Gus reached at the same time, and their hands collided. Again that galvanic shock, as if they were each connected to a low-voltage generator.

She dropped her cookie.

He crumbled his. As he jerked his hand back, his wrist hit his cup, slopping coffee over the table.

"Oh, dear!" She jumped to her feet. "Did you burn yourself? Are you all right?" She grabbed a dishtowel from the handle of a drawer by the sink and dropped it over the spreading puddle. "Let me see your hand." She caught his right hand, pulled it across the table.

The shock of her touch was not as great as before, but the effect was the same. His fingers burned with an intense fire, as if she were the conduit for a tremendous current. This time, he resisted the urge to pull his hand free. There was something strangely comforting about the electric warmth of her touch.

He looked into her eyes—blue-gray, with a ring of dark, velvety black around the iris. Bottomless. He fought the sensation of sinking…sinking deep into a season of indescribable delight.

Forcing his eyelids closed, he fought his way free of her spell. *She's a goddam witch, that's what she is!*

"I'm fine," he assured her. "Really. It wasn't even very hot."

"You're sure?" She clutched the towel to her chest, a plain, somewhat frowsy woman of indeterminate age. There was nothing witchy or mysterious about her. *Just a woman, Gus, and you've been a monk for too long.*

"Let me see."

He held up both hands, showed her palms and backs.

"Not even pink." Again he forced a smile, and this time it felt almost natural. He stood abruptly and went after the coffeepot.

"Warm yours up?" He held it above her cup.

"Oh, dear!" Her hands fluttered like sparrows in winter, not quite touching anything but gesturing at the coffeepot, the plate of cookies, the discarded towel and the table. "I'm sorry. How could I… I mean, I'm the hostess…Let me…"

"I've got it." He poured their cups full, replaced the pot on its warmer. Back at the table, he slid the plate toward her. "Have a cookie?"

She took one and nibbled it. Her teeth were small and white, her lips soft and pink. He wondered if they would taste of chocolate if he were to lean across the table and sample them.

Before his body could react to that thought, he said, "Ms. Carruthers, if I frighten you, why did you invite me in?"

"You don't… I'm not… You seemed…" She licked her lips again.

His body tightened at the sight of her quick, pink tongue.

"I was lonely." The last two words were little more than a sigh as she met his eyes with naked longing.

Oh, God! Not again!

Shoving his chair back until it banged against the wall, he stood and leaned his fists on the table. "You picked the wrong guy, then." Angry, because she was just like Marilyn, he snarled like a cornered animal. "You want company, lady, go buy yourself a dog."

He stalked out, raging inwardly with the inequity of it all. Why did women look to him to fill their needs? Couldn't she see that there was nothing inside the empty shell he showed the world? No heart, no soul? Nothing!

How could he fill her loneliness if he couldn't find surcease from his own?

Sally poured the rest of the coffee down the sink. It tasted bitter, nasty. Worse than Georgina's. The cookies she put into a fancy tin, set them aside to give to Ernie Green tomorrow morning on her way to the Post Office. She was cleaning the counters, postponing her retreat upstairs when a crash sounded from the front room.

"Oh, no," she sighed, wondering which of her mother's collection of china cats had been destroyed this time. She hoped it wasn't the Cheshire, with its purple and red stripes and its wicked grin. Of all the fragile little dust catchers, she liked the Cheshire cat best. She tossed the dishrag into the sink and went to see what new havoc her father had created.

"I DON'T KNOW, WILMA," SALLY SAID, WHILE IDLY LEAFING THROUGH the collection of envelopes on the counter. "Some days he seems almost intelligent, but most of the time he's like, well, some sort of enraged beast."

"Is he still tearin' things up?" The postmistress waved at someone behind Sally.

"No, he hasn't shredded a magazine for a couple of weeks. Now he's pounding on the walls." She rubbed her eyes, wondering how long she could go without sleep. "Last night I was afraid he'd put a fist through the window in his bedroom, but he managed to miss it." Slumping, she sighed in defeat. "This morning his hands were bloody and the Sargent print—you know, that one he always liked because it reminded him of England when he was there on his junior year abroad—was all broken. Even the frame."

Wilma reached across the counter and took Sally's hands, stilling their restive plucking at the pages of her copy of *Dress*, the journal from the Costume Society of America that was her only connection with her former life.

"When are you gonna face facts, Sally? Your pa needs to be put away. You can't keep on like you're doing."

"Oh, Wilma, I have to. I promised Mother I'd take care of him. And I promised Pop, too. He'd die if I ever took him away from the house. He loves it so."

Her father had been born in the big old Carruthers house, had returned to it after he was discharged from the Army, and had brought her mother there, to live happily for nearly forty years. He'd always said if it hadn't been for the house he'd have sought his fortune elsewhere, for God only knew there were few enough fortunes to be had in Whiterock.

"It might be a blessing if he did—" Wilma patted Sally's hand one last time before releasing it. "—before he turns you into a sour old maid."

Agreeing, and hating herself for it, Sally essayed a laugh. It came out as fragile as her attempted smile.

"I can't be an old maid, Wilma. I'm a gay divorcee, remember?"

"Whatever." Wilma shoved the stapler into place, straightened the tape dispenser and otherwise showed her feelings with abrupt, angry motions. "All I know is you need to get someone in there to watch him once in a while, or you're going to wear yourself to a frazzle. You looked in a mirror lately?"

She had, just yesterday. After the laundry man left. Gus. What she'd seen explained his abrupt departure—a middle-aged woman with frizzled hair and deep brackets about her mouth, drooping shoulders and empty eyes.

"I don't like to ask anyone to watch him. He's so unpredictable."

"Ask Milly Kemp. After what she went through with Jerry, nothin' your pa could do would faze her."

Sally checked her watch. It was past time for her to get back. "I'll think about it."

If only she didn't have to go home.

Gus forgot his intention of taking the scenic route back to Ontario after he stomped out of the Carruthers house. He finished his deliveries and pickups with dispatch and got back to the shop a little before three. For a moment, he thought about telling Frank he was moving on. The last place he wanted to be was where a woman whose haunting eyes pleaded with him to fill the empty spaces in her life.

He filled out his route sheet with half his mind, the other half thinking about what to take and what to discard. With each of his moves, he'd carried less of his past with him.

Less physical evidence, that is. He couldn't seem to discard those reminders of his past he would most eagerly part with. Guilt could never be left behind. He had assumed a responsibility for another human being—for two others, ultimately—and he had failed in his duty. Failed in the worst possible way because he hadn't cared enough to cherish and protect them as he had promised.

"How'd it go today?" Frank Tsugawa again perched himself on the corner of the table. "You getting acquainted with your customers?"

"Most of them," Gus said. "Especially on today's route, There are so few, it's easy to remember who they are."

"There's some interesting people out there, all right." Picking up a pencil, Frank rolled it between his palms. "They may seem a little standoffish at first, but all-in-all, they're worth knowing."

"I guess so." He wondered what his boss was getting at.

"Take Whiterock, for instance."

Gus couldn't think of anywhere he'd want to take a town as dismal as Whiterock, but he tried to look interested.

"It used to be a thriving little place, before the mine closed." Putting the pencil down, Frank began stacking the money wrappers into neat piles.

"Mine?" He knew a little about mining, and he hadn't seen anything around Whiterock that looked like a mine.

"The Carruthers Chalk Mine," Frank said. "It was out south of town, about three miles. At one time it shipped more diatomaceous earth than any other mine in the country. Closed down in the eighties."

Gus shrugged. He'd been mildly curious where the money came from to build a big, fancy house like the one Ms. Carruthers lived in. Now he knew. He began sorting the bills in his moneybag, stacking them into neat piles of ones, five, tens and twenties, each smoothed and facing in the same direction as those beneath it.

"The Carrutherses had their fingers in a lot of pies—cattle ranches, the mine, a shipping company, even an aerial spray service, until Eddie, the younger brother, was killed in a crash up Willow Creek way."

Gus sorted coins into nickels, dimes and quarters, stacked coins of like value into columns of ten.

"Uh-huh." As long as Frank was his boss, he'd listen to what he was trying to say, but that didn't mean he'd pay any attention to what he didn't care about.

Like a woman with eyes as deep as infinity.

Gus cursed silently and forced his attention back to Frank.

"The older brother, Will, and I were in the County Boosters together. He was always one to volunteer his time when we had a community improvement project. One year he even played Santa Claus and flew in on a helicopter." Frank stared off into space. "Paid for it, too, as I recall."

"What happened to him?" Gus really didn't care, but it seemed polite to ask.

"Oh, Will's still alive. At least his body is." With an easy hop, Frank was on his feet and at the door. "Awful waste. Him losing his mind like that and Sally breaking her heart over it." He shook his head—sadly, it seemed to Gus. "Alzheimer's" he added as he turned away.

Gus wondered what Frank had been trying to tell him. Was his boss playing at matchmaking? Between him and a shy, lonely woman who looked to be a good five years older than he was?

Of course, age only mattered to the older, more mature member of a relationship. The person who had to take care of the younger one, the dependent one, the child-wife, who could refuse responsibility because she believed it was her privilege to be cared for, protected, pampered.

Gus clenched his teeth so hard his jaw knotted. He had known what Marilyn was when he'd married her. Her helplessness, her dependence had been part of what attracted him to her in the first place. For the first few years of their marriage, he'd been completely content with her. Her total femininity had strengthened his masculine self-esteem.

Then he and Roger had opened their own firm. He had quickly discovered that owning his own business left little time for anything else. Marilyn had simply not been able to adjust, and he should have taken that into consideration instead of being so single-minded. In his quest for success, he had walked away from his responsibilities.

And he would never forgive himself.

INTERVAL

Introduced component affecting events. Useful?
Consider ramifications.

FOUR

For the next few days, Sally spent quite a few hours taking a long, hard look at what her life had become.

Empty.

Hopeless.

Wasted.

And whose fault is that, Sarah Elaine Carruthers? Not Pop's. He can't help what he's become. Put the blame squarely where it belongs, girl. On your own head.

She started with the kitchen, cleaning the cobwebs from the high corners of the ceiling, washing the windows inside and out, scrubbing the walls and woodwork. The cupboards still wore the dark cream paint her mother had favored, a color that offended Sally's artistic soul. They never looked quite clean.

Redecorating was out of the question. It wouldn't do any good, for as soon as she had the walls clean Pop would smear food on them. If she put the still-beautiful oriental rugs back on the hardwood floors in the living room and library, he would soil them, one way or another. Or worse yet, he might trip and fall, might break his hip. She just couldn't handle having him bedridden in addition to being senile.

But she could wash windows and curtains throughout the house, open the blinds and let the springtime light brighten the high-ceilinged rooms and the dark inner hallway. She could get out there and clean up her mother's rose garden, pulling last year's dead sow-thistle and wild lettuce, pigweed and bindweed. She could call in young Buster Jones to mow the lawn and prune the hedges, something she hadn't seemed to find time to do as often as she should have last summer.

Sally stood on the back porch, looking out over the yard. Both black locusts needed pruning, too, a job beyond Buster. A branch had blown off, narrowly missing her car, during the windstorm in January. It still lay where it fell, with last fall's unraked leaves piled around it by the gentler, more capricious winds of March. She just parked a little farther from the back door these days.

Running her hands through her hair, she wondered again if she should get Milly Kemp in to stay with Pop for a day. She hadn't had a haircut for nearly two years. It hadn't seemed to matter, for who saw her anyway, besides the people who'd known her all her life? They'd seen her spotted with chicken pox and chuckled at her skin peeling in sheets after a long nap in the noonday sun the July she turned sixteen. They'd smiled at her, glowing in her wedding gown. Then they'd looked at her with pity when she came home, feeling like a failure, to recover from a divorce she'd wanted as much as Jeff. And they'd mourned with her at her mother's funeral, when she had no more of herself to give, yet was already suspecting that her father would be her next patient.

Lately she seemed to be seeing her life in a brand-new perspective. Yesterday, she'd noticed Georgina wearing a new shade of lipstick, a bright pink instead of the ghastly fuchsia she usually favored, and Wilma's hair had been suspiciously lavender. Grip had almost seemed to gambol when he came to the fence to bark his obligatory warning.

And the rain last week had washed the worst of the bird droppings off the elk.

The least she could do was spruce the place up a bit, in keeping with the town's springtime reawakening.

INTERVAL

Energy dissipating at greater rate than accumulating…

Carruthers resource weakens, dwindles. Only two remain. One is obsolete, and therefore useless. The other is disoriented and nonfunctional…

Alternatives? Other available energy sources are weak and unfocused…

Supplementary sources are needed…

Increase glamour? Enhance environment?

Anticipated alternative is eventual termination…

Worthwhile gamble?

Affirmative!

FIVE

WINTER HAD LINGERED MUCH LONGER THAN USUAL, EVERYONE said. March was cold, windy and bleak. When the wind howled around the wooden eaves of his upstairs apartment, Gus thought about howling with it, except he hadn't the energy.

Or the interest.

Life was easier if you gave people nothing to complain about, so he did a good job, even for minimum wage. Avoiding hassles wasn't the same as caring.

Neither did he care about the woman in the big house in Whiterock. Never mind that she'd insinuated herself into his dreams more than once. She was needy. Far too needy, with her big, lonely eyes, her soft, wistful voice.

April brought rain, even in arid eastern Oregon. More than once Gus considered the gray-brown landscape and wondered if May flowers would actually follow. Not that he cared. He felt at one with lowering clouds and sad little drizzles.

The drizzle was turning to authentic rain when his truck topped the ridge outside Whiterock. The town was half-concealed in wind-blown gray curtains, with shabby structures lurking darkly among still-leafless trees.

He pulled up before the Carruthers house, once again acknowledging its foursquare tenacity. The cold rain had washed its drab clapboards cleanly white. Its black shutters glistened as though newly painted. Grabbing seven plastic-protected garments and three paper-wrapped parcels, he ducked his head and ran to the front porch, squinting against wind-driven droplets. He jabbed his finger against the doorbell and heard the Westminster chimes echoing inside. But no footsteps approached. Again, he pressed the bell. Waited.

He waited a good two minutes. There was no place on the porch where he could safely leave the dry cleaning. Most of the floor and the front wall of the house shone with blown-in moisture. Perhaps there was a back porch.

He removed his jacket and wrapped it around the already water-spotted parcels. A little rain wouldn't shrink him, but it might damage the garments he'd brought for alterations.

By the time he reached the screened back porch, he was soaked. Fortunately, the door was unlatched. He slipped inside. A handy coat hook beside the door would hold the hangers, and the floor was dry, so the parcels could sit there. He had to assume Ms. Carruthers would look out here when she realized she'd missed him. Next time he saw her, he'd make sure they had an understanding about what he should do if she wasn't here to take them in.

He was at the rear corner of the house when he heard the plaintive sound. It seemed to come from the shrubbery massed against the old barn. He paused, decided he was mistaken when he heard nothing more. He headed on toward the front yard and the dry sanctuary of his truck.

"Damn it, Pop!" This time the voice was a full shout. "You're gonna die of pneumonia if you don't get inside."

He hesitated. Whatever was going on, it was none of his business.

"Please, Pop, stand up!"

Oh, hell, I can't get any wetter.

He found a path into the shrub thicket, followed it. Around the second sharp turn, he came upon Sally Carruthers crouched in the mud beside an old man. Both were drenched. Ms. Carruthers, clad in a wet, clinging chenille robe, was sobbing and swearing as she tried to force the old man to stand. Not resisting, but not cooperating either, he sat like a lump. His face, what Gus could see of it, was slack, expressionless. His gray hair hung in dripping strands across his face, and his flannel pajamas clung to him, soaked through.

Gus shivered in sympathy.

Sally looked up and Gus was there.

"Help me, please. He must have been out here for hours. He's so cold—"

All her tugging and shoving at Pop hadn't moved him.

Bless the man, he wasted no time in pulling Pop to his feet. Although her father was not a small man, Gus handled him as if he were, lifting him easily in a fireman's carry.

She ran ahead to open the back door.

"Let's take him into the bathroom." She shivered as a gust of wind caught her wet robe.

"Where?"

"Straight through the kitchen, the second door on the left." She slipped around him to push the kitchen door open, then again to lead him to the bathroom. By the time he was there with her father, she had the water running in the shower, was holding one hand in it to test the temperature.

"Look out." Letting Pop slide from his shoulder, he hauled him upright with both arms. He let go for a moment to unhook the chain that held his wallet to his belt. "Keep this dry, will you?" As soon as she took it, he pulled Pop tight against his chest and walked him into the shower stall.

"Your shoes!" Sally protested.

"They'll wash," Gus said. "Hotter." His arms were wrapped around her father, supporting him. Pop's teeth were chattering and his body was wracked with shivers, but his vacuous expression didn't change.

Sally shut the door when water splashed out onto the linoleum, but she didn't move away. Through the frosted glass, she could see Gus's uniform, Pop's tan pajamas. Their shapes and colors were indistinct, but she could see that Gus held Pop still, in spite of his increasing struggles.

I wonder what he'd look like in tights and a leather jerkin.

As soon as the thought emerged, Sally quashed it, horrified. Pop could be halfway to pneumonia, and here she was drooling over a hunk in a wet Tsugawa Linen Supply uniform.

"Go make some coffee," he said, interrupting her shameful thoughts. Reminding her that he was the dark, bitter man who'd stomped out of her house a few weeks ago.

She went.

When the water began cooling, Gus shut it off. He had to fight to get the still-struggling old man out of the shower stall, stripped of his wet pajamas and dried off. The old fart had to be completely around the bend. He hadn't seemed to give a damn about being cold, hadn't cooperated in his own warming up and was putting up a good fight against donning the robe Gus found hanging on the back of the bathroom door.

At least he no longer in the grip of those awful, bone-deep shivers.

There was a tap on the door.

"Are you decent?"

"C'mon in," Gus said, while trying to force the old man's hand into the other sleeve.

"Oh, Pop," she said as soon as she saw the difficulty he was having, holding the old man while tying his sash. "Can't you cooperate, just this once?" She grabbed the loose sash end and tied him into the robe while Gus held him. "Pop, let's go watch TV, shall we?"

Her father grunted, and tried to pull free. Sally looked up at Gus, grimacing.

"Can you hold him just one more minute?"

"As long as you need," he said, all too conscious that she was still in her wet robe. He felt suddenly guilty for being warm.

"Take him into the parlor." she said, and gestured vaguely toward the front of the house. "I'll get his tea."

She disappeared into the gloom of the hallway.

Gus half-carried, half-shoved the old man into the room where the TV stood. He switched it on, saw that the picture rolled as it had the first time he was here. The old man immediately calmed, offering little resistance as Gus guided him to the shabby overstuffed chair.

"Pop?" Sally's voice came from behind him as he settled an afghan around the old man's legs. "Here's your tea."

She handed her father an insulated lidded cup and he immediately began sipping at it. Gus saw rather than heard her sigh, saw her shoulders relax, saw her bottom lip released from her teeth.

"Thank heaven," she breathed. "Sometimes that calms him, sometimes it doesn't."

He followed her into the dark hall. "Frank said he has Alzheimer's."

"And he's getting worse."

They emerged into the kitchen, bright now with fluorescent light reflected from clean white appliances and pale cream walls. She turned, seemed to see him for the first time. "Oh, my goodness. You're soaked."

It was the understatement of the century.

"So are you." He was surprised by a stab of desire when he realized how her wet robe outlined long, lean thighs and high, full breasts. A memorable body, and one that didn't match her bracketed mouth and tired eyes.

"Let me get you a robe." She scurried past him as if she'd heard his thoughts and was afraid of them. "I'll spin your uniform in the washer and toss it in the dryer. It won't take long."

Her last words drifted back from the long hallway, and the next sound he heard was her feet on the bare wood of the stairs.

Gus stood alone in the kitchen, shivering again as the water in his clothing evaporated. *Damn!* If he'd had any sense, he'd have just dropped the delivery on the front porch and to hell with the blowing rain. He could have been through with Whiterock by now and on the way to Juntura.

Yeah, and her father could have died of pneumonia, too, you selfish bastard.

Her feet thudded again on the stairs. Seconds later she was back, and shoving a dark green terry robe at him.

"Here. Let me have those wet clothes and I'll get them in the dryer."

He took the robe. "Let me get them dry while you get into dry clothes yourself." He was not being entirely altruistic. Her nipples were hard pebbles under her robe and just the sight of them made his loins tighten. *Hell!* An extended spell of abstinence was bound to make a man horny. Any woman would have affected him this way. "Point me at the dryer. I'll be fine."

As if to emphasize his words, a long, violent shiver swept through her.

"In th–th–there." She pointed to a door in the wall opposite the sink, hesitated in the doorway.

"Go on," he said. "I'll be fine."

The door opened into a small laundry, obviously a recent addition to the old house. To his immense appreciation, a couple of thick towels hung on a rack beside the washer. He stripped his soggy clothing off and dumped it into the washer. While the washer spun, he rubbed himself briskly, doing his best to ignore his slight, residual arousal. He'd been without a woman for far too long.

Since he'd killed his wife.

Gus was drinking coffee when Sally returned, still cold but at least clothed in dry garments. Pop's green robe brought out a matching shade in his eyes and brightened the fire in his hair. She hadn't realized just how red it was before. Richly scarlet, with highlights of gold and copper, it blazed in the white light from the fluorescent fixture.

He looked at her over the coffee cup, a question in his eyes.

"He's completely passive," she said. "I don't know what it is about the TV, but it works better than anything else. Most of the time."

"What happened this morning?" He seemed almost reluctantly curious.

She poured herself more coffee, topped off his cup. Sitting across from him, she was reminded of her temporary insanity the last time he'd been here. *He's just being neighborly. Don't scare him off again.*

"Last night was bad. He was restless, out of bed at least five times, wandering the house, opening cupboards and closets, apparently looking for something. He was relatively tractable, thank heaven. Sometimes he gets violent and I just can't do a thing with him. So far, though, I've been able to prevent his hurting himself too seriously."

"Living with his condition must be painful for you. I had a great-aunt who had Alzheimer's. Watching her go downhill just about broke my heart."

"It does." She shook her head, reminding herself he didn't care about her problems. But she did owe him an explanation. "I hate to give him sedatives unless he gets really violent. Last night he went back to bed each time I found him, so I kept putting it off. But he was up again soon, looking for whatever it was he thought he wanted. Finally, toward morning, he seemed to calm down." She grimaced. "I went to bed."

Exhausted, she'd slept until well past eight.

"When I went in to take him to the bathroom, he wasn't there." She heard the quaver in her voice and took a deep, calming breath. "I wasted nearly a half-hour searching the house."

"You didn't call for help?"

She shook her head. "I know I should have. I kept telling myself I'd find him soon. He's never..." Another breath, this one catching on the lump in her throat. "I was dialing the phone in the library when I saw him through the window."

She'd dropped the phone with a surge of relief—relief laced with anger and fear.

"He'll usually do what I tell him, but not this time. He was dead stubborn about staying in the rose garden."

"He's too big for you to handle. What if I hadn't come along?"

"I'd have had to leave him long enough to call for help, I guess." She reached for the coffee carafe, avoiding his eyes. "Thank you for helping."

Gus found himself wanting to yell at her for her passive acceptance of an impossible situation.

"What are you going to do when it happens again?"

Damn it, Loring, what difference does it make to you? You don't care.

"I don't know," she admitted. "I'd like to find someone who'll live in." Her shrug showed how unlikely she considered that possibility. "I hate to ask any more favors of the neighbors. I already owe them more than I'll ever be able to repay."

Speaking from personal experience, Gus said, "Sometimes it's pretty stupid to let pride dictate what you do."

"It's not pride," she snapped, with more life in her voice than he'd yet heard. "People get tired of always giving, when they get nothing in return."

"That they do." He set his empty cup down and stood. "My clothes should be dry enough to wear by now. I've got to be going." He went into the laundry room, carefully pulling the door closed behind him—slamming it would have been an admission that she'd gotten under his skin. His shoes were still wet, although the washer's spin cycle had taken all the squish out of them. The dryer was still working, but he removed his clothes anyway. They were damp, but not so much he couldn't wear them.

God preserve him from helpless women. He'd had entirely too many in his life. Grandmother Taylor had been so dependent on his grandfather she was completely helpless after his death. For thirteen years, she'd lived on, a contentious, whining, weak and demanding old woman. Gus's mother, her only surviving child, had done her duty, had all but displaced her children in doing so. Elise Taylor Loring had alienated her husband with her devotion to the old witch, until, after five years of hell, his father had left.

Gus had detested his grandmother. He'd come very close to detesting Marilyn for being so much like her, for all he'd loved her. For a while, his emotions had been in total confusion until he acknowledged that he'd made the choice—unconsciously perhaps—and it was his to live with.

Marilyn had been a good wife. She'd made a comfortable home for him, charmed his business associates, endeared herself to his family. Yes, he'd loved her, even as he found himself resenting her inability to make decisions, her insecurity about being left alone at night. Worst of all, her absolute helplessness in the face of any kind of trouble, from a dripping faucet to a child's ear infection.

Determined not to follow in his father's footsteps, Gus had done his best to be a devoted, dutiful husband and father, but once in a while it had been too much. He'd sometimes tried to force Marilyn to stand on her own two feet.

And the last time he had lived to regret it.

He jerked the laces of his sneaker tighter. After shouldering into his jacket—much clammier than the lightweight shirt or twill pants—he hung the towels carefully back onto their bar.

In his opinion, Ms. Carruthers should put the old man into a nursing home where he could get full-time care. The next time he escaped her supervision might prove fatal. One thing sure, Gus wouldn't be here to help her out. He was going to give notice as soon as he got in tonight.

He'd give Frank a week or two to find a replacement, and he'd be on the road again.

"Are you dry?" she said, when he reentered the kitchen.

"Dry enough," he growled.

She was standing by the table, clutching a bowl in white-fingered hands. "It's almost noon. I've got some leftover vegetable soup here..."

"I've got work to do." He made a beeline for the back door.

"But it won't take long. I can put it in the microwave."

"Lady, I've wasted most of the morning picking up your marbles. I've got customers waiting."

As he stepped out onto the back porch, he noticed the packages he'd delivered. Bending to retrieve the brown-paper-wrapped parcels, he handed them to her. Then he lifted the garments from the hook. "Where do you want these?"

She dropped the parcels onto the table, almost upsetting her coffee cup.

"I'll take them."

He held the plastic-encased garments out of her reach, not wanting to experience again that galvanic shock he'd felt each time she touched him.

"Just tell me where you want them, Ms. Carruthers," he said, letting impatience show in his voice.

Silently, she led him along the hall and opened a door. As she flicked on a light, he saw a modern, well-equipped sewing room, an oasis of light and color in this house of gloom and defeat. He hooked the hangers on a portable clothes rack and turned around.

She was standing directly behind him.

For one brief, insane moment, he wanted to catch her close, to kiss her.

INTERVAL

Glimmer of energy. Whence?

There...

Vital, but damped...

Potential great. Initiate?

Experience indicates greatest energy surge occurs with synergy...

How achieve? Method?

Concatenation? Aggregation?

Yes!

Nudge useless Carruthers. Associate new energy source with inept Carruthers...

Ingenious!

SIX

GUS FINISHED THE REST OF HIS DELIVERIES IN WHITEROCK A little after one. Although helping Sally Carruthers had put him behind schedule by a couple of hours, he decided to stop for lunch anyway.

The same crowd was in the same seats at the Bite-A-Wee Cafe, as if they hadn't moved since early morning a week ago. His seat, at the apex of the counter's arc, was empty, waiting for him.

"Missed ya this mornin'," Georgina said, and set a cup of battery acid before him. "The special's short ribs." She was gone before he could ask if he could get a sandwich to go.

"Blazers lost." The Old Duffer handed him the sports page.

Gus took it, feeling he had no choice. He picked up the menu.

"Don't bother with that," Stocky Man told him. "Georgina's short ribs'll make you think you died and went to heaven."

Gus buried his face in the paper, trying to pretend a fascination with the Portland Trail Blazers' loss to Phoenix last night.

The door behind him opened, sending a damp draft down his neck, reminding him that his jacket still held residual moisture from this morning's misadventure. As the newcomer passed behind him, the hair at his nape stood on end. He didn't need to turn around to see the reason, because nearly every voice in the café was raised in greeting.

"Hey, Sally, how's your pa?"

"You're late today, Miz Carruthers."

"Hi, Sal!"

"I decided to treat myself to lunch, since I never had time for breakfast," she explained to all and sundry, sounding almost guilty. "My father's sleeping now. Sedated."

Gus kept his face buried in the paper. From the comments around him, he gathered she hadn't done anything so daring as going out for lunch for a long time.

"This rain oughta green up the park good for the May Fest," someone said, about the time Georgina slapped Gus's salad before him.

"The May Fest?" Sally's voice sounded as if she'd forgotten there was such a thing.

"Only six weeks to go." Another voice, this one a deep baritone. "Maybe you can get out to it this year."

Gus stole a look to the side. She was in the last booth, her back to him, sitting with a big fellow in some kind of uniform. A cop? He looked like it.

"But I thought…"

"My Rhoda's Queen of the May this year," a middle-aged woman in a polyester pantsuit said with pride.

"Better keep an eye on her, what with Ben Kemp being her Consort," someone warned.

"I don't remember…" Her uncertain voice was drowned out in the general laughter.

Nearly everyone in the café had something to say about Ben Kemp, who seemed to be the town's bad boy, but a favorite one.

She lifted a slender hand to smooth back her hair. Gus hadn't noticed before how thick and heavy it was, nor how it gleamed with golden highlights.

"I really haven't much time, Georgina," she was saying. "Maybe just a sandwich…" She chewed her bottom lip. "Pop's alone…"

The cop reached across the table and laid a hand on hers.

"I'll be going out that way anyhow, Sal. I can look in, and if there's a problem, I'll call you."

"Short ribs today," Georgina said.

"How can I resist?"

She smiled up at Georgina, and Gus revised his estimate of her age downward by ten years. Not that it mattered, but he wished she'd smile more often, because it made her both young and lovely.

His short ribs appeared before him just then. He picked up his fork and began one of the best meals he'd ever eaten. As he ate, he eavesdropped.

Most was local gossip. Ms. Carruthers occasionally asked questions that showed she knew all the people but was out of touch with what they were doing. How long had she been immured in that big old house with her father, anyhow?

A middle-aged woman—Rhoda's mother?—departed, holding the door while she visited with a newcomer.

"Hey, Bernie," the Old Duffer called out as the door swung shut once again, "what's this I hear about Leo Plum goin' back to Reno?"

A skinny old fellow dressed in grease-stained overalls took a seat at the counter just beyond the Old Duffer. His billed cap read Cowles Implement. Gus thought he remembered him from the garage, which was also a gas station, a tractor sales-and-service agency, an auto parts store—a typical small town business.

"Shit, yes." Bernie sipped the coffee Georgina set before him. "His old lady decided she has to stay down there with her ma, so Leo gave his notice today."

"Whatcha gonna do for a pump jockey?"

"How's Pete Gomez workin' out?"

"Pete's doin' fine, but he can't run the shop *and* the gas pumps." Bernie looked glum. "Guess I'll have to put an ad in the paper."

Gus's plate was empty. Although full, he could have kept eating, just for the sensual pleasure of tasting the rich brown gravy, of gnawing the tender meat from the bones. Even the occasional lumps in the real, hand-mashed potatoes had appealed to him, and the steamed carrots had been worthy of a gourmet restaurant anywhere in the country.

Georgina snatched his plate away with one hand, refilled his cup with the other. "Pie? We got peanut butter cream, blackberry, pecan and lemon meringue."

"The pecan's to die for." The soft, familiar voice came from behind him.

Again the hairs at his nape stirred, and he barely stopped himself from spinning around on his stool.

Georgina looked back at the rear booth. "You didn't clean up your plate, Sally."

"I did the best I could." Laughter hovered at the edge of her words. "Honest, I did. And I've really got to go. I've already been gone too long."

She slipped out the door, and Gus felt the room's warmth go with her. When Georgina repeated her question about the pie, he gave her a curt "No, thanks," and dug into his wallet.

"See ya next week," Georgina called, as he followed Sally out the door.

Maybe. Maybe not.

He stood on the sidewalk and tried to decide which way Sally Carruthers had gone. How had she disappeared so quickly?

What was this strong pull he felt toward her, anyhow? It felt like more than lust. A lot more. Whenever she was near, the world looked brighter, more vital. She made him feel alive in a way he hadn't for more than three years. Yet she didn't flirt, didn't even smile much. It was more her—well, if he was into touchy-feely, he'd call it an aura. But he wasn't, so he didn't have a word for the way he always knew when she was anywhere nearby.

He'd work the week out, no more. This time next week, he would be far, far away from Whiterock, Oregon.

FOR THE FIRST TIME IN MORE THAN FIVE YEARS, SALLY FELT GLAD TO be back in Whiterock. Pop's escape this morning had been the worst episode yet. Without the kind of emotional support she'd gotten today at the café, she didn't think she could have faced returning to the house.

Oh, God, if only I didn't feel so damn guilty! Today's quick lunch with Lyle had been her first true escape for nearly a year.

It wouldn't be neglecting Pop to get Milly Kemp to care for him one afternoon a week. She knew she'd be justified; but knowing it, and believing it deep down, where the guilt lived, were two very different things. As long as she devoted her every waking hour—well, except for the time it took her to go to the Post Office—to Pop, she could forgive herself for sometimes wishing him dead.

No, that was wrong. She couldn't forgive herself, but she could live with herself.

She took her time going home, for all she'd given Wilma the impression she was in a hurry to get there. Any more discussion of her appearance, her state of mind, or the May Fest—*the last thing I need is a party!*—and she'd scream. What she really needed was a day off. A week would be better. A little time to remember that she'd had a life once upon a time, and a career.

The sedative she'd given Pop was usually good for four hours, and it had been less than two since he'd finally drifted off to sleep. With luck, she had another hour of freedom.

What she should do was go home, do last night's dishes and get a start on the new mending Gus had brought her.

Gus.

It had been a long time since she'd felt such an attraction to a man. Since the early days with Jeff, before they'd discovered that all they had was physical attraction. But there had to be more between a man and a woman than lust. Surely a strong love like her parents' was based on mutual interests, mutual goals, mutual respect.

Not just sex.

Perhaps that was why she didn't trust her feelings about the dark, brooding, short-tempered deliveryman. All she felt for Gus Loring was lust. Hot, steamy, mouth-watering lust.

Instead of turning south on Fifth, she turned north. It had been a long time since she'd walked through the park, and today she needed solitude and the silence.

I wonder who cleaned the elk. For as long as she could remember, white bird droppings had frosted its bronze back. Too bad the antlers had been lost to vandalism, back when she was a child. Now it looked like a hermaphroditic deer with a weight problem.

The path wound between weeping willows, still bare of leaves, but bright yellow-green with buds and full of twittering birds. Not the usual starlings, she noted, but some less common, less obnoxious birds, with flashes of white tail feathers as they flitted from branch to branch. Juncos? She didn't know, but they weren't the nuisancy house sparrows who devoured the seeds she occasionally tossed onto the driveway.

Why didn't she remember last year's May Fest? Or any of them, for years? Mom or Pop must have written about the town's annual spring party at least once while she was away at college and, later, when she'd worked in Seattle. She'd subscribed to the *Whiterock Banner* all the time she'd been away but had seldom read it, any more than she did now—there was a pile of them on the back porch, waiting to be taken to the recycling center in Vale.

The paper was much smaller than it had been back when Sally was in high school—two, sometimes three sheets, where it used to be twice that, and chock full of news and ads. Although it would last as long as Phyllia Everingham was alive and able to edit it, the *Banner* didn't attract many advertisers anymore.

Was she suffering from the same dread mental deterioration as Pop? Her stomach clenched at the thought, but cool reason quickly told her that if the May Fest was all she couldn't remember, she was guilty of inattention, not suffering from early senile dementia.

The old arched bridge across Little Hackberry Creek needed paint, but it didn't seem as dilapidated as she remembered. The last time she'd walked in the park she had hesitated to cross it. Now the floorboards seemed solid and strong, the wooden railings firm and protective. Someone must have taken it on himself to fix it up. She knew there was no money in the city budget anymore for park maintenance. Even the mowing was done by volunteers.

She checked her watch. A few more minutes and she would have to start home. But she wanted to follow the creek, half-full of water now, after three days of rain, and see if there was watercress in the spring-fed pond behind the bandshell. Last fall, the pond had been almost dry, as had the creek, but if the creek was flowing, maybe the spring was, too.

When she was a child, she'd often gathered the watercress for sandwiches, a favorite of her mother's. Would they still taste as good as they had then?

Following the creek bank, she came to the marshy area just below the pond. Cattails had invaded and spread, until the short path was almost blocked. When she pushed through, she saw that only a green scum covered the rocks lining the pond. The spring had disappeared. She almost wept.

Why did everything have to change, to die?

She cut across the weedy lawn in front of the bandshell. One more instance of death and decay, she thought, keeping her head lowered. The last thing she wanted to see was how the old structure, its stucco coating falling away, its rough timber beams exposed to the elements, was deteriorating. She hadn't been here since the afternoon of her mother's funeral, when she'd walked this way to escape the smothering sympathy of her friends and neighbors. That day she'd seen how the bandshell had fallen into disuse, and had wept for a fading town as much as for her own loss.

Sally wished she could have seen Whiterock in the '50s, before so many of its young people had gone away to war—and afterward found new lives elsewhere. Pop had told her of the Whiterock of his childhood, and it had sounded like something out of a Judy Garland movie. Now it was a sad little, tired little town slowly eroding away as its elderly died and its young departed.

As she would go, the first chance she got.

After Pop died.

GUS UNLOADED HIS LAST FEW DELIVERIES IN JUNTURA AND FOUND A flat parcel with Sally Carruthers's name on it.

"Damn!" He checked his watch. Four o'clock, and he had a seventy-mile drive ahead of him, even without a detour into Whiterock. For a moment, he was tempted to leave it where it was—he could deliver it next Wednesday.

Or his replacement could.

On the other hand, what did he have to do this evening? Watch TV and guzzle beer. And he'd done too bloody much of both already.

Knowing there was no cell service in Juntura, he went to the pay phone on the outside wall of the general store, dropped a quarter into the slot. When Frank answered, he said, "This is Gus. I'm running a little late, so I'll call you when I get to town."

He didn't have a key—didn't want one—so Frank had to be there to let him in. That, or let him hold on to his money and charge slips overnight.

"Don't bother. I'll see you in the morning."

Gus agreed and hung up. He couldn't decide whether Frank trusted him because of Roger's recommendation, or because there wasn't enough cash on this route to worry about.

All the way back to Whiterock, he wondered why he was being so damn obliging. He couldn't imagine mending or dry cleaning important enough that it couldn't wait a week.

She didn't answer the front door, even when he rang a second, and then a third time. He pounded on it, and this time, he heard, faintly, "Hold your horses. I'm coming!" It seemed to come from overhead, rather than from inside.

He waited a good two minutes before he saw her through the narrow side windows. She was scampering down the wide stairs, wearing something long, flowing and pale.

The door flew open.

"Lyle, what are you—you're not Lyle!"

He held out the forgotten parcel.

"Nope. Thought you might need this before next week."

"Oh." She drew the monosyllable out into a breathy sigh. "It's you."

Patiently, he lifted the parcel a little higher, raised his eyebrows in matching inquiry.

"Oh. Yes. Just let me…" She unhooked the screen, pushed it open.

Pushed it farther, until it was wide enough for him to enter.

"Come in," she said. "You're just in time for supper."

Gus looked into her eyes, wide and blue and plaintive. She needed him.

He didn't want to be needed.

Being needed carried a price he wasn't willing to pay.

He drew a deep breath full of the hurtful words he would batter her with…

And smelled lemon oil polish and rose sachet, honeysuckle perfume and warm, freshly bathed woman.

He couldn't help himself. He stepped over the threshold. With one hesitant hand, he reached out and touched her cheek. It was warm, slightly damp, soft as milkweed silk.

Her head turned, just a fraction, but enough to let him touch her lips.

The jolt of sensual electricity was so strong this time that it destroyed his thoughts. All he knew was that he had to have more of her, had to taste her, hold her, fill his hands and his mouth and his soul with her.

He pulled her to him, feeling pliant woman, yielding woman, scented, earthy woman along the hard length of his body. His mouth found hers and devoured it. His tongue found the hard ivory of her teeth, the rich, humid surface of her underlip, the seeking strength of her tongue. He swallowed her moans, and gave her his to consume. He drew her tongue into his mouth and played with it, exchanging his for it with thrusts telling her what he wanted. His hands found her bottom, covered only by the silky fabric of her drifting robe and grasped, kneaded, cupped. Lifted.

Sally swayed with the wind of his passion, with an intensity of her own. Her breasts crushed against his powerful chest, her pelvis cradling his erection, her feet dangling inches above the floor, she was conscious of nothing but the taste and feel and scent of him. Yet, she was aware of every sound, every smell, every sight in her surroundings.

She was terrified.

She was exhilarated.

She wanted him. She wanted to lead him down the wide hall to her lonely bedroom and ravish his body until he begged for mercy, until he died from sexual exhaustion. His calluses were hard and rough on her breast, even through the light tricot of her robe, the fragile fabric of her nightgown. He touched her gently, cupping and supporting, one finger drifting gently across the tight, beaded nipple until she wanted to cry out with the exquisite pain of it.

Slowly, he let her slide down, against his belly and thighs, letting her feel his rigid tumescence. As her feet found the floor, he bent over her, clasped her in both arms and held her, gently, yet with unbreakable bonds, against his chest.

Her heart pounded in her ears...or was it his? His broad frame trembled, or were the vibrations hers? His lips nipped at the lobe of her ear and she shivered—and felt an answering shiver in him.

He lifted his head against her clinging hands. She didn't want to let him go, didn't want this incredible interlude to end.

"What's happening?" His voice was hoarse, breathless. "How did we…"

"I…I don't know." She pushed him away. Her knees wobbled.

"I want you, damn it!" He shook her slightly, hands tight on her upper arms. "And I don't want to!"

Sally looked into his face, saw raw anger fighting with desperate hunger. The one frightened her, the other ignited her blood.

"Wait," she said, and pushed him away. "We've got to talk about this. To understand…"

He released her and took a step back, mouth twisting into a cynical half-smile.

"What's to talk about?"

"Why are you so angry?" Sally retreated until she felt the edge of the bottom step pressing against her ankle. "I didn't—"

He cut her off with a sharp gesture. She grabbed his arm as he turned to the door.

"Damn it, you will listen to me!" she yelled, and jerked him back to face her. "You started this, I didn't." Still holding on to his arm, she pulled him closer, until they were nose to nose. "I was just being neighborly—"

"Crap! You were coming on to me."

"I was… Why, you conceited ass!" Sally caught at the frayed edges of her temper, held on tight. "Look, Gus, you helped me this morning when I really needed it. So, when you showed up… went out of your way to come back… I was just trying to show my gratitude."

He stopped trying to pull free. The flat green of his gaze seemed to bore right into her. She lowered her lashes, hiding eyes that never had been able to keep a secret.

Carefully arranging a friendly smile on her lips and in her eyes, she looked up at him and said, "I've made potato soup. Would you like some?"

For an instant, she thought she saw a hunger she recognized—for companionship, for shared laughter, for comfortable silences. The stone in the lines and angles of his face softened ever so slightly.

"Got any oyster crackers?"

She let her eyes close in relief. He wasn't going to storm out, wasn't going to go away mad. And forever.

"Is there any other way to eat potato soup?"

INTERVAL

Reserves exhausted. Simple to nudge useless Carruthers...

Brief encounter of last Carruthers, new potential energy source, proved energy-rich...

Not reliable. Source—name...? label...? cognomen...?—Loring? Loring. Loring...

Inner confusion. Strong craving to escape...

Impossible. Not tolerate!

Possible methodology required for enticement...

May Fest incomprehensible, but evidently of great importance...

Worthwhile endeavor?

Nudge non-sensitive humans energy consuming...

Yet rewarding?

Conceivable...

Implement!

SEVEN

"More soup?"

Gus considered the possibility for a moment, even though he'd emptied two bowls. Then the thought of his still-expanding waistline occurred to him and he shook his head.

"I've had plenty. I haven't had potato soup since I left...for a long time."

"Would you like dessert? I've got frozen yogurt." She seemed hesitant, unsure of herself, as she had been last week when she invited him in for cookies.

He forced himself to rise, even though his body wanted to relax in the warmth of the kitchen and just sit there, comfortable and at peace. "I really can't. I've got to get back to Ontario."

"Oh, of course." She glanced at the clock. "I didn't think. It is late, isn't it?" Again she was twisting her hands together, as she had last week. What had happened to the passionate, demanding woman who'd met him at the door less than two hours ago?

Without thought, Gus placed his hands on her shoulders and pulled her toward him. When she was so close the tips of her breasts burned his chest, he bent and dropped a quick kiss on her parted lips. Before he could lose his resistance to the immediate and dazzling reaction of his traitorous body, he released her and stepped back.

"Thanks for supper. It was delicious."

"You're welcome." Her voice trailed after him as he strode along the hall. Within seconds he was outside, taking the high stone front steps in two descending leaps, trotting along the sidewalk until he was safely between the rangy climbing roses that bent along the rusty iron arch over the front gate.

As he opened his truck door, she called to him. For an instant, he considered pretending he hadn't heard. Then, slowly he turned.

She was framed in the front door, backlit with the golden light from the hall. With all his willpower, he forced himself to stand where he was. Forbade himself to stride back up the walk, to leap onto the porch, to take her in his arms and tell her he wanted her. Now!

"Goodnight," he called back instead. Waving, he climbed into the truck and started the engine.

He was at the edge of town before he remembered to fasten his seatbelt.

"NOW DON'T YOU ARGUE WITH ME, SARAH ELAINE CARRUTHERS," the diminutive white-haired woman commanded. "I haven't anything better to do with my time. Can't babysit any longer—those youngsters just run too fast for me—and I need to feel useful."

Sally let her inside. "Did Wilma send you, Milly? Or Georgina?"

"Well, now, maybe I just took it into my own head to come over here." Milly Kemp hung her dark blue cloth coat on the hall tree and laid her hat and gloves on the narrow table beside it. "I've been bored out of my mind this winter—I swear I can't remember one so long and so cold—and I was wracking my brain for something to keep me out of mischief."

"What about the Altar Guild? The library? And aren't you on the town council this year?"

"Pshaw! None of them take more than a few hours a week. Besides, it's high time some of the younger women got involved in them. As long as I'm around, they just sit back and let me do all the work."

Since Sally knew this last to be true, she couldn't argue. After Mom's death, she'd even thought about volunteering in the library once or twice a week, but she never had. Then Pop had gotten worse, and, well…

"But, Milly, if you're not able to keep up with children, how can you…I mean, Pop sometimes gets really agitated, and I… well, sometimes *I'm* not even strong enough to manage him."

"If that happens." Milly shooed Sally ahead of her into the kitchen. "I'll call Lyle and he can come over here and be my muscle. That's what I used to do when my Jerry acted up. Now, just show me where everything is—I'm sure you've changed the kitchen around since your mother's time—and I'll start on his lunch." She whipped an apron off its hook next to the refrigerator and slipped it over her head. "And I don't want to see you before suppertime, you hear me?"

Sally couldn't believe her ears. An entire afternoon—to do with as she pleased.

No. She just couldn't go. *What if Pop needs me?* But oh, how she wanted to!

"Milly, are you sure…?"

"Go on with you." Milly made shooing motions. "Go get a manicure, or buy a new dress." She tilted her head to one side and looked at Sally. "I'd say the first thing on your list should be the beauty shop, wouldn't you?" She opened the refrigerator and inspected its contents. After a long moment's perusal, she turned around. "Are you still here? Scat!"

Sally scatted.

IT WAS FRIDAY AFTERNOON, AND GUS STILL HADN'T GIVEN NOTICE. Frank hadn't been around yesterday at all. The bookkeeper said he'd gone to Boise to some kind of trade meeting. So today, just as soon as he got checked in, he would hunt him up and tell him to start looking for a new route man.

His check-in sheet didn't balance, and he spent fifteen minutes looking for the error. When he finally found it—thirty-four written as forty-three—the other two route men had left for the weekend.

Frank looked up as Gus entered his office.

"Roger Blakely told me you worked on cars when you were a kid," he said.

Damn! His ex-partner had a big mouth, but until now he'd been fairly discreet whenever one of Gus's employers had checked with him.

"Yeah, why?"

"Today was the Chamber luncheon," Frank said, looking down again at the paper he held in his hands. "I sat next to Bernie Cowles."

Bernie Cowles? The name was familiar. Gus waited. Frank liked to work his way into a subject, and Gus didn't have to be anyplace soon. He could wait.

"He's losing his mechanic. Oh, he's got a young fellow who's sharp as a tack and willing to learn, but Bernie thinks he's too green yet to take over the garage."

Gus remembered the talk in the Bite-A-Wee Cafe on Wednesday.

"So?"

"So, Bernie's looking for someone to help out while Pete grows up a bit. Someone who's got a little experience, a little maturity, but who doesn't want to make a career of it."

"What's that got to do with me?"

Frank looked as innocent as a newborn babe.

"Nothing, I guess." He laid the paper down, and Gus saw it was an employment application. Not his. "Unless you want it to."

"You firing me?" For all he'd intended to give notice, the feeling of being replaceable was galling.

"Not unless you want me to. You're doing okay. I just thought you might be interested in something a little more…" He shrugged. "…challenging."

"Cut the crap, Frank," he snarled. "If you want me out of here, just tell me. I can be gone in thirty seconds." Snatching the paper off the desk, he skimmed it. Some young punk, whose only prior experience was helping on a Pepsi truck one summer. "Who is this? A cousin?"

"My wife's sister's nephew-by-marriage." Frank wore a sheepish expression.

"Give him the damn job, then. I don't care!" Gus tossed the sheet of paper back onto the desk. "He can start Monday! I'm gone."

By the time he reached his furnished efficiency apartment above the hardware store, he was merely seething instead of feeling ready to explode. He'd never been fired in his life. Dammit, Frank had said he wished he could get *more* people of Gus's caliber for what he was able to pay them. He could probably sue, if he were so inclined. It had to be illegal to fire someone without cause.

A shower barely cooled him down. He stomped down the narrow wooden stairs, ducked his head as he jogged along the sidewalk to the steamy little greasy spoon at the corner. Frank hadn't actually fired him. What would happen if he turned up for work on Monday? He had every right to.

Or did he? Frank might have taken his angry words as the equivalent of saying "I quit."

He'd been going to anyway, hadn't he? Made up his mind to move on. Someplace where there wasn't a woman with a flowery scent and a musical voice who needed him.

He'd planned to tell Frank tonight, but Frank had beat him to the punch, damn him. And now he had a whole new understanding of the often-impotent rage he'd seen in so many faces, in so many employment agencies. Being fired hurt like hell.

He shoved the plate aside, most of the too-salty stew and the soggy biscuits still uneaten. Was the Bite-A-Wee Cafe open for dinner? Too bad it was so far away. If Georgina's stew was anywhere near as good as her short ribs, she was wasting her time in a dying little burg like Whiterock.

Tomorrow he'd pack his few possessions into his pickup and head on down the road. There was a quarter change from his dinner check. He held it on his thumb. Heads, he'd go north, up I-84; tails he'd go south into Nevada. Maybe stop over a few days in Winnemucca or Reno. He flipped the coin into the air, waited impatiently as it rose, then fell.

His fingers touched the spinning coin, knocking it sideways. He heard rather than saw it hit the sidewalk. He lost sight of the quarter until it glinted in the blue light of a mercury vapor street lamp, just before it rolled into a storm drain.

SALLY SAW THE DARK-BLUE PICKUP AS IT GLIDED SLOWLY ALONG Main Street late Tuesday morning. Since Whiterock was off the beaten path, few vehicles drove its streets she didn't recognize. This one she didn't know.

She couldn't see the driver because of the bright sunshine reflected from the passenger window. Watching until the truck pulled into Cowles Implement, across from the Post Office, she continued to sip her coffee.

This morning she'd given in to temptation and stopped for coffee and a cinnamon roll. Pop was docile, had been ever since last Wednesday. He'd gone into the front room without prompting, sitting quietly in his chair and staring at the rolling TV screen. Just to be safe, she'd set the monitor on the front hall table, turned on and tuned to the receiver in Milly's living room. She'd decided she couldn't leave him completely unattended anymore unless he was sedated. And she hated to do that, unless he was so agitated he was violent.

She really owed Lyle Curran for finding and hooking up the baby monitor, even if she had paid him for it. She hadn't been aware such things existed.

Such a sense of freedom. She didn't have to ration her minutes quite so strictly, and she didn't have to feel so totally imprisoned, just because a little electronic gadget sat there and let someone else listen to her father and call for help if he needed it.

"More coffee, hon?" Georgina was holding the carafe over her cup and Sally hadn't even seen her approach.

"I've really got to get back. Buster Jones came in Saturday and did some tilling, and now I've got to finish what he started. I thought I'd put in a garden."

"You want to try snow peas, I'll take all you can grow," Georgina said. "I can't get anybody to raise 'em for me, and the ones I can get from the restaurant supply are froze."

"Georgina, I am not going into the kitchen garden business. I just thought I'd put in a row of beets and one of carrots. Maybe a small patch of corn, when it warms up."

The door opened behind her. The hairs on her nape stood at attention.

"Morning, Georgina," Bernie Cowles said.

Another, deeper voice echoed his greeting. A familiar voice. She stood stock still as two masculine bodies edged past her to slide into the front booth. From the corner of her eye, she caught a glimpse of bright red hair, a dark-blue jacket, faded Levis.

Immediately, Georgina was there with her coffeepot. Sally tried to take advantage of the distraction to slip outside.

"Hold on, there, Sally!" Bernie called. "I want to introduce you to my new right hand."

She turned. Stared.

The right hand's smile was as full of canary feathers as any cat's.

Seeing his quarter disappear through the storm drain grate had somehow brought Gus to his senses. He didn't want to move on. For the first time in three years, he really didn't want to pack up the truck and head down the road.

He hadn't had a chance to explore this area, but the little he'd seen appealed to him, despite its emptiness.

Or maybe because it was so empty?

He'd walked around town for nearly two hours, listening to the quiet, catching a whiff now and then of wood smoke and damp soil, nodding at the occasional passerby. By the time he'd circled back to his apartment he'd pretty much made up his mind to stick around a while. If Frank was serious about letting him go, he'd look for another job on Monday. Construction work had picked up with the warmer weather—there was almost always an opening for someone who knew which end of a hammer to was the business end.

Frank was serious.

By noon on Monday, Gus had talked to three building contractors and the foreman of a trailer manufacturing plant. He could have had a job with any one of them, but each time he hesitated, told them he'd get back to them.

Not the usual behavior of a man needing work.

When he stopped at the bank to cash his paycheck, he discovered two other items in the envelope—a letter of recommendation from Frank and a newspaper clipping. The clipping was from the Help Wanted section of the Sunday paper, one Gus had already seen and ignored.

Cowles Implement in Whiterock needed a shop manager.

He'd wanted to see some of the country around Harper and Westfall, country he hadn't had a chance to explore while he was on his delivery route. So, while he was trying to make up his mind what he wanted to do, he headed out that way. He finally saw the badlands area, the white bluffs and quarries where diatomaceous earth had been—still was being—mined. He even stopped at the played-out Carruthers Chalk Mine, its entrance marked by a decrepit log gate and a faded wooden sign, but he hadn't entered.

After that he'd followed the unpaved, poorly maintained road along Hackberry Creek, through a shallow valley dotted with white-faced black cattle and bisected by a willow-bordered stream. When he emerged from the pastoral valley, he had seen Whiterock spread out before him, its windows sparkling in the sunlight, looking like every rustic small town Hollywood had ever portrayed.

That was when his tire went flat. When he discovered the spare was flat as well. Once he was through cursing, he hiked down into town and to the only place for miles where a tire could be repaired.

Cowles Implement.

When he walked in the door, Bernie had greeted him as if he'd expected Gus to drop in.

And then Bernie offered him the job of shop manager.

He hadn't wanted the job, didn't want the responsibility, never wanted to see Sally Carruthers again. Now he had two people depending directly on him—six if you counted Bernie's wife, Pete's wife and the two Garcia kids.

"Hello, Gus. Welcome to Whiterock." Sally's voice trembled, and the hand she held out to him shook, although he didn't think anyone noticed but him.

Her hand was like ice, and he wanted to hold it close to his chest, to warm it against the furnace heat of a body burning from the merest pressure of her palm against his. Instead, he released it. "Glad to be here." And wondered if he was.

With a fleeting smile, she was gone, hurrying up the street toward the Post Office. He turned back toward Georgina, aware he'd missed what she was saying. "I beg your pardon?"

"Just said I thought you'll find a lot about Whiterock to like." She added more vitriol to his cup.

SHE KNEW WHO WAS AT THE DOOR BEFORE SHE ANSWERED IT. Taking several deep breaths, Sally strengthened her resolve, stiffened her spine and squared off her heels. She was not—repeat, *not*—going to fall into his arms again. And she most certainly was not going to ask him to make love to...to have sex with her.

She couldn't forget the bone-melting desire she'd felt in his arms. Before common sense set in.

"May I come in?"

"It's late." She didn't let the door open more than five inches.

"Only eight-thirty," he said. His smile was white in the dim porch light, and his eyes were dark caverns with tiny, golden gleams in their depths. "Please."

His voice could melt a glacier.

She hesitated, and was lost. He pushed the door open, not forcing but with an inexorable strength, nonetheless. She had to step back to get out of its way.

"I came to see how your father was," he said.

"He's fine."

"And how you were."

"I'm fine."

"And to ask your help."

She imagined she heard in his voice the purr of a cat whose prey was securely caught.

"My help? How can I possibly help you?" She wasn't sure she wanted to know, but she couldn't not know, either.

"I need a place to live."

"A place...?" She took another step backwards and found her retreat halted by the wall. "I thought..."

"You thought what? That I was going to drive back and forth from Ontario every day?" He shook his head vigorously. "No way! Bernie said you might know of a place for rent. An apartment."

Sally closed her eyes a moment, banishing the fantasy that had leapt into her mind.

"When you were here before, we...I...you..." She gulped and tried again. "Last week, when you came back, I did some things I didn't mean to do."

Well, she had wanted him, desperately, for a brief, burning interval. But she didn't want him now. He had to understand that, to believe that she'd succumbed to loneliness and exhaustion for a moment.

"Is there any chance you can forget how I acted?"

His hand approached her face, and she found she could already feel the tingle of his touch. The brush of his finger against her cheek was as gentle as the brush of a spring zephyr, and warm as June sunlight.

"It's forgotten," he said, his voice low and throbbing, "if you're sure you want it to be."

Sure? She wasn't sure of anything at this point in her life. But in order to live with herself, she had to devote all her time and energy to Pop. She couldn't let herself look for the distracting excitement Gus Loring could bring to her life.

And she hadn't the fortitude to deal with the heartbreak when it was all over and she finally made her escape from Whiterock.

INTERVAL

Caution! Precipitate assumption of success dangerous...

Passion achieved, but not enduring; not yet permanent. Need assurance of continuity...

Generation of offspring optimum solution...

Experience indicates time and proximity necessary to task. Also love...

Proximity initiated with capture of Loring, but no assurance of duration. Need further enhancement of environment...

Humans gratified by visual stimuli. Peculiar concatenation of bronze minus appendages. Calcium carbonate and lignum structure deteriorating...

Translocate molecules, refurbish surroundings...

May Fest incomprehensible, but of significant importance to inhabitants, therefore requires facilitation...

EIGHT

Spring finally came to Whiterock, and it did so with an explosion of color. A singular fancy struck Sally that every bare tree in town had been waiting, quivering with embarrassment, for winter to turn its back. With the first warm rain of April, they stretched skyward, as if to loosen limbs stiffened with cold, and did their best to unfurl each leaf as quickly and completely as possible, to go from naked one day to fully clothed the next.

Had every spring been so fruitful, so pregnant with the promise of extravagant harvest? Had she been so blind, so insensitive to the shifting seasons in the past to have not noticed this prodigal expression of nature's bounty?

Perhaps her mood of expectancy was because she no longer felt so imprisoned. Just having Milly Kemp come in twice a week to care for Pop gave her such a sense of freedom. So far she hadn't gone anywhere on her free days, but knowing she could made all the difference.

If there were only some way she could take the good things about Whiterock with her when she went back to her life—the home she'd been born in; her wonderful, caring neighbors; the bucolic atmosphere. Although, come to think of it, hadn't the atmosphere been what stifled her, back when anywhere else in the world seemed more exciting than Whiterock, Oregon, population 639? And the neighbors often went beyond friendliness, all the way to nosy, so a person had no privacy whatsoever.

Of course, seeing Gus Loring each morning on her way into or out of the Post Office had absolutely nothing to do with her new, lighter mood.

Seeing him, but not speaking to him, not in the ten days since he'd come to ask her if she knew of available lodgings. She had heard—oh, last Friday or Saturday—that he'd persuaded Walt Kemp to rent him the long-unused apartment over the drugstore. He must now be a resident of Whiterock.

Every day as she emerged from the Post Office he had been standing just inside the large overhead door of Cowles Implement, or outside at the gas pumps. He always waved. She had more than once been tempted to cross Main Street and speak to him. If he'd called to her, even just an acknowledgement that it was a good morning, she might have. But he always just smiled—that heart-stopping smile he was so frugal with—and then turned 'round and went back to work.

Sally pulled her gaze from the view out the window and back to the ice pink satin in her lap. She really had to get this dress finished for Rhoda Garcia so she could begin on her regular sewing, no matter how sweetly spring called to her.

Sally had been Queen of the May her eighth-grade year. She remembered how excited she'd been when she was chosen by a vote of the entire student body in Whiterock School. Her mother had made her dress, a lace-covered, ruffled Victorian gown that had looked just like the fancy prom dresses she'd seen in *Seventeen*. Bill Holmes had been her reluctant Consort. He'd worn a wide-sleeved French peasant's smock, also made by her mother from a folklore pattern they'd found in Boise, and had complained loudly about looking dumb. Pop had told her all thirteen-year-old boys were embarrassed by dressing up, unless they could wear a sword or cowboy boots.

Milly stuck her head in.

"Lunch," she said.

"I'll be right there." Sally finished basting the bodice seam and laid the dress aside.

"I hope Kate Garcia knows what she's doing, letting Rhoda have that dress," she said to Milly as she entered the kitchen. "When did little girls start wearing skintight, strapless satin gowns?"

Milly passed her the salad dressing. "I seem to remember a certain young lady who wasn't allowed to wear her swimsuit in public the summer after she was Queen of the May."

Sally grimaced.

"Oh, lordy, I'd forgotten that." She could feel her face burn. "It really was skimpy, wasn't it?"

The bikini in question had been little more than strings and a trio of tiny fabric scraps. She'd bought it with her carefully saved allowance. Her mother's initial reaction had been to tell her to return it, but when told that bathing suits weren't returnable, she'd forbidden Sally to wear it anywhere outside her own yard.

That summer the corner of Fifth Avenue and Jasper Street had been the busiest intersection in Whiterock.

"Walt says that new fella is all settled in." Milly slipped into the chair across the table. "According to Walt, he travels real light. A few books, a fancy coffee maker, a little bitty TV and a microwave oven." She stirred blue sugar into her iced tea.

Sally pretended to have her mouth too full for speech.

"Walt's going to try to get him to work on the booths for the May Fest. Since Leo Plum went back to Reno, he's short a man on the committee."

"That's nice." Sally was not sure she wanted to have a conversation about Gus Loring. She'd forgotten how much of a gossip Milly was. The woman knew as much about what was going on in Whiterock as Georgina did, but was much less discreet about telling what she knew than the café owner.

"He's a good-looking man," Milly went on between bites. "I swear, I've never seen hair that red in all my born days. Have you?"

"It certainly is unusual," Sally agreed.

Her lunch inhaled, Milly started clearing the table.

"Ardith Cowles called. She wants to bring over the ribbons for the maypole today. Maybe you could help me get them all measured and rolled?" Sally's mother had always cut the ribbons, because her dining room table could be extended with leaves to nearly fifteen feet long. It was a simple matter to measure the wide ribbons when they could be laid out almost flat.

Sally choked down one last bite of salad, feeling her entire too-quickly-eaten lunch congeal into a hard lump in her stomach.

"I'm pretty busy." Hearing her voice, she winced at the slight whine in it, "but I guess I could help you set up the table." She didn't want to get pulled into the rhythm of everyday life in Whiterock, didn't want people thinking she was any more than a visitor.

After helping Milly, she escaped into her sewing room. She really was busier than usual, what with Rhoda's dress and Ben Kemp's fancy shirt of matching fabric. She had to smile. If Bill Holmes had been embarrassed to wear a loose, flowing shirt made of natural cotton, plain and unadorned, how did Ben feel about a pink satin, ruffled-sleeved, flamenco-styled shirt? Had he had any say in the matter?

GUS PAID LITTLE ATTENTION TO ALL THE TALK ABOUT THE MAY Fest. There was seldom reference to any held after 2006, and he gathered the most recent ones had been less exciting and successful than those held in the past.

One day at lunch, Roy Gilbert—Gus still thought of him as Stocky Man—who always sat on his right in the café, mentioned that Walt Kemp was looking for volunteers.

"They'll help build and set up the food and game booths," Roy said. "Nothing fancy. Just plastic stretched over wooden frames."

"I'll think about it." Gus had no intention of volunteering for anything. The last thing he needed was to get sucked up into civic activities.

Within a couple of days, he realized he had no choice in the matter. If you lived and worked in Whiterock, you worked on the May Fest.

"I can swing a hammer," he told Roy, the next time the subject came up, "but that's about all."

"How about the prizes committee?" Roy said, as he dug into a slice of rhubarb-strawberry pie. "We need somebody to canvass the merchants in Ontario for donations."

"You're kidding! Roy, there are probably a few folks in town with worse people skills than I have but not many."

It stung that Roy simply nodded his agreement. Once Gus had been fairly successful at marketing, although never as good as Roger.

"Well, we'll find a place for you. There's never enough willing hands." Roy pushed his empty plate away and left.

But Gus was not to be left in peace. A few minutes later Walt Kemp slid into Roy's seat.

"I've got a vacancy on the clean-up committee." He nodded at Georgina, who was holding up the coffee carafe. "Seeing as how you're new in town, I figured you'd want to be free during the day, so you could take in the May Fest."

"Walt, I can't—"

"That maypole dance is something to see. The kids work real hard to get it right." He addressed the plate Georgina set in front of him. After a few bites, he said, "We're gettin' together after work tonight at the Chalk Pit, to get the committees set up. You might find something else you'd rather do."

Gus tried again. "Walt, I'm not much at—"

"Bernie tells me you're the best shop manager he's ever had. Glad to hear that. It's time he had somebody around to depend on. Now he can get a little fishing in, come summer."

Gus gave up. "I'll see you this evening." *As if I had a choice.*

Whether he liked it or not, he was being caught up into community life, something he'd managed to avoid for three years. There was no quicker route to being needed than to belong.

Well, he'd help out at the May Fest, since it was for a good cause. And he'd do a good job for Bernie. But otherwise, he'd keep to himself, stay well out of the social life of Whiterock. Folks around here would learn soon enough that there wasn't much of the milk of human kindness in him.

"OWWW! POP, PLEASE! DON'T FIGHT ME." SALLY DID HER BEST TO hold her father in his bed, but it was like trying to hold a wild animal. He pulled away and rolled out the other side of the high hospital bed, landing with a solid thump. Sounds poured from his mouth in an obscene stream, unconnected syllables mixed with curses.

As he scrabbled across the floor, she caught him by one ankle. His other foot whacked her on the cheek, making her head ring. She held on, soon caught his wrist.

"Pop! Pop, damn it, calm down. Please!" With both arms around him, she tried to hold him still.

He caught her under the chin with his shoulder as he made one last lunge before going completely limp in her arms. She held him while she caught her breath and worked her tongue gingerly over her molars. They all seemed unbroken, thank goodness.

Although he had lost considerable weight, it still took all her strength to get him into bed.

"Why couldn't you have relaxed ten minutes ago," she muttered, tucking a leg under the covers. She pulled the blanket up under his chin and gave it a pat. "I sure hope you sleep well tonight. I don't think I could do that again."

At the door she paused, looking back. In the beam of light from the hall, his face seemed younger, as if the signs of age were disappearing along with his memories.

"Oh, Pop," she murmured, "I wish…"

Sally left the wish unspoken. Some wishes should never be made.

Later, she sat on the front steps and just listened to the stillness. It helped her to deal with her resentment and the guilt it caused.

She had made the choice to stay with Pop, freely and with love. She was still here out of love—and duty. No one was forcing her to keep him in his beloved home. No one forbade her to go back and pick up her career. There was enough money. She could put Pop in a home—there were some well-run, almost luxurious ones in Vale and Ontario—and close up the house.

The only reason she didn't was that she loved him and believed he was better off in the place he'd always called home.

So why did she resent his every demand on her time?

Tonight he'd been little more than a lump, having to be fed, drooling every other bite out over his chin. She'd practically had to carry him to his bed. Getting him into his pajamas had been like pushing a rope. And as soon as his head had hit the pillow, he'd become frenetic.

While she was fighting him, she'd wanted to scream, to strike out at him, to go away and leave him alone and unattended.

My God! No wonder some people abuse or abandon their parents.

She buried her face in her hands, shocked at her thoughts, and ashamed. She did love Pop. She would never mistreat him, never abandon him. No matter how long he lived, she would always be here, keeping him in the family home, giving him the best care she could.

Because she owed him.

Because he was her father.

Because she loved him.

She removed the cloth from her face, twisting it to wring out the water from the melting ice cubes. Prodding the swollen flesh with a gentle finger, she decided it had stopped swelling. With luck her eye would be open enough to allow her to see to sew tomorrow.

If it wasn't, she'd just have to call Frank Tsugawa and tell him why the three prom dresses he'd sent her for hemming weren't ready. And she hated to do that, since they weren't ready because she'd chosen to work on Rhoda's dress instead. It had been months since she'd had an entire garment to work on, so she'd decided to treat herself. There was nothing quite so boring as taking in and letting out waistlines, lengthening and shortening skirts and pants.

Sally had kept on with her mother's little mending business because she needed something to do. The first year she'd been home she'd also helped with the junior class play over at Vale High School. While designing and making the costumes for a small-town production of *Auntie Mame* wasn't quite the same as designing the entire wardrobe for a Seattle Opera production, she'd enjoyed herself. And the kids had been a lot of fun—enthusiastic and innovative.

The next year Pop had been just bad enough she couldn't leave him for any extended period, and she'd been reluctant to call on her neighbors, who'd already been so unselfish during her mother's final weeks. When the drama coach again asked for help, she'd reluctantly refused.

By the time she got back to her career, would she even have the spark of creativity necessary to lift her above the ordinary? With each year that passed, she felt it slipping away, fading from lack of use.

She raised her head at a faint sound from the road. Listening, she heard another, then a third. For a brief moment, she felt the urge to flee indoors, as she would have in Seattle, where the night was no longer safe.

But this was Whiterock. Anyone walking along its gravel streets was a resident, someone she'd probably known all her life. She was all but invisible, hidden in the shadows of her front porch. The gibbous moon's pale light could reach only halfway up the steps.

He appeared out of the night, silhouetted against the star-studded sky. She recognized the profile, sharp, with a strong nose and stubborn chin, and the shoulders, wider than most men's. She would have known it was Gus, even if she hadn't seen him, for his very presence sped her heart's pace, robbed her of breath, sent waves of heat through her body until each nerve ending quivered, waiting to be stimulated.

Her mouth went into motion before her brain was in gear.

"Nice night for a walk," she called.

He stopped, dead still. Turned. Peered into the dark, although she didn't know who else he expected to see sitting on her front steps at eleven at night.

"Come walk with me." His voice was velvety, enticing. "It's too nice a night to waste."

Sally didn't acknowledge the mental voice that told her she was setting herself up for a fall. She just smiled. "Just a minute, while I check on my father."

Pop was sleeping soundly. Surely he'd be all right if she escaped for a little while. He'd never awakened once his pill took effect.

She grabbed a sweater from the hall tree and stepped back outside.

"The creek's running high," Gus said when she joined him at the edge of the road, "and the bats are hunting in the park."

He took her hand, and once again the contact shot through her body like a jolt from a live electric wire. She did her best to ignore it, and forced her voice to remain steady.

"I used to go down to the park when I was a kid and listen to the creek sing."

"We had a brook," he said, as they walked along Fifth Avenue, "on my grandfather's farm. It had some ordinary name—Hayden's or Hardin's or something—but to me it was always the Singing Brook because of the way it sounded as it bounced along on its rocky bed."

His voice was soft, thick with memories. It lacked the harsh note she'd often heard in it before.

"Hackberry Creek used to be dammed for a small grain mill," she told him. "My great-grandfather built it. The rocks that make it sing are all that's left."

The mill had been torn down long before she was born, but somewhere, in a box in the attic, were old sepia-toned photographs of it when it ground all the grain for Whiterock, Harper and Westfall.

Their footsteps slowed as they approached Main Street. At this time of night there was no need to watch for traffic, but both stopped and looked both ways before crossing.

The elk's antlers held sparkles of moonlight at their tips. It stood tall and stalwart, guarding the entrance to the park as it had for almost three-quarters of a century. Sally was glad someone had decided to restore it.

I wonder why I didn't hear about it.

"Do they ever have concerts there in the summer?" Gus waved in the direction of the old bandshell.

"No, not anymore. It's not…" Sally looked again. She would have sworn she'd seen gaping holes in the stucco facade the last time she'd been here, but the roof was intact, the facade unbroken. Oh, the paint was streaked, and the two old-fashioned light sconces held only broken globes and gaping sockets, but those could be easily fixed. "Not for a long time," she amended.

I'm not crazy! I just wasn't paying attention. She hadn't really looked closely at the bandshell the last time she'd walked here, that was all. And who was to say her own sense of devastation hadn't colored her perception of the world around her?

She looked again.

"Gus, you're around town more than I am. Has anyone said anything about fixing up the park?"

"Just that they had a work party a couple of weekends ago, to spruce up after the winter."

That must be it. They'd fixed the elk, patched the bandshell. She really hadn't been imagining the deterioration.

They walked the twisting path until they came to the arched bridge across Little Hackberry Creek. The intermittent stream chuckled and gurgled to itself in a quiet little song whose notes were almost lost in the unrestrained hilarity of the larger stream as it tumbled over the rocks. Instead of continuing, Gus stopped at the top of the arch. He released her hand and leaned on the rail.

Bats swooped between the trees, briefly appearing in the light from the ornate lampposts along the path. She imagined she heard their almost inaudible calls as they hunted, dipped into the creek to drink and returned to pursue yet another insect attracted by the lights.

She leaned beside Gus, not quite touching him but comfortable in his nearness. The powerful awareness she felt whenever she was anywhere close to him had not faded but was simmering, just beneath the surface. Ready to burst into full boil with the slightest incentive.

"Tell me about this May Fest," he said, his voice still quiet and soft.

"It used to be really grand." Closing her eyes, she pictured the May Fest as she remembered it. "When I was a little girl, I could hardly wait until I was in first grade, so I'd be old enough to dance around the maypole. One year—oh, I guess it was my second or third year of dancing—the TV station in Boise sent a crew over to film us. We were on the evening news."

She still remembered how thrilled everyone had been. They'd closed the carnival for an hour so everyone could go home or to the street in front of Peterson's Furniture, with its window full of a dozen TV sets, and watch the news.

And now Peterson's Furniture was boarded up, and the children she'd danced with were grown and gone—away from Whiterock.

Gus turned sideways and leaned one elbow on the rail. "I've read about maypole dancing, but I've never seen it."

She felt his gaze on her face and was glad her bruised cheek was on the other side. He hadn't noticed it yet and perhaps he wouldn't in the dark.

"It's practically a lost art. I don't know if we did it right, but we did have fun." In spite of herself, she was almost looking forward to the May Fest. "I haven't been to one for a long time, since I was in high school, I guess." That had to be why she couldn't remember hearing about recent celebrations. She hadn't been in the mood for fun, so she simply blanked them out of her mind. "But I don't imagine they've changed any. Everyone takes turns working the booths, so nobody misses too much. We get a lot of people from nearby towns, and a few from farther away, like Burns and Boise."

"Are you going this year?" He'd moved closer, until he was looming over her, almost touching her.

She shrugged. "I don't know. A lot depends on how Pop is that day." She allowed her head to fall forward, her back to relax, until she was slumped over the rail. "I still don't feel much like a party, and that's what the May Fest is. A big party."

"Any chance of your changing your mind?" Now his voice was even softer. It tempted her, even as his arm slipped around her waist. "Show a little hospitality to a stranger in town, perhaps?"

His fingers tilted her chin up, and she had not the strength—nor the inclination—to resist.

"I…Pop…I'll see if someone can come in…" She stopped stammering her capitulation as his fingers tightened on her chin and he turned her head to the side.

"Who did that to you?" he demanded, his voice no longer soft, but hard and insistent. His fingers touched her swollen cheek, soothing rather than hurting. A faint tingle seemed to radiate from the point of contact.

"Pop," she said. "Pop did it."

INTERVAL

Useless Carruthers deterioration virtually complete, no further benefit obtainable. Difficult to maintain contact.

Potential hazard to replacement?

Terminate association?

Energy trickle from Loring anger. Inadequate for survival, but advantageous to environmental enhancement.

Long term use contraindicated. Undependable and erratic...

Possible reserve for translocation of mineral salts, however. Consider...

Utilize all feasible resources to prevent dissociation...

NINE

Your own father blacked your eye?" Gus felt murderous rage that a father could so abuse his own daughter.

"Wait!" She fought to free her chin from his grasp. "Please. Listen to me. He didn't mean to."

Aware that he held her tightly enough to leave a few bruises himself, he released her, but he wrapped his arms around her and pulled her close to his chest. While all he'd wanted from her a few minutes ago was a kiss or two, now he wanted her trust. Senile or not, if her father was abusing her, she needed his help.

"Tell me," he commanded, and wondered why he cared so much.

"Sometimes Pop gets violent." Her words vibrated against his chest. "He's a gentle man. You know, he never spanked me when I was growing up, rarely even scolded me."

She was silent for several minutes, until he began to believe she would tell him no more.

"I think the irritability was the first indication I saw that there was something wrong." Her voice became even huskier. "That and the forgetfulness."

Gus stroked her hair, tangling his fingers in its silky length. Once again he felt a ghostly tingle.

"He couldn't sit still, and little things bothered him. He began to swear a lot." Pulling away, she looked up at him, and the bruise was darker than a shadow on her pale cheek. "You've got to understand that Pop was an old-fashioned gentleman. He believed that swearing was a sign of ignorance—people who swore showed their lack of a better vocabulary. So, while he might let loose with an occasional 'damn' at work, he never, *never* used bad language at home."

Her eyes looked into the distance—or the past. Gus saw upwelling tears glimmering in the moonlight.

"He started to use a lot of really gross language, just a word or two at first, then nearly all the time." Again that shaken head. "That's when I finally accepted that something more than grief for my mother was affecting him and took him to the doctor."

"Just how violent does he get?" He didn't care why her father was abusing her, but he was certain it had to be stopped.

"He's wild, rather than violent. He'll throw things, or pound on the walls, but he's never raised a hand to me."

"Until tonight?"

"Not even tonight. I was trying to get him into bed, and he was struggling. This…" She touched her cheek. "…was as much my fault as his. I walked right into it."

"The truth?" He was still skeptical and let it show in his voice.

"Absolutely. I can't believe Pop would ever strike me on purpose, no matter how bad he gets."

The certainty in her voice told him more than her words. Gus relaxed and let her pull free of his loose embrace when she tried.

"We've been gone too long. I've got to get back."

He followed when she turned toward the park, content to watch pale light and deep shadow defining her slim shape as she walked ahead of him. How could he have ever thought she was middle-aged? Her skin was soft and firm, her body lithe, her hair molten bronze. He could dive into her bottomless blue-gray eyes and never come up.

"I hope you'll think about going to the May Fest with me," he said as they slowly walked the last little way to her home. "After all, you're a native, and I'm a newcomer." He did his best to look forlorn.

She chuckled. It was tentative, as if her chuckle muscles were out of practice.

"I'll tell you what. If I can get Milly to stay with Pop for a couple of hours, I'll go. But I won't be able to stay long, because she'll want to see Ben holding court."

"Ben?"

"Ben Kemp. Your landlord's son. He's a real live wire. I think the teachers might have nominated him as Consort out of desperation to get him involved in something harmless." Again that unpracticed chuckle. "At Halloween, a lot of the farm families bring their kids into town to trick-or-treat. One year— Ben couldn't have been more than ten or eleven—he and some of the older boys set up a speaker downtown and played a tape of shrieks, groans and howls at the highest volume. Most of the littlest trick-or-treaters were too frightened to go anywhere.

"Last year Ben and his friends ran around in sheets and glow-in-the-dark skeleton costumes, scaring the wits out of those kids who were brave enough to be out." They were at her gate, and she turned to look up at him, a smile on her face. "I shudder to think what they'll do next." She held out her hand, as if expecting him to shake it. "Thank you for walking with me. I hadn't realized how lonely I was."

Without a second thought, Gus pulled her into his arms.

Her face lifted, flower to his sun, ready for his kiss. Gently, he tasted her lips, wondering if she was as sweet as his memory told him. As he took her mouth, she sighed, the whisper of sound an aphrodisiac of the highest order. Her breasts against his chest were full and tempting, bringing him to immediate readiness.

He had to have her! Gus deepened the kiss.

Instead of pulling away, she pressed herself to him, cradling his male flesh against her soft belly. Her fingers dug into his shoulders, pulling him closer. He clasped her bottom in his big hands, lifting her. With his tongue, he explored her mouth, the slick ivory of her teeth, the thrusting arrow of her tongue, the hot, wet depths of inner cheeks. He felt her hands sliding beneath the collar of his shirt, tunneling through his hair. Her legs wrapped around his, bringing the feminine center of her hard against him, so close that, without their clothing, they would join in an instant.

As he lost himself in her, Gus was only peripherally aware of light sweeping across the yard. But she noticed, and immediately pulled away, unwrapping her glorious legs and leaving off her frantic search for entry under his shirt. He released her at once.

She took one step backwards and turned, leaning against the post beside her front gate.

"I can't believe this," she said, her voice a thready imitation of its usually husky contralto. As she spoke, headlights swept over them again and a car approached slowly, its tires rasping against the gravel.

Gus looked over his shoulder, recognized the roof silhouette of Lyle Curran's patrol car.

"You'd best go in," he said, not sure just how possessive Lyle might be of Sally. They'd seemed pretty close that day they'd been together in the café.

He was aware he was still an outsider, no matter that his help had been accepted with the May Fest.

Sally waved as Lyle cruised slowly past.

"I will," she said, "but not before I've said something."

He sensed, rather than saw, the nervous twisting of her hands. This time he recognized it as merely a symptom of her uncertainty, not as a sign of anxiety.

"I'm listening."

"I don't want you to do that—kiss me—again. I can't handle it. Not now, with everything else I have to deal with."

"I hadn't expected it to be like that. Not the first time," he said, "and not tonight, either." He sought the words to make her understand he was as confounded as she at what happened every time they touched. "Oh, I wanted to kiss you, I won't deny. But just a kiss. Not an explosion."

She shook her head, her hair swirling around her shoulders.

His fingers remembered the feel of it, his nose the scent of it.

"I'm scared," she whispered. "You...it...this...this hunger I feel. It frightens me." Lifting her head, she stared at him, although the darkness kept him from reading whatever message her eyes held. She sounded puzzled. "I'm not widely experienced, but I don't think most people ever feel anything like an electrical shock whenever they touch."

"Yeah. Me, too." He was probably as experienced as the average guy, and he'd never reacted to a woman as he did to her. As he was reacting now, at this very moment. Her voice tickled his ears, her faint scent tempted his nostrils, and her nearness made his arms long to hold her.

"Will you promise?"

"Promise?" He had all he could do to hold his desire in check. How could he follow what she was talking about?

"Not to kiss me again like that? Please?"

"I'll try," he said, thinking that the only way he would be able to leave her alone was to go away. "Good night." He went down one step, then another. "Good night." He took one last look back at her before he forced himself to turn and walk away.

Hands in pockets, Gus headed back toward downtown, while doing his best not to think about Sally Carruthers.

He'd managed to escape the group indulging in a post-meeting beer at the Chalk Pit after the May Fest meeting. But he'd been too restless to return to his adequately comfortable apartment above Kemp's Drugs. For the past three years he had deliberately avoided interacting with many people at one time. Ever since leaving Hartford, he'd deliberately sought jobs where he could work alone, or with only one or two other people. A drifter was always on the outside anyway, so it had been easy for him to remain socially and emotionally isolated.

Tonight, at the meeting, he'd found himself being sucked into the town's social structure like it was so much quicksand. His halfhearted objection had been to no avail. Before they adjourned to the tavern, he was counted as part of the town's movers and shakers.

Entirely without one word of assent from him. All he'd agreed to do was help police up the park after the crowds went home. Without being aware of it, he was appointed Clean-up Committee chairman, with responsibility for getting volunteers to help him.

The funny thing was, for the first time since he'd started running, he wanted to stay.

SALLY WOKE SOMETIME IN THE NIGHT, STIFF, ACHING AND IN TEARS. The awful tragedy of a dream clung to her until she could not stop the shuddering sobs.

A long time she wept, not even sure of what she was mourning, until shreds of the dream came back.

Momma had been there, and both her grandmothers. Her Grandfather Carruthers, Uncle Eddie and Jackie Fisher, who'd drowned when he and Sally were in the third grade. Each had appeared, stared at her with sad eyes, and turned to walk slowly away until they disappeared into a glowing, cloud-streaked horizon.

When she stood alone on a featureless plain Jeff, her ex-husband, appeared. He, too, stared at her, but he didn't walk after the others. Instead, he shook his head, as if to apologize, and stepped around her to walk in the other direction.

Feeling as if her feet were caught in cold molasses, Sally turned to see where he was going.

In that direction was another glowing horizon, but verdant, broken by the profiles of tall trees and snow-covered mountains. Jeff never looked back as he approached it, and soon he was gone and she was alone.

Alone and filled with a sense of abandonment. That must have been when the tears began, for she still felt the residue of that terrible emptiness. She closed her eyes in the darkness, knowing there had been more to the dream but unable to remember.

Perhaps she should not try, because whatever had followed had only intensified the soul-searing grief she was feeling. She forced herself to relax, working on one muscle group at a time, the way she'd learned in a meditation class she'd taken in college. Slowly, the inner ache let go, and slowly, she drifted toward sleep.

This time she knew what was happening. It was almost as if she were awake, watching herself in a film projected on the ceiling. She still stood on the plain, still felt more alone than she would have thought possible. Movement caught her attention— two movements, one to each side.

First, to her left, a figure approached as if carried on a moving walkway. Pop. Dear Pop, looking young and vital as he still did in her memories. As he approached, he aged, until the man she saw was the shambling shell she cared for every day. But his eyes—his eyes were still intelligent, not empty and blank.

He came very close, until she could almost touch him with the hand she instinctively reached out. He smiled, shook his head.

"I'll be going soon," he said, but his lips were not moving, his smile was undisturbed. "You're a good girl, and I love you." And in the blink of an eye, he was swept off in the direction all the others except Jeff had gone.

Before she could react, another figure advanced on her right. This one was formless, its shape shifting and flowing, until she wasn't sure which of the many streams of glowing light belonged to it and which were part of the background. The light creature came close, surrounded her, enveloping her within its rainbow nucleus, suffusing her with its essence.

It enfolded her, cherished her, sheltered her. And then it spoke, voicelessly, yet she heard in every cell of her body.

"Stay…sojourn…linger…bide…stay. STAY!" it said. "Carruthers…need. Carruthers…essential. Stay. Remain. Fundamental. Belong. Carruthers belong…belong…belo-o-o-ng-g-g…"

Sally knew when the hallucination ended and true sleep began because she felt it overtake her and surround her. The light creature was gone, but its essence remained, filling the emptiness within her. She knew, without a doubt, that as long as she stayed within the luminous entity—as long as its essence stayed within her—she would never be alone again.

But in the morning, she had the real world to deal with. Pop couldn't seem to move his right arm or leg. His face, lately slack unless he was in one of his violent spells, seemed even slacker, and his breathing was…different. He plucked at the sheets with his left hand, mouthed meaningless syllables along with saliva.

Sally called Dr. Berman, who was in surgery and unavailable. His office would have him call back as soon as possible.

"Oh, God, Pop, I don't know what to do," she muttered as she rolled him to one side so she could get clean bedding beneath him. She spread a fresh sheet over him and laid a light blanket on top. "There. Will you be all right until I can figure out what to do?"

Her father lay unspeaking, more oblivious than ever to his surroundings.

She was certain he'd had a stroke, but knew there was nothing she could do. Dr. Berman had warned her this could happen, had told her that anything medical science could do would only prolong his life, not make it better. Not restore her father to what he had been.

But I have to do something!

She tried to remember if there was anyone in town with medical training of any kind and came up blank. If only she'd stayed home last night. Although, Pop had seemed all right when she'd checked on him before she went to bed.

She should've gotten up to check again when she awoke from that nightmare.

"I'll be going soon." She remembered those words, and the peace they'd seemed to bring her. Now they scared her.

Was he dying at last? Was that why he was so different this morning?

If he died, she'd be free. She could go back to her job, go back and try to pick up the pieces of her life. She could…

Oh, God! What am I thinking? She should be worrying about her father instead of wishing him into his grave.

Sally nearly jumped out of her skin at the sound of the doorbell. She gave Pop one last look to make sure he was quiet and dashed to the door.

"Good morning," Gus said over the top of an enormous box. "Ardith had car trouble yesterday and didn't get these delivered. Where do you want them?"

"What? Ardith? I didn't order…Oh, yeah, the ribbons." She remembered Milly asking for the use of her dining room table again. Stepping aside, she motioned him inside. "In the dining room, I guess. I'll let Milly take care of them."

She led him through the parlor and into the dining room, turning on lights as she went. Although she'd begun leaving the blinds open, the windows were so overgrown with Virginia creeper on the north side of the house that little light entered.

He set the box on the floor beside the big table.

"There you go." He straightened and waited, as if expecting something.

Sally started out of her worried daze.

"Oh. Thanks." She looked at him, wondering if his hair actually glowed from within. Whenever he came into her house, he brought light and life with him.

He smiled, that heart-stopping smile he rationed so carefully. "I've got time for coffee."

Somehow, those innocent words were the final straw. She burst into tears.

Immediately, Gus had her in his arms, holding her safe, protecting her with his strength and his warmth. "What is it, Sally? What's the matter?"

"Pop," she sobbed. "It's Pop. Something's wrong."

"Where is he?"

She led him to Pop's room, controlling her sobs now but still aware of a painful tightness in her chest.

Gus walked to her father's bedside and looked at him. He touched Pop's slack cheek, lifted his right hand and let it drop a few inches to the bed.

"Has he ever been like this before?"

She shook her head.

"He's sometimes lethargic, occasionally uncoordinated, but he's never been so…so limp before."

"You've called the doctor." It was an assumption, not a question.

"He's at the hospital, in surgery. He'll call when he can." She wrung her hands. "I couldn't really say it was an emergency. I mean, Pop doesn't seem to be in pain, and his pulse is steady and he doesn't—"

"Hush," he said. With one arm he pulled her close while he held her hands until they stilled their nervous clutching. "Isn't there anyone here in town with some sort of medical training?"

"Not since Mildred Jones died. She was a nurse."

Gus seemed lost in thought. Finally, he said, "Stay with your father. I'll see what I can do."

For what seemed like forever, Sally sat beside Pop's bed, holding his limp hand and staring at him. He lay without moving, his breath stertorous, his skin pale and waxy. She wanted to do something, anything, but was afraid to leave him for more than a few minutes. If only she'd checked on him in the night.

When Gus finally returned she jumped to her feet, almost knocking the coffee cup from his hands.

"Where did you go? What did you do?"

"Drink this." He thrust the cup into her faintly trembling hands. When she'd taken a careful sip, he told her, "I called Lyle Curran. He'll be here in a few minutes. He's a certified EMT."

"I didn't know that." Why had Lyle never told her?

"Drink your coffee." Gus pushed her back into her chair. "You look like you need it."

Sally had handled her mother's lingering illness, her painful, drawn-out death. For five years and a little more, she'd watched Pop deteriorate, seen him lose, bit-by-bit, everything that made him human. And she'd coped, because she had to. Because she chose to.

Suddenly, she couldn't seem to cope anymore.

She looked up at Gus Loring, thinking how strong and dependable he appeared.

INTERVAL

Carruthers contemplates departure when useless genitor discorporates...

Remedy required. Passive collaboration undesirable. Inducement entails cooperation...

Concentrate energy attempt communication...

Contact!

Rejoicing!

TEN

G US STAYED WITH SALLY. HE DROVE HER TO ONTARIO BEHIND the ambulance that eventually arrived for her father, held her hand while Dr. Berman examined Will Carruthers and, later, while she waited for the doctor's diagnosis. Wishing he were anywhere else, he stayed because he couldn't abandon her when she needed him. Not and live with himself.

"I'd like to keep him for two or three days," the doctor said when he joined Gus and Sally in the small lounge at the end of the hall. "Long enough to see him stabilized, anyway."

"Is he going to be all right, Jim?" Gus heard the tears hovering at the edge of Sally's voice, but she was in control, as she had been ever since she recovered from that one brief, intense storm of weeping this morning.

"It's hard to say. He could recover almost completely from this CVA—stroke—but you know he's not going to get any better." Dr. Berman rubbed his upper lip several times, as if trying to come to a decision. "It's more likely he'll have some debility. I think it's time you considered putting him where he can get professional care."

Gus saw Sally stiffen.

"I can take care of him. I took care of Mom."

"Sure you can," Berman said. "That's why you look like something the cat dragged in."

Gus glared. Where'd he get off, saying things like that about Sally?

"I didn't sleep well last night." Sally's square little chin set and her magnificent eyes glowed with determination. "And I didn't have time for a shower this morning."

Berman sat down on the other side of her and slipped an arm around her. If he hadn't been close to sixty, Gus might have been tempted to question his actions.

"Sally, you've lost a good ten pounds since I last saw you, and you look twenty years older..."

Was the man blind? Sally's figure was perfect, and her face was as young and unlined as a girl's.

"...and so tired one good puff would blow you onto your knees. Not to mention the fact that Will's getting more uncontrollable." He touched the bruise on her cheek.

"I'm fine," she insisted.

Gus couldn't argue with the doctor's concern about her father's violence. He'd lain awake for hours last night, wondering if there was anything he could do to keep her from being injured again. And if he did, wouldn't she depend on him even more? He forced his attention back to the argument between her and the doctor.

"I'll make a deal with you," Berman said. "If Will's condition stabilizes, I'll let you take him home..." He held up a hand as Sally started to respond. "Let me finish. I'll let you take him home, on one condition."

"Anything. You know how Pop would hate being anywhere else."

"I doubt he'd notice."

Based on his own observations, Gus silently agreed.

"Don't say that! Pop knows where he belongs. He'd...he'd die if he had to live anywhere else."

"Sally, he's going to die anyway." Berman's voice was gentle, patient. "Sooner or later."

She squeezed her eyes shut for a moment, shook her head. "Not soon." she said. Her voice was strong, firm, as she looked the doctor in the eye. "Not soon."

Gus wondered if it was a prayer or a cry of defiance.

"What's the condition?"

"That you'll get someone in for at least eight hours a day." Shaking his finger in her face, Berman repeated, "Eight hours a day, not just overnight, Sally. I want you to have help with him so you can have a life of your own. You need to be getting outdoors, being with people, instead of walling yourself up in that dark old house and spending your youth on what's left of Will."

"I've called the employment agency. They sent me two people to interview. The first one was a tiny little woman who'd never be able to handle Pop when he's upset. The other...well, let's just say she wasn't what I was looking for."

Dr. Berman held up his hand. "Juana Dominguez is a practical nurse. She's about my age, and strong. She used to work here, but when her husband died, she decided she wanted a job that would let her live in. The man she was taking care of went into a nursing home just last week, and I know she's looking for another situation. She'll take good care of your father, Sally. I promise you."

Sally chewed her lower lip and wrung her hands.

Gus wanted to take them in his and stop their nervous twisting. Instead he said, "Do you want to meet Ms. Dominguez before you decide?"

"Yes," she said. "Yes, I'd like that."

Berman went to call the practical nurse and arrange for the meeting.

Sally looked up. Her eyes were wide and troubled, her hands clasped tightly together, knuckles white. "I really don't have any choice, do I?"

"It's the right thing to do," he said, knowing she needed reassurance.

Hell! I don't know what's the right thing to do any more now than I ever did! Maybe taking him home is the worst thing she could do. What if he hurts her again?

POP HAD BEEN HOME FROM THE HOSPITAL FOR THREE DAYS WHEN Sally finally decided to take advantage of having someone in the house. Although Juana was competent, compassionate, cheerful and all those other qualities that describe the perfect nurse, Sally still worried about neglecting her father. Look what had happened when she'd ignored him for just one night.

But this morning, the last Friday in April, was simply too glorious to spend indoors. She'd gone out in the dew-wet dawn and begun washing windows. This afternoon after school, Buster was coming by to help trim the hedges. Yesterday she'd made a hurried trip to the Post Office and had noticed how spiffy the rest of the town looked. Even the boarded-up stores on Main Street looked fresh, as if the whole town was putting on its Sunday clothes for the May Fest, only eleven days away.

Today, since she didn't have to hurry home, she planned to treat herself to a long, leisurely lunch. Perhaps Gus would be there. She wanted to thank him for his help the day of Pop's stroke.

He wasn't.

Lyle was in his usual seat, the front-facing bench of the last booth. Both Roy Gilbert and Arne Lundquist were on their stools, where they'd been sitting every time Sally had come in to the café for almost six years. Roy and Arne hadn't spoken for four times that long—ever since Arne's daughter Erma and Roy's son Randy had gotten divorced—so the seat between them was empty.

"How's that nurse workin' out?" Georgina said when Sally slid into the booth with Lyle. The constable wasn't in uniform this morning, but he still was handsome as the day was long. Just because she couldn't feel more than brotherly love for him didn't mean she couldn't enjoy his good looks.

"I think she's going to be a godsend," she admitted, although it had taken her a couple of days to reach that conclusion. "Having her in the house, even when she's not officially on duty—well, let's just say I sleep better than I have for a long time."

"Milly said she's some kind of kin to Pete Gomez's wife," Lyle said, after Sally had ordered the beef stew.

"A great-aunt, I think. Lupe Gomez called yesterday to invite her to Sunday dinner." Grimacing, Sally set her coffee cup down after a single bitter sip.

The door opened. She didn't need to turn around to know that Gus Loring had come in. She felt his presence as if he'd reached out and touched her.

Lyle waved him to join them. "I've got to be on my way, and Sally shouldn't have to eat alone." He stood, letting Gus slide into his place. "The liver and onions are good today."

With a touch to the brim of his western hat, he was gone.

"I haven't had liver and onions in years," Gus said.

"I never have. I'm not even sure I want to sit at the same table as someone who'd eat them."

"You sat with Lyle." His almost-grin raised her internal temperature about ten degrees.

She pulled herself together. "He was eating pie when I sat down." For lack of anything else to do with her hands, she sipped her coffee again. Immediately, she regretted it—the bitter brew burned all the way down. "I was hoping to see you," she said, as soon as she could speak.

He raised his eyebrow but didn't reply. There was something different—something distant—about him, for all his superficial friendliness.

"I wanted to thank you for your help the other day. I don't know what I would have done without you."

"You'd have managed." He sounded almost angry. "If I hadn't been there, you would have done just fine."

"Well, of course I would have," she said, irritated at his rejection of her gratitude, "sooner or later. But having you there meant a lot to me."

Georgina set her lunch before her, and she used the interruption to deal with her irritation. After the first bite of the stew, she said, "No matter what you think, I couldn't have coped as well without your help. I'll be glad to do whatever I can to return the favor."

"You don't owe me anything," he said, his voice harsh, "so let's just forget about it." He set his coffee cup down so hard some sloshed over onto the table.

Sally stared, confused. "But, Gus—"

"Forget it, I said." He stuck the menu back behind the napkin holder. "Liver and onions," he said to Georgina. He stood, reached for the copy of *The Oregonian* that lay on the counter and sat back down, opening the newspaper between them.

Sally wondered why she'd ever thought him a nice man.

Gus knew he was being a real bastard. He could have politely accepted her thanks and simply said he'd be too busy to have much time for a social life for a while.

Or something—anything—to make damned sure she didn't ask him for any more favors. Instead, he'd probably made her so mad she'd stay as far away as she could from him.

Well, wasn't that what he wanted?

No. What he wanted was to take her to bed and make love… have sex with her until neither of them could do more than lie in a boneless heap of satiation. She was under his skin, that was for sure. And the only way to get her out was—

Georgina batted at the newspaper, startling him.

"Here's your dinner. Now put that paper down and pay attention to your food."

Sally still sat across from him, but she was looking at her plate, not at him. Her fingers were crumbling her roll, making a pile on top of the nearly untouched stew.

Gus ignored her and picked up his knife and fork. Liver and onions had never smelled so good before.

Just as he lifted a forkful of the first delectable bite to his mouth, Sally looked up at him. Her huge eyes shimmered with unshed tears.

"I really feel sorry for you," she said. "You must be in incredible pain to want to hurt other people so much."

While Gus stared, she tossed her napkin beside her plate and slid out of the booth.

"Gotta run, Georgina," she said, her voice too high and too carefree. Waving and speaking briefly to others in the café, she made her quick escape.

The forkful of liver and onions was still suspended just before Gus's mouth. He took it in.

Was it shame that made it taste bitter as gall?

Sally honestly didn't know why she even bothered to be nice to Gus Loring. He was the crankiest man!

Well, she wasn't going to worry about it. Now that Juana was here to take care of Pop, she had a lot of catching up to do, and not just with her work for Frank Tsugawa.

She was really ashamed to have the house looking so bad. Everyone else in Whiterock made an effort to keep the town presentable, even when they had to close their businesses. Look at the hardware store, for instance. When it came time for Gene Alpin to retire, none of his children had been interested in returning to become the fourth generation in the family business. Gene hadn't found a buyer, although he'd advertised. So on the day last year when he turned sixty-five, he'd simply walked out the door and locked it behind him.

But Gene must still be paying for upkeep on the building because its painted façade wasn't too faded. Behind clean windows, a display still invited people to buy hammers and cake pans and ladders. She looked inside as she passed, seeing that no dust dimmed the shiny tools and utensils.

And look at Max Guthrie's law office, with its red door and the purple-and-gold trim around the long, narrow windows. She had to smile. Max would have been happier a hundred years ago, when his velvet-collared jackets and paisley ascots wouldn't have been so startling. His legal secretary, Edna Wallace, waved from behind her typewriter as Sally walked by. She returned the wave but didn't stop. Until she was certain Juana could handle Pop, she didn't want to stay away from the house too long.

Grip greeted her with a fake-fierce growl as she passed his yard, and Elizabeth Alpin waved from her seat at the front window. Again she waved back, reminding herself to get over to see Mrs. Alpin soon.

"My, but your roses look good this year," she told the bulldog. "I don't think I've ever seen that red bush so full of flowers."

Her roses—her mother's roses, actually—had been paltry the past couple of years. They'd never been a match for Mrs. Alpin's, but they didn't deserve to be neglected, either. That was something she could remedy.

She worked in the yard all afternoon, making discouragingly little progress at turning the bramble patch in the backyard into a semblance of a rose garden while Buster attacked the hedge. The fence surrounding it sagged in places, the paint on its pickets scaling and weathered. Half a dozen of the pickets had fallen off and others were held in place only by the tangled thicket of long-unpruned canes. In the center, the gazebo sat like a raddled *grande dame* whose beauty was fled, fortune wasted and hopes dead.

This had been her childhood secret place where she'd gone to dream of a bright future.

Stop that! You've been wallowing in self-pity so long it's become a habit. You chose to stay. Now think about someone besides yourself for a change.

Twice when she went inside for a drink Juana was sitting with Pop, holding his hand while they watched soap operas.

The second time, the practical nurse explained, "He's more quiet when I touch him. I think he gets lonely."

Sally felt the acid burn of Juana's innocent words the rest of the afternoon.

I think he gets lonely.

She hacked at a particularly long rose cane, not caring when it whipped back and caught the skin of her upper arm—she was already a bloody mess from her war with the roses. *And you deserve to be*, a niggling little voice told her, *the way you neglected your father.*

She couldn't even argue with the voice. When had she forgotten that it was as important to show Pop how much she loved him as it was to keep him clean and well-fed?

"I won't ask who's winning."

The words came from behind her, but she didn't turn around. She'd be damned if she'd let him have another try at battering her emotions. Before she was more than coldly polite to Gus Loring, he was going to have to apologize.

Grovel, even.

If she had any sense, no amount of groveling would get him back into her good graces.

She aimed the loppers at another rose cane, shoving them into the twisted, tangled mass and gaining herself another long scratch on the back of her hand.

"Sally?" His voice was low, gentle. Pleading.

"Go away." *Why should I let you mess with my head?* For that was just what he'd been doing, with his ax-handle-wide shoulders, his voice as sensuous as the feel of fur on naked skin. She cut viciously, and saw she had taken a branch bud she'd intended to keep.

"I came to apologize." He sounded as if he was right behind her.

"Huh!" she said, grabbing the severed cane and pulling, never mind that she also had hold of a monster thorn. "You've got a lot to apologize—" The cane came free and she staggered backward, full into him. "—for!"

His arms went around her, even as he fell backward. He managed to twist as they fell so she ended up lying atop him, nose-to-nose, chest-to-chest.

Thigh-to…

"Don't move!" he cried as she brought her leg up for leverage.

She stopped the motion as she heard his words, but she didn't get off him. He felt too good, all hard muscles and warm, hard man.

"Oh, God," she sighed, just before she gave in to the urge she felt every time she saw him.

She kissed him, tasting the faint scent of gasoline on him, feeling the slight, gritty film of sweat from his day's work in an environment full of dust and oil.

She liked it. He smelled like a man ought to smell—not like a garden or a pine forest or a civet cat in heat.

"I wasn't going to speak to you until you groveled," she said, and nipped his lower lip.

"Grovel?" He settled her more comfortably along his body.

"Something like that." She laid a line of kisses across his cheek, enjoying the slight prickle of his day's growth of beard against her lips. Her husband had always been well-groomed, immaculate and scented with spices and musk. She'd once thought him sexy, but never so exciting as Gus was, right here, right now.

His hand stroked up and down her back. His leg had somehow insinuated itself between hers.

"So, do I have to crawl, or will a little writhing do the trick?" As he spoke, he moved his hips, thrusting himself hard against her, holding her bottom so she could do nothing but respond.

"Ah!" A bolt of desire went through her, so intense, so irresistible she could feel her body shake with its force. Even as she cried out, his hand slipped around her nape, holding her tied-back hair with a firm grasp, bringing her mouth down to his again, this time with no teasing, no tantalizing. There was no play in his kiss, only promise. He showed her, with his tongue, what he wanted, what he intended.

His hand slid up under the loose sweatshirt she wore, stopped at the back fastener of her bra. With practiced ease, he opened the hooks. One quick movement and he had her on her side, was looming over her, his big hand hot on her back, her midriff. The undersides of her breasts.

He teased, now. His fingers stroked the tender flesh of her breasts, approaching but never touching her straining nipples. Releasing her hair, he swept her shirt up and pushed her loosened bra aside, revealing her breasts to the spring breeze and his eyes. His hands kneaded and caressed her, and his mouth explored her, starting at the elastic waist of her canvas pants, nibbling its way up the sensitive skin of her midriff. He laved the undersides of her breasts, first one then the other, and worked his way up the center.

Sally knew she was the one writhing, and didn't care. She didn't want him to stop, wanted him to discover nipples aching with the need to be touched, to be taken into his hot mouth and suckled.

When he finally answered her wordless demand, she thought she'd die with the pleasure of it. Her whole being concentrated in her breasts as he gave each his whole attention. A sense of waiting germinated in her belly, until she heard herself chanting, over and over, "Now. Now. Now."

"Not yet," he growled, laying one last kiss on her wet nipple. He rose onto his elbow, leaving her lying boneless beside him. "Why does this always happen?" he said, and stroked one lone finger down the valley between her breasts.

She felt it tremble, as if he was holding himself under tight control.

A line of goose bumps followed his touch and grew into shivers all over her body.

"I don't know," she whispered, unable to find the strength to be louder. "I was furious with you. I—I still am, but…"

"Yeah. But." He rolled over onto his back, not quite touching her. Lifting one arm as if it weighed a ton, he laid it over his eyes.

After a long silence, he said, "It's almost as if there's some... some *force*, pushing us together..."

"I know. It's like a switch gets turned on. Or something." Sally was suddenly aware that the sun was almost gone, and the grass beneath her was cold and damp. Her shivers increased and became real. She sat up and pulled her sweatshirt down, not bothering to refasten her bra. "I wanted you the first time I saw you," she confessed.

"You had on those shapeless sweats and your hair needed washing." His mouth twitched. "I thought you were a dumpy middle-aged lady."

Before she could be insulted, he finally smiled and she forgave him almost everything.

"I figured I wanted you because I hadn't been with a woman for a long time. But it's more than that."

"And I thought it was because I haven't... Well, I've been divorced more than six years." She heard the wistfulness in her voice. She and Jeff had had many problems, but sex had never been one of them. She had missed that part of her marriage more than any other, but never enough to seek just any available man as a substitute.

Never before, anyway.

"I don't want to get involved," she said, and wondered if he would understand how little of her there was to share. Taking care of her parents had stripped her emotionally until she was dry and empty.

He lowered his arm and rolled onto his side again, facing her. With compelling green eyes he caught and held her gaze. "Neither do I, but that doesn't stop the wanting."

She closed her eyes because she knew the desire flaming in his would burn her to the core.

The next instant they opened involuntarily when he said, "So. How about it, Sally Carruthers? Do you want to see just how it could be, this passion we seem to excite in each other?"

She looked at him. Looked at his bright red hair, his eyes burning with an emerald flame. She let her gaze drift over his wide shoulders and deep chest, along the hard strength of his thighs and back to the ridge of flesh that still, incredibly, distorted his trousers.

I want to. I want to make love with this man and see what I've been missing. For she knew that making love with Gus Loring would be more than she'd ever known before, more than she could ever know again.

INTERVAL

Success! Yet energy usage extravagant!

Endurance indicated. Passion must continue, result in progeny...

Individual Carruthers ephemeral...

Perpetual energy accumulation dependent on recurring progeny...

ELEVEN

I WANT TO…" SHE ADMITTED.

"But."

"Exactly. But." She knew her smile was as wry as his. "All we've done since we met is climb all over each other or snarl." She reached toward him, wanting the security of his touch, but pulled her hand back. His touch gave her more than security, and she didn't need that kind of confusion right now. "There's so much I don't know about you."

It was as if shutters closed over his eyes. "What you see is what you get." All warmth was gone from his voice. "A delivery man. A mechanic."

"An Easterner." It wasn't really a question. Few people in this part of Oregon spoke with that fast, clipped style.

"Ayup," he said. "Once."

"What brought you to Oregon?"

He was silent for a long moment.

"Just lucky, I guess." With a single movement, he rolled to his feet. "Come on. You're going to catch your death, sitting on the damp ground." He pulled her up but didn't relinquish her hand once she was on her feet. Instead, he lifted it to his mouth and nibbled gently on her knuckles. "What happened to me before I came to Oregon hasn't anything to do with us. Can you trust me enough to believe that?"

She looked deep into his eyes. Not sure whether she was responding to the desire she read there or to the loneliness, she said, "Yes, Gus Loring, I trust you."

He turned her hand in his and kissed the palm, sending tremors throughout her body. "I can't offer you any promises, except that I'll try not to hurt you."

Hot breath warmed the wetted center of her hand.

"Right now, that's enough," she said, and was glad he wasn't asking for any sort of commitment.

I am glad. I really am. I've too much on my plate right now to get into a relationship.

"Where, then?" His expression told her he wasn't a patient man. "And when?"

"Here?"

As soon as she said it, she saw his refusal, and Sally wouldn't…couldn't go to his apartment. Not where anyone walking or driving down Main Street would see her entering the narrow stairway between the drugstore and the beauty shop. While she had no intention of hiding her feelings for him, her neighbors were entirely too interested in minding everyone else's business.

"I don't know, then." Suddenly the gist of their conversation felt all wrong to her. "Listen to us," she said, disgusted with herself. With him. "This isn't what I want. I won't make love with you just to scratch an itch."

"Why not?" He dropped her hand and stepped back.

She tried to read him again, but the lowering sun had cast them into shadow.

"I warned you, Sally Carruthers. I'm not making any promises. If you come to my bed, that's all it will be. Just to scratch an itch."

"Then I won't be there, Gus. I want at least friendship."

Friendship? He'd never be able to be friends with Sally Carruthers, Gus realized. The sparks between them would burn away any friendship before it could develop. What they had was passion, pure and simple, and she was kidding herself if she thought otherwise.

"You want me," he said, daring her to disagree.

"Yes," she admitted. "Yes, I want you. I ache with wanting you. I dream of you at night and wonder what your hands, your body would feel like against my skin." Her mouth twisted in a grimace of pain. "But unless we can go beyond simple lust, I can't have you."

"What do you want, then? You agreed we needed no promises, no commitments." He realized he was still holding her hand when she tried to pull it free. "Tell me!"

She led him around the corner of the house, to the front steps. "Sit down. Let's talk about this."

"There's nothing to talk about," he growled, wondering how he could sit. Her effect on him was strong and lasting.

"Then let's talk about us," she said, seemingly not put off by his growl. "What do you do for fun?"

He looked sideways at her. They were in the shadow of the house, since it faced east, and he really couldn't make out her expression. Out of the corner of his eye, he could see a young fellow hacking at the shaggy hedge with long-bladed shears. A good thing they'd had second thoughts. For now, anyway.

"Read." He shrugged. "Watch TV." What did he do for fun? He wasn't sure, since it had been a long time since he'd really had fun.

"What do you read?"

117

Damn, she was persistent.

"*Road and Track*," he said. "*Time* and *National Geographic*."

She was leaning back on the steps, her elbows propping her. His hands itched in memory of the soft wealth of her breasts, thrown into prominence by her position.

"And what TV shows do you watch?"

"Whatever's on." Again he shrugged. He honestly couldn't remember the last show he watched, although the TV had been on just last night. "Old movies. Sitcoms."

"Damn it, Gus! Don't just answer my questions! Tell me about yourself. Who is Gus Loring? What made you the way you are?"

"Enough!" He grabbed her upper arms and jerked her to him. "You want to know who I am? Okay, I'll tell you."

He shoved her back until she was at arms' length, but he didn't release her.

With enormous eyes—great blue-gray eyes that seemed to glow with an inner luminescence—she stared at him, her lips slightly parted.

"I killed my wife." Pain flooded his entire being.

Her eyes went even wider with shock.

Gus stood and turned his back on her. Forcing the words through a throat grown impossibly tight, he said, "Is there anything else you want to know about me?"

She didn't answer.

He walked away, down the sidewalk and into the road.

Stunned, Sally let him go. She couldn't lie to him and say his confession hadn't shaken her. Hadn't frightened her.

She knew, as she watched him disappear into the twilight, shoulders bowed in defeat, that he must have had a very good reason for whatever he did. Even killing his wife.

"My God!" she said when she heard her own thoughts, "I must be insane." There could never be an excuse for murder. Never.

Yet in the next instant, she understood the reason behind her outrageous thought. Gus Loring had asked her to trust him, and she did. For some reason, she trusted him enough to believe that he couldn't possibly have killed anyone, especially not his wife.

SALLY LET THE WEEKEND GO BY. SUNDAY AND MONDAY WERE Juana's days off, so she was too busy to do much more than care for Pop. Even though bedfast, he took enormously more attention than he had before his stroke. He was also calmer, although she wasn't sure that was necessarily a plus. He lay in his bed like a vegetable most of the time, his breathing shallow, his skin sallow and waxy.

This was what he would look like in his coffin, she realized. And while part of her—the selfish part—wished he would just go, and be done with an existence that couldn't matter to him anymore, the daughter who loved him hated seeing the vegetable her beloved father had become.

The following Tuesday she made sure she was in the Bite-A-Wee Cafe at noon, perched on a high stool in the kitchen, where she could see but not be easily seen. Sure enough, Gus came in about ten after twelve, taking the empty place between Arne and Roy. She sipped her iced tea and watched him, thinking how thick and strong the walls he'd built about him were.

He nodded to his neighbors, accepted the sports pages when Arne offered them, nodded when Georgina suggested the special. Then he buried himself behind the newspaper and ignored the conversation going on around him.

Sally listened. Most of the exchanges had to do with the May Fest. Who was working in which booth. Whose children or grandchildren were dancing. And especially, what the odds were that Ben Kemp would manage to pull something crazy before the day was over.

"Well, now, he's gonna be stuck on that throne most of the morning," Arne said, while picking his teeth, "but I'll give you dollars to doughnuts he's into some kind of mischief before sundown."

"Go on, now, Arne," Georgina said. "Benny wouldn't be half so ornery if you old fogies didn't expect him to be."

"My Rhoda says he's been just as meek as pie lately," Kate Garcia said. "Maybe he's outgrowing his wildness."

"I wouldn't put my money on it," Bob Larkin scoffed. Since Bob was well known to bet on anything and everything, it wasn't hard to see what he believed.

Gus seemed oblivious to the debate.

"Hey, d'ja hear Bill Holmes bought the old Anderson place?" Keith Rasmussen said. The apple grower wasn't one of the regulars in the café, but he dropped in every week or two.

"Bill Holmes?"

"Well, I'll be!"

"When'd that happen?"

"Hush up, everybody," Georgina called out. "Let the man talk." She grabbed a fresh carafe of coffee and began refilling cups.

The Anderson place had been sitting empty since Marvin's widow, Bertha, passed away the previous fall. There were no children. Their son had died in Viet Nam and their daughter in an auto accident a few years later. The only heirs were distant cousins who hadn't wanted an unprofitable truck farm in a dying little town in Oregon. The household goods had been sold at auction and the house, with its surrounding twenty acres, put on the market. No one in Whiterock had thought it would sell.

Sally strained her ears to hear what Keith had to say. So, Bill was coming home. She couldn't imagine why.

In the middle of the speculation about whether Bill would continue in his job as a heavy equipment manufacturer's rep or would find something that would keep him home nights—it was generally believed that his new young wife Mandy was a good reason for him to do the latter—Gus got up and left.

Sally had been listening so hard she almost missed his departure. She jumped off the stool and rushed after him. Surprised comments followed her, but she didn't care.

"Wait," she called once she was on the street. "Wait, Gus!"

He slowed but didn't stop. Neither did he turn around.

Sally caught up with him and had to walk around him so she could look at him.

"Do you still want me to go to the May Fest with you?" She'd thought a lot about everything that had happened during their last encounter and had decided the next move was up to her.

She was making it.

Gus stared at her, standing slightly breathless and flushed. How had he ever thought her plain?

He stared at her a long time, trying to understand where she was coming from. Finally he said, "Didn't you hear what I told you? I killed my wife."

"Yes, well, I'm sure you had a very good reason to," she said primly. And smiled.

"Lady, you are crazier than a loon," He felt an almost irresistible urge to smile back.

"That's why I'm here," she agreed. "Now, are you going to answer me?"

Gus had no choice. One way or another, he had to get this woman out of his system. Until he did, he would have no peace. He couldn't even run again as long as she held him here.

If only he knew what she wanted from him. After his confession, she should detest him, hate him, fear him.

Instead, she'd asked him for a date.

"Yes," he said, bowing to the inevitable. "I'd like that." As soon as he said the words, he knew they were the truest ones he'd ever spoken.

"Good," she said, her smile brilliant and heart-stopping. "Be at my house at nine Saturday morning."

And without another word, she turned and walked away, her walk free and swinging.

ARE YOU SURE YOU DON'T MIND MISSING THE MAY FEST, JUANA?"

"I'd rather have tomorrow off to spoil Lupe's babies, Sally. I'm too old to sit on the ground and eat junk food."

"Well, if you're sure." Sally stopped protesting, admitting to herself she was almost as excited as she used to be on Christmas morning. She would have the entire day with Gus.

They would have the night as well.

Feeling young and carefree, she walked along the hall to the front door and peeked out to see if he had arrived. The morning sun woke rainbows in the prisms she had hung in the narrow windows on either side of the door. She touched one and then the other, giving them a slight spin, and the shattered light flittered around the bright front hall like insubstantial butterflies.

Too excited to wait, she went outside and stood on the porch, breathing deeply. Lilacs, in purple and while masses all over town, perfumed the air. She caught a faint hint of cinnamon, probably from the bitterbrush that scattered its pale yellow bloom across the hillside behind the barn. And something else was there, too, a subtle mixture of mold and damp earth and new, green shoots.

She spread her arms wide, feeling as if she wanted to embrace the day. This morning the world felt new and full of promise.

She could almost feel that someday her life would be her own again.

"Good morning."

Sally started.

"Oh!" She laughed. "I was so wrapped up in nature I didn't even see you coming." How could any woman with life in her body fail to see his masculine beauty.

The high desert sun had given his normally pale skin a gentle golden tan, until his faint freckles had all but disappeared. For a moment, she had the fanciful notion he was sculpted of an exotic alloy of gold and copper and silver, with the green fire of his construction still burning in his eyes. Then he moved, and she knew that no cold metal could ever have the beauty of warm flesh and hot blood.

He wore a short-sleeved knit shirt of russet, tan slacks that hugged his tight buttocks and hid nothing of his strong thighs. Even the dark brown Docksiders on his feet spoke of something other than the deliveryman or mechanic he claimed to be. She almost asked him what he'd done in the East, but the memory of how he'd closed up earlier stopped the words before they could spill from her mouth.

Today she wouldn't worry about the past or the future. She would relish each moment as it came, with no expectations, no regrets.

He stood at the bottom of the steps, looking up at her. "You look like springtime itself." His voice was soft, just a little more than a whisper.

For the first time, Gus realized what a change spring had brought to Whiterock. It wasn't the lilacs, blooming in great masses all over town, or the apple orchards, whose pink-clad branches he could see from his apartment's window. It was Sally. She reminded him of a daffodil this morning, lifting her face to the sun. He held out his hand. "Let's go."

She came down the steps, smiling. Slipping her hand into his, she said, "I hope you haven't eaten breakfast."

"I meant to, but the café was closed."

"Of course, it was. Georgina and Jack let the town feed *them* one day a year."

"Jack?"

"Jack Maye, Georgina's cook. You mean you've never met him, after all the meals he's cooked for you?" She took his hand as they strolled along Fifth Avenue. When she waved at someone in the house on the corner, Gus looked in that direction. A gruff bark warned him to be cautious.

"Good morning, Grip," Sally said. "Your tulips are lovely this year."

The dog, a fat, elderly bulldog, barked again, this time more gently, as if acknowledging her compliment.

"You talk to dogs?" he said.

"Only to Grip. He's so proud of his yard. Wait until you see his roses."

He decided not to comment.

He snapped off a richly purple lilac spray as they passed the library and tucked it into the lemon-yellow band Sally wore around her head. "Since the café's closed, where are we eating?"

"At the Legion Hall." She plucked a sprig from the double white lilac at the corner and buried her nose in it. "Ummm. These are the sweetest ones in town. We got a start from this bush when I was a kid, but it just doesn't smell as good in our yard." Stopping him with a gentle hand on his chest, she worked the stem into his second buttonhole. "There! Now we're a pair."

Gus almost wished she could be right.

They turned down Main Street in comfortable silence, broken only when Sally greeted one or another of the people they met. He found he was enjoying the walk. Whiterock was becoming a special place to him, try as he might to resist its charm. It had a vitality most towns, big or little, lacked. The empty stores were surprisingly well-kept, their paint fresh and their windows sparkling clean. Most of them had some sort of arrangement behind the glass—displays of library books, exquisite examples of the Community Church Quilters' craft, even a mannequin wearing clothing of the early 70s. He wondered if that had been the last time the dress shop was open.

There was no litter on Whiterock's streets, and the trash barrels scattered along the few blocks of the business district were painted in whimsical designs. The people they met were friendly. Gus had never been anywhere he felt so welcome.

Oh, hell. Pretty soon you're going to decide this is some kind of modern Shangri-La.

Whiterock was just a town, like a thousand others in rural America. The only thing that made it special was Sally.

INTERVAL

Maintenance of glamour taxes capacity to utmost, may require additional concentration of scant resources...

Energy surge timely but inadequate.

TWELVE

I'M SURPRISED THEY DIDN'T GET YOU TO HELP WITH BREAKFAST," Sally said as she and Gus walked from the Legion Hall to the park, stuffed to the gills with home-cured ham, sourdough pancakes and coffee that tasted like coffee instead of diesel fuel.

"Nobody said anything," Gus told her, but he didn't go on to say that if they had, they would have come up short. He was a pretty fair hand with a spatula, but his involvement in Whiterock's May Fest was already too deep. He still wasn't quite sure how he'd let himself be appointed chairman of the clean-up committee.

"Look! They've got the pole up!" Sally pulled at his hand. All around them people were streaming along Main Street, laughing and calling greetings to each other. She led him through the gathering crowd to an open space on the open lawn halfway between the elk and the bandshell.

Everyone was gathered around a tall pole, topped by what looked like an old wagon wheel. Falling from the wheel were the colored ribbons he'd delivered to her house a couple of weeks ago, dozens of them.

"Isn't it lovely!"

Gus agreed, although he still wasn't sure exactly what a maypole dance consisted of. He followed Sally until she stopped under a big weeping willow.

"This is where we always sit, as far back as I can remember." Her expression sobered, and something darkened the happy expression in her eyes. "My grandfather planted this tree when I was too young to remember him doing it. See?" She pointed to a plaque almost buried in the grass close to the trunk.

Gus bent to read the words on stained, oxidized metal.

"Sally's Tree. In memory of her grandmother, Sara Marget Heineke Carruthers, 1910-1985."

He looked up to see tears in her eyes.

"She died when I was three days old." She was biting her lip.

He wanted to pull her close and comfort her, but instead he said, "Are you planning on sitting on the grass? You'll ruin your dress."

With a quick headshake, Sally recovered. "No, I was going to leave you here to save the place while I go back to the house for a blanket and our lunch."

"Lunch? You've got to be kidding!" He couldn't believe he'd eaten eight pancakes, but they'd been like nothing he'd ever tasted.

"Once the dancing starts, I won't want to leave. Will you stay here?"

Gus looked around. Recognizing a boy he'd seen hanging around the shop, he beckoned. "You want to earn a couple of bucks?"

The kid nodded, his eyes wide and his grin wider.

"Okay. You sit here and don't let anybody move in. We'll be back in a little while."

The kid flopped down on the ground, obviously not worried about grass stains on his jeans.

"Now—" Gus took Sally's arm. "—let's go get that blanket."

Sally enjoyed every step of the few minutes' walk back to her house. Nobody in her whole life had ever treated her as if she were too fragile and delicate to carry a blanket, cushions and a picnic cooler five blocks. Gus would have taken the entire burden if she hadn't insisted on carrying the blanket.

Its prickly nap was harsh against her arms, but she wouldn't have considered using anything else. As far back as she could remember they had used this old square of khaki wool whenever they went to the park. She'd had the dickens of a time finding it yesterday, for it had been a long time since she had picnicked. Finally she'd unearthed it in the attic, packed in a trunk with old wool comforters and her grandmother's afghans. It still smelled of mothballs, even though she'd hung it outdoors overnight, and then tumbled it on the dryer's air setting with a couple of fabric softener sheets.

The park was almost overflowing when they got back, but young Freddy Larkin was still holding their place under her tree. Gus made a big production out of searching his wallet. He finally handed Freddy a five-dollar bill.

"Thanks, mister," Freddy called over his shoulder as he sped away, running in the direction of the food booths.

"You're a nice guy, Gus Loring," she said, smiling.

He shrugged, as if to deny her statement. "The kid doesn't look like he has much fun." With an economy of motion, he soon had the blanket doubled and spread, with the two tasseled cushions at one end leaning against the squat little cooler full of sandwiches, veggies and fruit.

"How soon do the festivities begin?" he said, while reclining on his side and pulling one cushion under his head.

Sally checked her watch. "A half-hour or so, if they're on schedule." They never had been, but one could always hope.

Gus yawned. "Time for my morning nap. You want to wake me when something happens?"

His eyes closed, and his breathing slowly grew regular. She was both piqued that he would so rudely withdraw into sleep and flattered that he was comfortable enough with her to do so. She wasn't a bit sleepy, in spite of the enormous breakfast. After so many years of missing the May Fest, she wanted to see everything.

Gus looked younger asleep. His mouth lost its downward trend and the lines bracketing it softened, making him appear almost to smile. She found she wanted to touch him, to run a finger along his sensuous lips and down the straight line of his nose. Her fingers tingled, remembering how wiry and clinging his hair was as she'd combed through it.

Enjoying the view, she let her attention wander down his body, seeing the breadth of his shoulders and the flatness of his belly. He was unmistakably masculine, even in sleep. She tried to imagine what he looked like naked. Was his skin warm ivory with pale tan freckles, or pinkish, with the freckles only slightly darker?

She wondered if he would want the light on or off when they made love tonight.

As prickles ran down her arms, she turned half away, knowing that if she didn't she wouldn't be able to keep her hands off his sleeping body. What a sensation that would create.

In the next forty-five minutes, she saw people she hadn't seen for years, people she'd forgotten and people she'd just as soon forget. The turnout had to have exceeded the planners' wildest hopes.

I wonder why I can't remember any May Fests since the one when I was a sophomore in college. I must be getting old.

An icy shiver ran up her spine. Would she someday be like her father—all memories, good and bad, lost? *Don't think about it! Not now.*

In an effort to send her thoughts in a different direction, she forced her memories back to that earlier May Fest. The town had already lost many of its younger people, and a handful of the older ones as well. With no prospect of jobs locally and an hour's commute to Ontario, Whiterock simply wasn't a practical place to live.

Her parents had been optimistic about the situation.

"This won't last," her father had insisted.

But their faith had been misplaced. More than a decade had passed since then, and every year had seen more empty storefronts on Main Street, more abandoned houses in town. Before too much longer Whiterock would be little better than a ghost town.

A clash of cymbals and an extended drum roll told her that it was time. She turned to wake Gus, but he was already rolling upright and rubbing his eyes. She stood, knowing what was coming.

With the first notes of the National Anthem, he rose quickly. They stood together, not quite touching, while the flag was raised on the pole beside the bandshell. A new flag, without the frayed end she remembered.

The Whiterock Drum and Bugle Corps led the procession. There were far fewer members than when she'd played the cymbals—only two snare drums, the cymbals, the bass drum, five assorted horns and a single flute. Buster Holmes carried the flag, and three girls in red shorts and red-white-and-blue striped shirts carried a banner proclaiming this to be the 82nd Annual Whiterock, Oregon, May Fest.

Behind the corps, a black surrey carried Ben Kemp and Rhoda Garcia, both looking proud and excited and so grown up that Sally suddenly felt ancient. Rhoda's pink satin dress, as unsuitable as she still believed it to be, was perfect for her dark Latin coloring. The matching ruffled, flamenco-style shirt somehow made golden-haired Ben look dashing and debonair. Two white horses with pink bows on their harnesses pulled the surrey, and a huge spray of Mrs. Alpin's early pink roses decorated the back of it.

The American Legion was in the procession, with members from every branch of the armed services, and from every war since 1941. Jethro Kemp, in his powered wheelchair, led them. The Quilters' Guild marched two abreast, each of the four pairs carrying a beautiful quilt. There were two Red Cross volunteers in uniform, five members of the Malheur Mounted Sheriff's Posse and a red-nosed clown pushing a wheelbarrow, ready to pick up the inevitable results of horses in a parade.

The procession halted before the bandshell, and Mayor Maribelle Grayhawk stepped to the side of the surrey. With one on either arm, she escorted Rhoda and Ben up the decorated steps to the floor of the bandshell, where bunting decorated a low platform on which a velvet-draped throne sat. She curtsied to Rhoda and stepped back to let Ben hand the May Queen onto her throne. As Ben took his seat on a cushion at Rhoda's feet, the mayor handed her a scepter.

Rhoda smiled at the mayor, at Ben, and at her cheering subjects. She waved the scepter. "Let the festivities begin."

Maribelle and several other adults went to sit in folding chairs on either side of the throne. The paraders scattered to join friends and family all over the park. Soon, the crowed stilled, waiting.

Sally bit her lip as high, clear voices sounded somewhere off in the distance. The melody was "Greensleeves," but the words were those from a long-ago movie. Sally's throat burned as she heard the children sing of a "wondrous land" and a "home in the valley." As they approached the bandshell, they segued into "America the Beautiful."

Twenty-odd first-through-fourth graders from Whiterock Elementary School wove through the crowd, carrying a garland fashioned of native juniper and lilac clusters. As they reached the maypole, they circled around it. Boys and girls from the fifth and sixth grades came running from behind the bandshell, each pulling a long-tailed delta kite. The brightly colored kites fluttered like exotic flowers above the crowd. They, too, circled the maypole before leading the little ones back to the bandshell. They all sat along its apron, their legs and the garland dangling.

Gus nudged her. "Where did they all come from?"

"The children?"

He nodded.

"Every child who goes to Whiterock Elementary is expected to take part in the May Fest. The seventh and eighth graders are in the Drum and Bugle Corps. These are the other grades."

"I've never seen anything like this."

She had to agree. There were some things about Whiterock that were unique.

His sense of anticipation, small at first, and easily contained, grew as the day advanced. Gus was initially content to enjoy Sally's company, to feed his desire with small touches. While they watched the ceremonies in the bandshell, they sat close together, shoulders and hips brushing. Once she dug into the cooler and pulled out juice boxes. When he reached for his, he deliberately took her hand for a long, delicious moment. She looked into his eyes, her smoldering gaze full of promises.

The first maypole dance involved the children in the first four grades. Gus laughed, along with everyone else, as they wound ribbons haphazardly around the pole, the steps they'd practiced all week forgotten in their excitement.

While several adults were untangling the ribbons for the next dance, Mayor Maribelle called for the crowd's attention.

"I didn't realize Whiterock had a mayor," he said.

She chuckled, and this time sounded as if she was getting back into practice doing so. "Of course, we do! We're civilized."

Again she chuckled, and Gus felt his heart warming at the sound.

"Of course, it's mostly a ceremonial position," she said, "like now."

Maribelle announced the winners of the school spelling bee, the math bee and the reading competition. The winners—and there seemed to be one from each grade—proudly marched up onto the stage and received certificates from the mayor and kisses from either the May Queen or her Consort. Gus thought how his daughter would have loved to be among them.

It was the first time he had willingly thought of Emily since coming to Whiterock—and the first time he'd thought of her with anything but pain since—

He chopped off the thought before it could develop.

After applauding the winners as energetically as anyone, he murmured to Sally, "This is unusual. I guess I expected to be entertained."

She turned around, stared at him with surprise. "I can't think of anything more entertaining than watching the children being recognized for their accomplishments. I thought you understood. This is their day."

He held up his hands, delighted at the fire in her eyes. "Hey! I didn't mean I wasn't enjoying myself. I've just never seen a town do anything like this for its children before."

The music began just then, so he didn't quite catch her reply, but it sounded something like "More's the pity." She was just a little bit stiff as she sat beside him while the older schoolchildren did marginally better at the maypole dance. About halfway through, he slid closer to her and draped his arm across her shoulders. After an initial start, she softened and relaxed.

The lilac he'd tucked into her headband was wilted now, but its sweet scent blended with the honeysuckle of her perfume, filling his nose and eventually his whole being.

Again there was a ceremony. This time it was for athletic excellence. Gus wondered at a town that rewarded Frisbee-throwing and hopscotch right along with running and jumping.

"We used to have swimming awards," Sally told him, her breath warm on his ear, "until the state tested the creek and said it wasn't clean enough."

Considering how he'd driven through upstream pastures filled with cattle, Gus wasn't at all surprised. "You really need a pool."

"I think there's a savings account sitting in the bank at Vale, earmarked for just that purpose." She stopped to applaud a jug-eared boy's award of a blue ribbon for the baseball toss. "That's Jason Holmes, Buster's youngest brother. He'll probably make the major leagues someday."

She rolled to one side, leaning on her elbow and stretching her legs out in front of him. "Anyway, the swimming pool fund drive just seemed to peter out after they had about half the money. Harald Alpin—he was the chairman—died, and nobody seemed to care enough to take over. It's really too bad."

More dances and more award ceremonies went on until mid-afternoon. In between times, people familiar and strange stopped by their blanket to visit. Sally seemed to know almost everyone, even those who'd long since moved away. Gus was surprised at how many ex-residents had come back for the May Fest. He said as much.

"I'm surprised, too. I wouldn't have thought so many people would come back."

Eventually, all the children had danced, all the awards had been presented. He imagined that every child in the grade school must have been recognized for something. The sky was so blue it hurt the eyes, and the overhead sun heated already relaxed bodies into somnolence. People who'd been standing sat, while those already sitting on blankets slid into more comfortable positions.

Both Gus and Sally were reclining on the blanket, and when the ceremonies ended, she scooted even closer to him. With a quick inhalation, he commanded his wide-awake body to relax. She looked over her shoulder and smiled, so that he knew her movement had been calculated. She moved again, bringing her sweet little bottom even tighter against his burgeoning arousal.

"Stop that," he muttered between clenched teeth.

She peeked again over her shoulder, and her smile was just plain evil. "You really want me to?" Again that sassy little wiggle.

"No!" God, but she felt good against him. "But I think you'd better, before we shock everyone."

"Pooh! Nobody's watching."

Gus glanced around. She was right. Nobody seemed interested in them.

"What's on the program next?" He heard the hoarseness of desire in his voice.

She shrugged, the motion again pushing her bottom against him.

"Nothing much until supper time. The committee is probably setting up the barbecue, but mostly people nap or visit."

With her first word, he was rolling upright, hoping he wouldn't have to keep his hand in his pocket for long. "Let's go."

"Where?"

"To your house. My apartment. I don't give a damn. But let's go!"

She smiled a secret, satisfied little smile and pushed to her feet. "Your apartment is closer."

"You're sure?"

"Absolutely."

Without another word, they walked together toward Main Street. Gus was afraid to touch her for fear he would burst into flame at the slightest contact.

INTERVAL

At last!

THIRTEEN

THEY SAW NO ONE ON THEIR WAY TO HIS APARTMENT. SALLY noticed, through a haze of anticipation, that the empty town seemed different, somehow. With none of the people she was used to seeing on the streets, it was almost like a stage, waiting for the actors to walk on and give it life.

She shivered. Was that all she and Gus were—actors on a very large, slightly shabby stage? Were they going through the motions the script called for instead of following their hearts?

She shook her head slightly, banishing the fancy. There were no hearts involved in this afternoon's interlude. Just bodies, too long alone. She had nothing to give Gus, for she'd already given too much of herself away.

And all he wanted from her was sex.

She looked up at him from the sides of her eyes, saw the twitching muscle in his jaw. She knew how he felt, for she was as tight as an E-string herself.

Their steps seemed to echo off the blank faces of the empty stores lining Main Street. Sally found herself wanting to look over her shoulder, to see who was watching. When they finally reached the recessed entry to the stairs beside the drugstore, her spine was stiff as an iron rod and the back of her neck prickled.

Gus grabbed her as soon as they were in the stairwell.

"The park never seemed so far away before," he murmured into her ear as he nipped the lobe. His big hands were on her back, on her bottom, pulling her tight against him. The ridge of his erection pressed against her. "Thank God, we didn't meet anybody. I'm in no shape to be sociable."

For a delicious time, she enjoyed his hunger as he covered her face and neck with hot, wet kisses. She allowed the enlarging core of passion within her to feed on his muttered words of desire. This time there was no need for her to wall it into a cold corner of her soul.

She heard him speak, his voice hoarse and distorted, but had no idea what he said. It was more important that she taste the salty tang of his skin, feel the shifting tendons and muscles under his light shirt, clutch at his tight buttocks until he was painfully hard against her soft belly. When he swung her into his arms, she let her tongue explore the underside of his chin, the line of his jaw and the complex curves of his ear.

The door at the top of the stairs stopped him, and he had to set her down. She was glad he kept one arm about her, for she wasn't certain her legs could support her. When the door swung open and he pushed her gently forward, she stumbled. He caught her immediately, and they went through the door together.

It slammed behind them, and Gus pulled her back against him.

"Sally. Sally. Sally." He spoke her name again and again as his hands, hot against her skin, found the fastenings of her dress, her bra. She could not move, for he held her captive in the fiery blaze of his desire.

Soon she stood before him, clad only in wispy yellow nylon panties and white strap sandals. With wonder in his eyes, he reached to touch her breasts, cupping gently and stroking her budded nipples with just his fingertips.

Sally gasped with the force of the now-familiar shock. She felt herself sway and was immediately lifted again. The room blurred about her as Gus carried her past a folding screen.

And then they were together on a bed. He covered her face with hot kisses, explored her with eager teeth and tongue. His hands were firm and knowing on her breasts, on her belly, on her thighs. She bucked against his hand when he lightly stroked the silky fabric of her panties, felt its heat when he cupped her. His fingers were rough against her skin as he hooked them in the elastic and slipped her last covering away.

Then his mouth was hot on her. The gathering storm within her broke, carrying her along on its winds. She heard its scream, felt its force. She knew the scream was her own, recognized the force from pale comparison.

Gradually, she returned to here and now, still buffeted with the aftermath of her passion. Gus knelt between her legs, fully clothed.

"Oh, no!" she said, embarrassed at her incredible selfishness.

Immediately, his smug grin changed into a concerned frown. "What?"

"I didn't…you didn't…you should have…"

He moved quickly, stretching beside her. Wrapping one arm about her, he pulled her close to him.

"I'll last about ten seconds, if I'm lucky." He kissed her, lightly, quickly. "There's plenty of time."

But there wasn't, because the afternoon was already half-spent, and they would be missed if they weren't at the barbecue. Sally wasn't ready for the whole town to know about her and Gus.

She touched his head, just above his ear, thinking how his hair still seemed as if it would burn her. "So bright. So red. I've never seen hair like yours before."

He smiled, but didn't answer. His hand was busy stroking along her body, from throat to navel, with occasional forays into the soft curls hiding her feminine core. Each time he almost touched her, she gasped, aware that her hunger had been merely teased, not fulfilled.

"Is all of your hair as red?" She tapped his belt buckle.

"Why don't you see for yourself?"

"I intend to." Flattening one hand against his chest, she pushed.

He resisted.

She rose to her knees. "It's my turn. I want to make you as crazy as you did me."

"You already have," he growled, but he let her push him onto his back.

Slowly, deliberately, she unfastened the two buttons at the neck of his shirt, loosened the buckle of his belt, and slipped the hook free on the waistband. A fraction of an inch at a time, she slid the zipper down, watched his erection force the fly open. She looked, admired, but did not touch.

His shoes were already gone, but he still wore socks, the same rich russet as his shirt. She pulled them off, letting her short fingernails rasp along his arches as she did.

His legs jerked in response.

"You'll have to sit up, now."

Obediently he rose onto his elbows. Sally, with the expertise of months spent undressing a non-cooperative man, removed his shirt. The dense triangle of impossibly red hair on his chest gleamed dark against ivory flesh. She paused to rub her cheek against it, inhaling his distinctive man-smell. She let her fingers explore, enjoying the minute quivers that followed her touch. He might be sitting rock-still, but he was not unaffected by her light caresses.

"Down," she commanded, and he lay back. She grasped the waistband of his trousers, rolling him slightly from side to side as she pulled them downward.

"Careful," he gasped, as her hand deliberately brushed against his woody.

"Oh, I'll be careful," she said, and smiled, cat-full-of-canary-like, at the power of her touch. When she brushed a butterfly kiss on the soft knit of his briefs, his breath hissed between clenched teeth.

He caught her wrists and began to pull her toward him.

"No," she commanded. "Turn me loose."

"Why?"

"So I can torture you some more." She trembled with anticipation, seeing the urgency, the barely controlled fire, in his eyes.

Sharing it.

When he released her, she finished working his trousers over his feet, and then ran her fingernails lightly up his legs, circling his knees and zigzagging along his thighs.

Again the hissing inhalation.

"I supposed I should take these, too." She slipped one finger under the leg band of his briefs, moved it to the side, back toward the center.

When it came into contact with delicate, pebbled skin, he cried out, his hips jerking in automatic response.

Sally took mercy on him and reached for the waistband.

He gave her no chance. With a quick movement, he was naked, magnificently naked. And the hair on all of him was that same incredible, flaming red.

He pulled her to lie atop him. His hands were urgent on her, kneading, caressing, stroking, smoothing. Again she had that stretched-to-the-limit feeling, as if his slightest touch would set her thrumming like a plucked violin.

"Do you have…" A long time had passed since she had played the dating game. Any man-woman game, at all. She no longer knew the moves, but she knew that unprotected sex was a far greater gamble now than it had been when she was in college.

Would he provide his own condom? Or should she have brought some?

"I have," he said, as if he'd read her mind. "I bought a dozen."

"That should be—" She gasped as he cupped her breasts and his thumbs flicked her turgid, tender nipples. "—enough!"

Then he kissed her and she forgot everything else.

His knee worked between her thighs, spreading them. Sally knew what he wanted. She pushed erect and straddled him. Sitting back on his thighs, she felt again a subtle quiver, telling of his tremendous need.

Deliberately, firmly, she moved her hands up, until they framed his narrow waist, down again, over his flanks and back, until her thumbs could reach across his abdomen and almost… almost touch him. She drew small circles on his skin, watching as his mouth open in a rictus of passion.

"Are you ready?" she said, knowing the answer already.

"Are you?" he challenged.

She had been so involved with bringing him to the verge of explosion, she had not paid attention to her own state. Now, with his question, she became aware of a heaviness in her belly, a tingle waiting to become an explosion.

"Almost."

He sheathed himself, tossing the torn foil aside. His fingers sought and found her. A purposeful stroke and she was at the brink.

"Gus," she cried, knowing that one more touch and she would lose all grasp on reality. "Oh! Please!"

He took her waist in his hands and lifted her, pulling her forward and down. And he rose to meet her, filling her as she had never been filled before. As the first waves of her completion broke, she felt his spasms begin. Then she was aware of nothing but the all-consuming, blazing heat of her own climax. And his.

She dozed in his arms until the afternoon sun sent a dusty beam across the bed, awaking her. From the angle, she knew it must be well after five.

"Gus!" She shook his inert body. "Wake up."

"Hmmm?" He nuzzled against her throat, tightened his arm around her waist.

"We have to go." How she wished they hadn't slept their precious time away.

"Why?"

"Because I want to be seen at the barbecue. If I'm not, Lyle might come looking for me."

"What business is it of his?" Gus said, definitely awake now. His frown brought back the grim, unsmiling man he'd first appeared.

"You've never lived in a small town," she said, while looking around for something to cover herself with, "or you wouldn't ask that."

Gus rolled out of the bed.

"Was Lyle your lover?" He tossed the words over his shoulder as he stalked, naked and unembarrassed, to a door that, when he opened it, revealed a small bathroom. From behind the door, he retrieved a dark green robe. He tossed it to her.

She hadn't asked him about his outrageous claim to have killed his wife. Why should he think he had the right to know about the men in her past? She answered anyway.

"No, although there was a time when he would have liked to have been." She had always regretted that she felt nothing beyond fondness for Lyle. He was such a good friend. "I don't love him that way."

His face closed like a steel trap.

"You're right," he said, and his voice was lifeless and cold. "We need to get back. Go ahead and take the first shower." He strode out of the bedroom, still naked.

Sally could have bitten her tongue off and ground it up for cat food. She didn't love him, but he'd read her answer that way. She'd have to make him understand she didn't expect any more from him than companionship, affection and sex. And only for as long as they were both in Whiterock.

Gus heard the shower go on as he stood at his front window looking down on a still-empty Main Street. Motion down by the Post Office caught his eye, but when he looked in that direction, he saw nothing. Probably a dog. Whiterock had no leash law.

He could not allow Sally Carruthers to fall in love with him. Love meant dependence, and dependence meant he would have to take the responsibility for her welfare and happiness.

He could not. He lacked the strength, the courage. He lacked whatever it took to be that kind of man. His apartment showed what a hollow man he was. There was nothing of him here. He could be gone in a couple of hours.

Damn! First he'd have to find Bernie and tell him he was losing a mechanic.

And he'd given his word to take charge of the cleanup after the May Fest. He couldn't walk out on that obligation.

Tomorrow. I'll leave tomorrow.

He wasn't aware Sally had finished her shower and dressed until her arms came around his from behind. He should have jerked her clasped hands apart and thrown her aside. Instead, he laid his hands over hers and for one last, brief moment enjoyed the sizzle of electricity her touch always brought to him.

"I didn't mean it the way it sounded," she whispered. "I like you, but…" She paused, rubbed her face against his shoulder blade. "Darn! There's just no good way to say this."

"Then don't."

"I have to."

He felt her voice vibrating in his chest, felt the soft fabric of her skirt on the back of his bare legs.

"I don't want you to misunderstand how I feel. I don't want you to go away scared."

"Scared?" How could she know?

Her quiet chuckle shook him slightly. "Pop once told me there are two kinds of men who say 'I love you' after sex."

He appreciated her choice of words. They hadn't made love. They'd had sex.

"So?"

"So, one kind is sincere, but he's already said it before. The other one…" Her fingers tightened on his hands. "The other kind is simply asking for a repeat performance."

Relief so strong it almost made him weak washed through him.

"Are there women like that?" he wondered aloud, knowing that once would never be enough, not with Sally.

"There must be," she said, and her words were a breathy whisper against his naked back, "because I want more." She released his hands, letting him turn to face her. "But later. Right now we've got to get back to the park. It's almost six."

Again relief, as Gus realized he needed time to think before experiencing another cataclysmic encounter with her.

"It won't take me long to shower." Taking her face between his hands, he kissed her—her eyes, her nose, her parted lips. "You're not alone," he said, his voice gruff with unwelcome tenderness. "I still want you, too."

Before he lost the strength to do so, he released her and walked into the bathroom.

Sally didn't need him for anything but great sex.

He didn't have to run again.

The sun was sinking toward Bendire Mountain when Gus and Sally returned to their blanket, replete with barbecued pork, baked beans and assorted picnic delectables. Many of the out-of-towners had gone home after eating, but those with roots in Whiterock were still here, waiting for the bonfire and dance.

Gus was pleasantly tired, and at peace as he had not been for a long time. He turned when someone tapped him on the shoulder. Lyle Curran was squatting behind him, his lips twisted in an effort not to laugh.

"What's up?" he said.

"You're not gonna believe this." Lyle allowed one small chuckle to break free. "C'mon."

He rose, and waited for Gus to do the same.

"I'm coming, too," Sally said.

"Fine with me," Lyle agreed before Gus could say no. Despite Lyle's amusement, anything that involved the police was not something he wanted Sally exposed to.

While leading them across the park, Lyle said over his shoulder, "I meant to keep my eye on those kids, but a couple of punks with their snoots full decided they should see who was the better man, and I got distracted."

"Who won?" Sally was half-trotting to keep up.

"They both lost. I put 'em where they could sober up before they did too much damage to each other." Lyle came to a halt a few feet short of the elk. "Now, I want you to close your eyes and let me lead you the rest of the way. So you'll get the full impact."

Obediently, they both closed their eyes and let Lyle pull them forward. Gus felt the roll of gravel beneath one foot just before the other trod on pavement. Three steps on pavement and Lyle stopped them.

"Okay. Open 'em."

There was a barricade—well, a couple of sawhorses with signs on them—across Main Street. The hand-painted signs read "Road Closed" and "Detour," with an arrow pointing up Fifth toward the Carruthers place.

"Oh, my," Sally said.

Gus was more emphatic. "Oh, shit!"

Lyle roared with contained laughter, and soon all three of them were laughing like fools, still standing in the middle of Main Street.

As far as Gus could see, bright ribbons stretched in a tangled maze, crossing and recrossing the street. Stretched from one anchor-point to another, the neon pink, orange, yellow and green ribbons wove back and forth, back and forth, from doorknob to lamp standard, from signpost to telephone pole. Bows hung on every upright, and the old cement-block library building was tied up like a Christmas present.

When Sally was finally able to stifle her laughter, she said, "Ben Kemp?"

"I can't imagine anyone else with this kind of devious sense of humor." Lyle wiped his mouth, but the smile remained.

Gus said, "I wonder where they got the flagging tape." The narrow plastic ribbon decorating Main Street was commonly used by construction workers, foresters and surveyors to mark sites and routes. "It must have cost them a fortune."

"Yeah, well, I hope they got their money's worth," Lyle said, "'cause they're going to have to take it down, if it takes them all night."

Gus agreed, because he believed it would do the boys more good to have to pick up their own marbles than have the cleanup committee do it for them.

"Do you know where they are?"

"I'll pick 'em up during the dance. You want to help?"

Oddly flattered he had asked, Gus said, "Sure. I'll have to take Sally home—"

"No, you won't," she said. "I have no intention of missing anything."

"But…"

"But nothing, Gus Loring. It's not as if those boys are desperate criminals, is it?"

"No, but…"

"She can come along," Lyle said, stopping Gus's continued protest. "It won't be the first time Sally's helped out. Besides," he said over his shoulder, as he led them back toward the park, "I have a hunch it wasn't just boys."

He showed them a hair ornament that, even in the early twilight, looked suspiciously like that worn by the May Queen.

INTERVAL

Energy.

Rich, lavish.

Pattern indicates ceremonial bonding follows physical bonding. Interim frequently protracted.

Potential dissipation of energy.

Perhaps additional nudge...

FOURTEEN

G US WALKED SALLY HOME ABOUT ELEVEN. SHE WAS SO TIRED, she felt as if she could fall asleep walking. She woke when he kissed her goodnight with thoroughness, a kiss that nearly buckled her knees.

She leaned against him, reluctant to let him leave. When he did, this wonderful, glorious day would end. "You and Lyle will probably be up half the night while those kids clean up their mess." She yawned, a real jaw-cracker. "I should feel guilty for not staying to help."

"You're already half-asleep. Go to bed." He kissed her again, this one a promise of passion to come. Without releasing her, he murmured against her mouth, "I'd like to come back and join you, but I think we've given the town enough to talk about for one day, don't you?"

So, he *had* heard Georgina. Sally could have strangled the café owner at supper when, in her usual straightforward way, she'd said, "From the looks of you, Sally, you've already had dessert."

Since Gus had been several people behind her in the line for baked beans, she'd assumed he hadn't heard it, or her own whispered, "Shut up, or I'll stuff a napkin in your mouth."

Georgina had shut up, but Sally knew several people had heard her and were smart enough to know exactly what she meant.

It wasn't that she was afraid of what her neighbors would say, but that she wanted to wait a while before giving them reason to say it.

She hesitated, her hand on the doorknob, remembering he'd told her earlier that he'd grown up in urban Boston. "Does it worry you, the way everyone in town is watching?"

"Not really bother, but I have to admit I'm not crazy about the way everybody's minding my business." He kissed her once more, a brief peck on her mouth. "See you tomorrow?"

"We'll have to stay close," she warned, "so I can hear Pop if he—"

"I know. But that doesn't mean we can't sit in the backyard and drink lemonade, does it?"

"Sounds wonderful," she said, and slipped inside.

Through the screen, she watched him stride away into the night. As he passed under the streetlight at the corner, she smiled. He still had the best rear view she could remember seeing, and she'd seen a fair sample, what with costuming dancers for so many musical productions.

Back on Main Street, Gus oversaw the removal of the flagging tape, and Lyle directed traffic as the remaining out-of-towners dispersed. While the teenagers were undoing their handiwork, Gus listened to their comments.

The flagging tape, he learned, had been found at a garage sale by Lucie, whose mother was an antique dealer of sorts.

Lucie had bought the entire box—worth close to a hundred dollars at a surveyor's supply—for seven bucks. Decorating the town with the brightly colored streamers had been Ben Kemp's idea, all right, but Gus wondered if he would have done quite so thorough a job of it without the encouragement of the other three.

From overheard comments, Gus had formed the impression that Buster was a quiet, hard-working boy and Rhoda an airhead; but the pretty little May Queen was actually the brains of the foursome, and Buster was the brawn. Ben was merely the most visible, because of his energy and his quick wit. While the other kids wanted to be the usual things—Rhoda a veterinarian, Lucie a dress designer and Buster a landscape architect, Ben wanted to be the next Billy Crystal.

Gus rather thought he might make it.

These kids needed adult mentors, he mused. He'd had one—old George Shaw, who'd done the engineering for many of Boston's tallest buildings. *And wouldn't George have a fit if he could see you now?*

He shoved that thought back to the deepest recess of his mind. While he wasn't intending to stick around forever, as long as he was here he might as well see what he could do to aim these kids in the right direction. They all had potential. Lots of it.

Maybe Sally, with her dressmaking skills, would be able to advise Lucie. He could take Buster under his wing. He'd worked with landscape architects on a fair number of projects at L/B Engineering.

Wait a minute! Since when was he going to be in Whiterock long enough to take anybody under his wing? If he had any brains at all he'd leave now, before he and Sally got too deeply involved.

Lyle returned while the kids were still working on the last block. Gus had to laugh at the way they'd decorated the constable's office, cattycorner from the Post Office, with shiny metallic bows from someone's stored Christmas wrap and a big sign that read "Abandon hope, all ye who enter here" stretched across its door and windows.

Lyle was obviously amused as well, although he did his best to hide it.

"I told your folks I'd bring you home," he said as Rhoda and Buster pulled the sign down. Lucie and Ben were across the street, taking the last of the neon yellow tape from the handrails on the Legion Hall steps. "But first I think we'd better have a little talk."

Both kids groaned.

"I've got a better idea," Gus said, checking his watch. It was past midnight, and he'd had a long and tiring day. He would be willing to bet Lyle's had been even longer. "Let's take these kids to Vale tomorrow morning and feed them breakfast. Then we can talk about what they'll need to do in restitution."

Lyle looked at him curiously, but he agreed.

"Eight o'clock? That way we can be back in time for church."

Again the groans, but this time from all four.

"It's Sunday!" Ben protested.

Lucie turned enormous, innocent blue eyes on Lyle. "I don't know if my folks will let me."

"Or mine," Buster echoed.

"We always go to early Mass," Rhoda said, piety strong in her voice.

"How early?" Gus said.

"Well, actually, nine."

"Fine," Lyle said. "Be at my office at seven. Lucie, I'll pick you up on the way to Vale, seven-fifteen." It was not a question.

While the kids were putting their garbage sacks into the dumpster behind the Town Hall, Lyle said to Gus," I don't know what you have in mind, but it had better be good. I usually sleep in Sunday morning."

"So do I," Gus admitted. "But they need to pay, and I think what I'm planning will be just the ticket."

He waved at Lyle as the police car pulled away, four not-very-repentant kids inside.

God! What had he let himself in for? Now he'd have to get hold of Roy Gilbert, or the May Fest chairman would think he'd skipped out on his responsibility of cleaning up the park and the town.

Tomorrow afternoon with Sally looked more and more like a couple of hours in the evening, if he was lucky.

"You did what?" Sally caught her breath, doing her best to contain her laughter.

"Well, I noticed that the old motel—you know, down behind the drugstore—was about the only place in town that looks like it hasn't been painted in years. So, after we picked up the park and along every street in town, I took 'em down there and explained what they were going to do next."

She wished she'd been there. Lucie McEwen was the most perfectly turned-out girl she'd ever seen. Sally remembered her own mother's comments, years ago. "Maureen McEwen is ruining that child. She sends her to school dressed up like a perfect little doll and has an absolute conniption fit if she comes home dirty. What kind of a prissy little twit is she going to make of that poor girl? I ask you?"

Sally had agreed with her mother, unable to imagine what a childhood in dresses rather than blue jeans would be like. And now she knew that, somehow, Lucie had managed to grow up full of life and mischief, and not at all prissy or twit-like.

She was still the best-dressed child in Whiterock, though.

"I can't imagine Maureen McEwen letting Lucie get covered with paint and ruining her manicure," she said, and smiled at the prospect. It would be good for Lucie. Too bad it would never happen.

"Trust me." Gus reached across the space between their lawn chairs. "I'll get some dirt under her fingernails. You know, this means I'll be busy after work for a while."

She extended her hand to meet his. "That's all right. Five-thirty of a weekday afternoon is probably not the most discreet time for a romantic tryst."

Catch her going up those stairs to his apartment at the time of day when there was more foot and automobile traffic on Main Street than any other hour!

The monitor on the wrought-iron table beside her emitted a sudden sound. Sally stiffened to attention, but when the sound was repeated, she relaxed. Pop was merely snoring.

"I thought I could bring you here sometime, Gus, but I don't think I'll be comfortable doing it. I don't mind Juana knowing about us, but I just don't want to…well, rub her nose in it, I guess."

"Are you having regrets, then?"

He sounded almost uncertain. It touched her. Before this she'd heard anger, resentment, impatience, and desire in his voice, but never before had she thought he might be as unsure about what they were doing as she was.

"No regrets." She tugged on his hand. "If you'd like to scoot a little closer, I can show you what I think about a return engagement."

Instead of bringing his chair closer to hers, he came to her. As he pulled her out of her chair, he said, "Arms are too wide." And before she knew it, he was sitting on the ornate white iron loveseat with her perched on his knees.

She had to bend slightly to kiss him, but she didn't mind. Starting at his forehead, she worked her way down, leaving a moist trail across his temple, down his cheek and to the corner of his mouth. Before he could capture her lips with his, she went back to her starting point and gave equal attention to the other temple, the other cheek.

Gus's arms tightened about her as she made her slow and provocative way toward his mouth. One hand stroked up and down her spine, the other crept under her shirt and found her breast, free of a bra this warm May evening. He kneaded and plucked until she forgot what she was doing and simply let her mouth slide along his cheek to its final goal. She felt a cool draft as he unbuttoned her shirt, and she arched her back to bring an eager nipple closer to his questing fingers.

When he at last released her mouth, she was jelly-like, shimmering and quaking in urgent need. She tangled her fingers in his thick hair, feeling the heat of him even there. His arousal pressed against her hip and she ground herself against it, loving his moan of pleasure-pain.

Seconds later, she responded with her own moan as he took her nipple into his mouth and suckled. Sally felt something inside her follow the pull on her breast, yearning to join with him now, not later.

"Gus," she gasped. "Oh, Gus."

"Oh, yes!" He lifted her, turned her until she was astride his legs. His fingers sought the hem of her cotton skirt and she was glad it was wide and full. "Can you…?"

He showed her what he wanted, and she cooperated, pulling her skirt up until her barely clad bottom was against the soft denim of his jeans.

While his hands stroked up and down her thighs, coming ever closer to her center with every cycle, she found the snap of his jeans, released it. Her fingers stumbled on his zipper, partly from her own blistering urgency, partly because his erection strained the limits of fabric and zipper alike.

When she finally released him, she felt herself lifted, positioned so that with one motion she could take him in.

And she did, feeling him slide slickly and tightly into her core. Conscious thought fled, leaving only indescribable sensation. Sally gave herself up to it, moving in concert with him, holding to him because she never wanted to be anywhere else ever again.

When she knew she could endure no more pleasure, she cried out. Her mouth might have formed words, or it might have emitted pure sound. All she knew was that his muffled shout of completion followed almost immediately, when he thrust against her one last time, holding himself rigidly as he found release.

Still gasping for breath, Sally collapsed against him.

"My God!" she said, when she finally could speak again, "That was incredible."

"Yeah," he agreed. "Incredible." His voice was faint, and he still breathed as if at the end of a marathon.

She relaxed against him, waiting while strength returned to both of them. He again stroked the length of her spine, gently, with affection but no passion. She felt him withdraw from her, but they might as well have been still joined.

Eventually she said, "I wasn't entirely kidding about timing, Gus. But I'm not sure I can come to you for my...uh, my sexual fix every day or so."

"Your 'sexual fix?' Are you sure you don't want to be a little more blunt?"

If she'd ever heard an outraged male, it was now.

"Well, what do you want me to call it?" she said, and reared back so she could look him in the face. In the deepening twilight, she couldn't make out much more than that he had two eyes, a nose and a mouth—a mouth that was a tight, straight line.

"In those terms," he growled, "how about a good f—"

Her hand over his mouth stopped the word.

"Gus, I'm not trying to put this…" She waved her hand, not entirely sure herself what to call the compelling attraction between them "…on a tawdry level. But we aren't making love. I don't love you. I can't love you."

"Nor I you," he agreed.

"And I certainly am not going to tell you lies about forever after. When Pop goes…" She bit her lip, not wanting to say aloud what she'd been saying to herself since her father's health had deteriorated so badly. She had finally admitted out loud—but only in the privacy of her bedroom—that he hadn't long to live. Swallowing, she forced herself to sound insouciant. "When that happens, I'm outta here." She slid her hands together, showing him exactly with what speed she would depart. "I'll stay long enough to close the house, then it's bye-bye, Sally."

"Fine with me." He sounded less affronted but not entirely won over. "I wasn't intending to settle here myself."

"Good. Then you shouldn't be insulted when I tell you that I've never had such great sex. As long as you're willing to cooperate, I'd like to be with you as often as I can."

She'd equated good sex with love once before, and when the haze of passion cleared she found there wasn't anything else. Jeff and she had been—still were—good friends who happened to turn each other on, but they hadn't found enough for a lifetime together. After three years of trying to make a marriage, they'd parted amicably.

She didn't regret the parting, but couldn't help feeling as if she'd failed. She should have been smart enough to see what was missing in their relationship before they made it official. Instead, she'd gotten caught up in the excitement of planning the wedding, never thinking very far beyond it.

Never again would she let her hormones tell her she was in love. Marriage was a lot more than great sex, and she hadn't given up on finding the man she could spend the rest of her life with. She was certain, though, that she wouldn't find him in Whiterock, Oregon.

Gus felt indescribable relief when Sally told him of her intentions to leave as soon as her father passed away. He was safe. She wouldn't come to depend on him to take care of her—outside of bed, that is.

He could handle that kind of need.

He pulled her back against his chest, liking how she felt in his arms.

"You're right," he said. "It was the greatest." He kissed her neck, burrowing against her, liking the honeysuckle smell of her, mixed with musky, satiated woman-scent. "How about more?" he said against her throat.

"More?" Her voice sounded slightly breathless. "Are you serious?"

"Never more so," he said, feeling himself tighten again. Impossibly, for he had never believed the tales of sexual stamina he'd heard and read. Never before.

Perhaps he'd never before met a woman who incited such passion in him. There was no question he wanted her still. Again. And yet again.

A harsh, wordless cry came from the monitor. Immediately, Sally was alert, her body tense. Again the cry, like an animal in pain, followed by a crash.

"Pop!" she said, pulling free of his embrace. Without closing her shirt she ran across the lawn and up the back steps.

Gus replaced their tipped-over lemonade glasses on the silver tray. With his free hand, he picked up the monitor and followed her at a slower pace. He would see if she needed his help with her father before he left.

Now that she wasn't so close that lust overpowered his better judgment, he knew it was time for him to step back and take a long look at what he might be getting himself into.

Great sex, indeed. But was there a woman in the world who could be satisfied with nothing more from a relationship than great sex?

Could he be, for that matter?

INTERVAL

Patience.

Carruthers and Loring procrastinate. Resisting formalization of bond, despite recognition of unique synergy.

Both contemplate departure.

Impediment? Obstacle? Deterrent?

What?

FIFTEEN

SALLY FOUND POP HALF IN, HALF OUT OF HIS BED, MOUTHING incomprehensible syllables and struggling to get out of the cage formed by the bedrails. Somehow, he had managed to scoot the wheeled hospital bed across the room, wedging it tight against the mahogany table where a photo of her mother had been.

Had been, for the photo lay on the floor in slivers of glass, soaked by water from the nosegay of lilacs she had just that morning set beside it.

It had been Pop's favorite image of his beloved wife, and now he didn't even know it was damaged beyond repair. Or care.

Gus was right behind her, and he helped get Pop back into the bed. Immediately, using his still strong left hand, Pop pulled himself back to the rail and reared against it. All the time the formless cry came from his mouth, broken only by gasping breaths.

"Lower the rails," Gus said, while holding him in the bed.

Sally complied, hoping Gus knew what he was doing.

Lifting the struggling old man, Gus carried him across the room and set him in the heavy oak rocking chair Sally had moved in for Juana to use. Pop became relatively quiet as soon as Gus released him. She tucked a blanket around him with shaking hands.

"Oh, Gus, what if he'd fallen?"

"I know," he said, pulling her close. "It's a good thing you had the monitor."

Sally felt his strength again, wished she could lean on him for a while instead of standing on her own two feet.

Pop rocked rapidly in the chair, seemingly oblivious to the world around him, his vacant eyes unfocused, his mouth slack. But he was calm, and seemed as content as he ever was.

"Do you want me to stay?" Gus's arms were loose about her. She looked up at him, hearing something in his voice she had heard once or twice before. Reluctance? Distaste? It was almost as if being around Pop made him uncomfortable.

Odd, because he was so good with Pop.

She shook her head, stepped back until she was entirely free of his embrace.

"No, I don't think so. I doubt if I could get him back into bed tonight, anyway."

Always before when he'd had one of these hyperactive spells at night they lasted well into the following morning. There was no reason to believe this would be any different.

"I can always call Lyle if there's a problem."

After Lyle had given her a very large piece of his mind the morning of Pop's stroke, she had no reservations about calling on him at any time of the day or night. If she wanted to remain his friend, she would allow him the privilege of helping whenever he could. Besides, it was, as he'd reminded her in no uncertain terms, also his job.

166

Sally had no doubt it was relief she saw on Gus's face as he kissed her goodnight.

"I'll call you tomorrow," he said as he pulled the front door closed behind him.

Standing in the door of Pop's room, she stared down the hall, as if seeing Gus still there. His ready departure had hurt, and she knew why.

It was one thing saying that all she wanted from him was great sex, but it was another thing entirely when that was all she got.

Pop suffered a series of mini-strokes during the next several weeks. No single episode was life-threatening, but taken together, they slowly, inexorably, carried him closer to his final moment.

Juana was a godsend. Sally couldn't have made it through the rest of May and the early part of June without her. Matter-of-fact, cheerful without being insensitive, she took care of Sally as much as she did of Pop. Sally hadn't realized how much she'd missed being hugged.

After she'd had time to come to grips with having exactly what she'd asked for, she was equally grateful to Gus for his deliberate non-involvement. When she was with him she could forget, for a little while, that her father really was dying.

The heat wave in mid-June had the mercury hovering around a hundred. If it weren't for the nights, when it sometimes grew cool enough to require a light sweater, she might have moved back downstairs. Her room had never seemed this hot when she was a child.

After the first night of the heat wave, Gus bought a window air conditioner for his apartment. All the warm air that entered the drugstore with each opening of the door gradually worked its way upstairs throughout the day until, by evening, his apartment was an oven. The air conditioner made it passably livable rather than a barbecue.

They were together nightly, except for Sundays and Mondays, Juana's days off. Sally went to him as to a spring. For refreshment...and to forget. Their sweat-slickened bodies writhed and tumbled on the warm sheets as they sought, and often found, new heights of passion, new crests of fulfillment.

She sometimes felt as if she were two people. One, the dutiful daughter, was exhausted, resentful, impatient and scared. The other was carefree—for an hour or so each evening—and hedonistic. Sally didn't like either one very much, but she didn't know what to do about changing, nor did she have the energy to care.

She tried to be discreet when she went to Gus's apartment at first, but her efforts were about as successful as her earlier intention of not getting involved with him. One night she arrived at eight instead of nine, and waved to Walt Kemp as he was locking up. Another time she met Georgina and Jack Maye, out for their evening walk.

Georgina said, "I told you he was a hunk," and winked.

"He's a good man," Jack added. "Been givin' Buster Jones some time every afternoon, showin' him how to tinker with engines."

Sally couldn't remember Jack ever saying so many words all at once. He must really be impressed with Gus. She waved to them as she turned into the stairwell, knowing neither Jack nor Georgina would ever gossip about her.

The very next morning, Ernie Green varied his conversation.

"How's your pa?" he said.

"About the same," she answered, as she always did, "and how are you?"

"Tickled pink you've finally got yourself a good man," he said, and his mouth widened in an approving grin. "It's about time."

Sally was so astonished she gave him a tentative smile and hurried on down Main Street. She didn't stop at the café, just waved at Georgina through the window as she wondered if there was anyone in town who didn't know about her and Gus.

Well, perhaps she wouldn't be expected to wear a big red A on her sweatshirt after all. So far, no one had said anything disapproving.

She slipped into the Post Office, opening the door only wide enough to get through.

"Whew!" she said to Wilma, who was sorting on the other side of the counter. "I thought it'd be cooler if I came early."

"It's supposed to get up to a hundred and ten today," the postmistress said. "I reckon I'll close down for a siesta about one. Nobody'll be comin' in till it cools off."

Sally pulled the bundle of mail out of her box and sifted through it. Down toward the bottom was a bright pamphlet, the announcement of the Portland Opera's upcoming season. She set the rest of her mail on the counter and leafed through it.

"They're doing *Parsifal*," she said, more to herself than to Wilma, "and *Aida. The Barber of Seville.* Oh, God! They're doing *Fidelio*." A hard knot grew in her throat and threatened to overwhelm her. "I wanted to design those costumes," she whispered, remembering the folio of drawings she'd been working on for years, ever since she first heard *Fidelio*.

"What are you talkin' about, girl?" Wilma demanded. "Speak up. You know my hearing's not what it used to be."

"Nothing, Wilma," she said, tucking the brochure in the middle of her stack of magazines and envelopes. "Just impossible dreams."

"There's no impossible dreams, Sally Carruthers. Just people too lazy to work for what they want most of all." She leaned on the counter, an ancient woman who'd been Sally's grandfather's playmate. "I can't believe any granddaughter of Archie's would lack the gumption and grit to go after what she wants, can you?"

Sally shook her head. How could she go after anything, as long as she didn't know from one day to the next what Pop's condition would be?

"I'll see you tomorrow, Wilma," she said. In about one minute she was going to weep, and she didn't want Wilma to see.

"WHAT HAPPENS AROUND HERE ON THE FOURTH?" GUS ASKED HER one night about a week before the Independence Day holiday. They were lying naked on his bed, letting the breeze from the fan cool the sweat of their recent passion. The air conditioner kept the living room end cool, the bedroom end merely endurable, so Sally had bought a little clip-on fan the last time she'd taken Pop in to Ontario to see the doctor.

"Nothing much." She was tracing patterns in the red pelt on his chest. It fascinated her. She'd never thought about body hair on a redhead—it made her fanciful impression of his being forged out of brass and copper seem less fantastic. "People generally go somewhere else. There are rodeos in Jordan Valley and Vale, fireworks in Ontario."

"And what about you? What are your plans?" His eyes were closed and his body totally relaxed.

Sally wondered if he really cared what she was planning, or if he was simply talking to keep himself awake.

"I haven't made any plans. Even if I wanted to go somewhere, I'd be afraid to be out of touch."

She had this awful feeling that if she went farther from home than the Post Office, something terrible would happen.

Pop was so much worse. He hadn't even objected to the bedrails for more than a week. All he did was lie in the bed and waste away.

No! She wouldn't think about Pop. Not while she was with Gus, the only time she felt as if she still had a life.

Desperately, she kissed him, crushing her mouth against his. "I've got a little while longer," she murmured. "Don't waste it talking."

Gus responded to her kiss automatically, even while he wanted to push her away. The desperation in her words, in her voice, was too much.

It wasn't physical need that was driving her tonight, but emotional. And he had nothing emotional to give her.

After a moment, he realized he had nothing physical, either.

She realized it at almost the same time. "You're tired, aren't you?"

It was a convenient excuse. "Long day." He shrugged one shoulder. "And the heat."

She rolled away from him. "Maybe I'd better go."

"Yeah. It's late." A pang of regret arrowed through him as he heard the hurt in her voice. It was followed quickly by resentment. Damn her! He'd told her what he could give, yet she kept wanting more.

She scooped her clothing from the floor and went into the bathroom. Gus lay on the rumpled bed and wondered if he'd finally driven her away. Always before she'd dressed in the bedroom, humoring his once-stated desire to watch her. It turned him on, he'd said, and it did. Her body was slimmer, firmer now than when they'd first met, her motions were graceful and sensuous.

He sighed, aware of a subliminal ache. He didn't love her, but his life was richer for knowing her. He often went for days at a time between black moods, rarely thought about leaving Whiterock.

Perhaps that was the problem. She had brought happiness back into his life, and he wasn't supposed to be happy.

As waves of remembered pain broke through him, Gus clenched his fists, his teeth, his whole body. He tried to visualize his wife, his child. Marilyn's image was hazy in his mind, but he could still see her dark hair, her petulant mouth, her yearning eyes. He could still feel the weight of her emotional neediness—a need he'd been unable to satisfy.

But where was Emily?

Oh, God! How could he have let this happen? It was not quite three years ago, and already her face was growing dim in his memory. He could no longer feel the delicate wiriness of her little body as he swung her onto his shoulders. He could no longer hear her happy "Quack-quack-quack!" at his command to duck as he carried her through her bedroom door. And he could no longer smell the sweet baby shampoo-strawberry soap scent of her as he hugged and kissed her after checking for monsters under the bed.

Why had he left all the photos of her behind, along with everything else he'd once thought important?

He rolled over and buried his face in his pillow, feeling the burn of tears behind his eyes, the aching lump in the back of his throat. He heard Sally open the bathroom door, hesitate, and then head for the apartment door. Her soft "Goodbye, Gus," only exacerbated his agony.

Sally let herself out without going to Gus as she longed to do. She didn't have to be slapped in the face with a dead fish to know when she wasn't wanted.

It was still hot, the sidewalk reflecting back its stored heat. She hurried across Main Street, knowing the gravel that began half a block up Third Avenue would be cooler than the pavement and concrete of Whiterock's narrow downtown.

The old-fashioned yellow streetlights, swinging in the middle of the intersections, cast sharp shadows. She watched hers catch up with her at the corner, lengthen before her as she turned onto Jasper, passing first Wilma's single-story bungalow, then the Jones house, untenanted since Mildred died.

She lingered by Mrs. Alpin's fence, smelling the hot, heavy scent of sun-warmed roses. Their watchdog, of course, was not about, but she whispered, anyway, "Your roses are lovely, Grip."

And at that moment, she could no longer contain the tears she had been denying since Gus's withdrawal.

Leaning against the fence, she laced her fingers into its chain links, needing the support. Sobs wracked her, no matter how she tried to contain them. She didn't know what she wept for, except that she had so much sorrow, so much regret and so much loneliness within her that this might be the only way it could come out.

"Pop," she gasped. "Please. Please, let go. I can't stand seeing you like this any longer."

Today he had caught her hand as she washed his chest, holding it tightly for a few seconds as if he'd known what he was doing. But most of the time he was like a vegetable in the bed—inert, oblivious, apart.

There, she'd said it out loud. Finally.

"Yes, Pop, I want you to die," she said, this time in a firm voice. "I'm so sick of seeing your body suffer, when I know that my father's not there anymore."

Her suspicion that he was hidden somewhere inside the failing husk of his body, unable to escape, had been defeated by reality. The father she'd loved and admired was long gone. It was time she accepted that.

Time to let Pop go.

The thought of living the rest of her life without his wise advice and uncritical love was almost more than she could bear, and the sobs renewed.

"Oh, Pop, I love you so, and I miss you so much," she told him, hoping that, wherever he was, he could hear.

Eventually, the ungovernable weeping passed, and she was able to continue toward her house, feeling drained and empty. Perhaps she could finally find peace, now that she had finally admitted to herself that wishing for Pop's death was infinitely more compassionate than praying for his continued imprisonment in a failing body.

Sally slipped inside to tell Juana she was home, and went back out to sit on the front steps. The moon wasn't up yet, but the streetlight at the corner of Fifth and Jasper kept the night from being totally dark. She perched her elbows on her knees, cradled her chin within them.

Weeping for Pop hadn't resolved her confusion about Gus Loring. She wasn't sure anything would, but she owed it to herself to examine her feelings about him.

Of course, there was the possibility, after his complete withdrawal tonight, that her feelings about him wouldn't matter anymore, except to be conquered and exiled. He'd gone back into that private place inside himself where all that showed was anger. Why?

She thought back over all the times he had withdrawn. At first he had done it whenever he seemed tempted to smile, to be comfortable, to be amused. After he took the job at Cowles Implement, he'd relaxed a little, although he still hadn't been exactly friendly.

No, that was wrong, He'd been friendly enough, but only in response to friendliness. Seldom had he initiated any kind of exchange beyond the necessary small talk of daily life. She'd listened to Roy Gilbert trying to talk him into helping with the

May Fest and had gathered from his responses he was reluctant to get involved in the town's social life.

It seemed like every time he let himself get close to someone, he went into automatic retreat. Like tonight. All she'd done was show him how much she needed him, and he'd withdrawn.

She hoped he would be as mercurial this time as he had before. While ordinarily she wouldn't give the time of day to someone as on-again-off-again as Gus, right now she needed him. Tomorrow night she would be at his door as if nothing had happened.

At least when she was in his arms, in his bed, she didn't feel so terribly alone. She didn't have to be strong.

INTERVAL

What is Emily?

SIXTEEN

BERNIE STUCK HIS HEAD OUT OF THE OFFICE AS GUS WAS returning from lunch. "Got a minute?"

"Sure." Gus entered the dimly lit office that looked as if nothing had been thrown away since the day Bernie's grandfather opened for business. He set a pile of parts catalogs onto the floor and sat in the rickety chair. "What's up?"

"Why are you wasting your time working for me?"

Gus shrugged. "I like it here. It's uncomplicated."

"That's no answer." Bernie's tone said he wasn't anybody's fool.

"It's the only one I have." He rose, done with a conversation that wasn't going anywhere.

Bernie said, "Hold on. I've got a deal for you." He opened the file cabinet behind his desk. "It's in here somewhere," he muttered while flipping through file folders.

Gus waited.

Finally Bernie pulled out a stapled-together sheaf of papers, dog-eared and coffee-stained. He looked at the top sheet.

"Good grief! Has it really been that long?" He held the papers out. "Take a look. It's a little out of date, but things haven't changed much."

Gus looked. Cowles Implement Company, Financial Statement. The date was more than three years ago. Curiosity got the better of him. He flipped to the balance sheet, skimmed down the right hand column. Where he halfway expected to see red, there was a nice, healthy black number.

"Why are you showing me this?"

"I talked to that fellow you used to work with. He said you've been drifting for more'n three years. It's time you settled down." Then more slowly, he said, "I'd like to sell the business to you."

Next time I get my hands on Roger Blakeley, I'm going to wring his scrawny neck! He laid the papers carefully on Bernie's desk.

"What I do is none of your goddam business, Bernie." He spun on his heel and walked out.

Interfering bastard. Always thinking he knows what's best. He's my partner, not my mother. Someone spoke a greeting but Gus didn't look around. He crossed Third Avenue and cut across the Lundquist Market parking lot into the abandoned fields behind. *Be damned if I'll settle down. There's nothing here for me. Not a damned thing!*

His pants leg caught on the barbwire of the fallen-down fence along Gypsum Street, and he cursed under his breath. *I should've left the first time I thought about it, instead of letting myself get suckered into working on that fool May Fest.*

This end of the park was unimproved, a mini-wilderness of sagebrush and cheatgrass, threaded with dusty paths. He followed the one that crossed Little Hackberry Creek, almost dry now. A pair of mallards burst into flight as he emerged from the sagebrush, startling him. *Stupid birds. Can't you find anything better than this godforsaken place?*

He jumped the narrow stream, continued along the path until it ended atop the steep bank of Hackberry Creek. Angular boulders stabilized the slope, prevented erosion. Gus found one with a flat surface and sat, staring out across the opposite hillside.

Below him, cattails surrounded a clear spring-fed pond. On one of them sat a yellow-headed bird, singing its heart out. He had to smile but quickly stifled it. *The only thing holding me here is in my britches. Like Sally said, there are no promises between us.*

It's just sex.

He didn't move.

Where would he run?

He'd traveled nearly ten thousand miles over the past three years, lived in a dozen different rooms, done whatever unskilled labor he could find.

And I still haven't found peace.

"I'm not looking for peace! I just want to forget!"

Bullshit! It's forgiveness I need, not forgetfulness.

He'd never forgiven himself for Marilyn's death, but lately he'd begun to think he could eventually come to accept that he might not have been able to prevent it. Oh, he was at fault, and he'd live with the sorrow all his life. He'd told her the steering was squirrelly, that he'd get it fixed as soon as he could. But he'd been in the middle of a project and had set everything else aside.

She could have taken her car to the shop—

"I should have done it." Yet for some reason, he'd lost some of the oppressive guilt that had weighed on his conscience for three years. Marilyn's death seemed somehow distant, an old ache rather than an immediate pain.

"What the hell's wrong with me?" He knew he could have prevented the tragedy that had robbed him of all he held dear. Knew he could have...

But could I? Short of staying home and watching over Marilyn every minute, could I have kept her from doing what she wanted when she wanted?

The answer came, with a total certainty.

No.

"No. She wouldn't listen to anyone when she had her mind made up. Even her mother admitted she acted first and thought later, if at all."

And I helped spoil her, just as everyone else did. She was so lovely, so easy to pamper, to indulge. And she always made me feel so special.

The world around him blurred, and Gus blinked rapidly to clear his vision. But it wouldn't clear. It swam. He tasted salt and realized he was weeping.

I loved her. I trusted her to take care of Emily. And she failed.

Gus realized that he was, for the first time, admitting he'd been blaming Marilyn as much as himself. *But I loved her. I really did. So I have to forgive her.*

As for Emily...

No. Don't go there. Not now. Not yet.

He was preternaturally aware of the tangy scent of sagebrush on the fitful breeze, the distant cries of playing children. The sun was hot on his bare arms, and heat waves shimmered above the desert, creating motion where there was none. He felt out of place, out of time. Slowly, he sank back to his rocky seat, no longer fighting the tears that flowed freely, no longer stifling the sobs that shook him.

Washing away the guilt, the anger. Leaving only an eternal emptiness in his heart.

GUS WAS SUBDUED THAT NIGHT WHEN SALLY ARRIVED AT HIS apartment. His kisses were nice, but that was all.

Gus's kisses had never been merely nice before.

She resisted the urge to cling. If she'd ever needed to be loved, it was tonight, but she'd be darned if she'd beg for it.

"Something's bothering you."

He shook his head. "A long day, that's all."

His hands, familiar, knowing, stroked down her spine, but in gentle affection, not in passion.

Yet Sally was comforted. If he would only hold her, just like this, in the days to come. Give her the strength to accept Dr. Berman's latest prognosis.

"Juana and I took Pop in to the doctor today."

Gus led her to the sofa. "Want to talk about it?"

"Not really. I'd rather not even think about it." She relaxed, for the first time all day. The regular rise and fall of his chest soothed her, the faint thump of his heart tranquilized. She tried to blank her mind.

It was impossible.

Finally she said, "I can't not think about it." With another sigh, she sat upright, slipping from under his sheltering arm.

Gus rose and went to the refrigerator, returned with a bottle of beer and a can of Fresca. "Your father's not getting better is he?" He sat on the other end of the sofa.

Sally stretched her legs out so she could tuck her feet under his thigh. She didn't want to cuddle while she unburdened her mind, but she needed the reassurance of his touch.

"He is going to die. Soon." She said finally, straight out, flatly, forcing herself to accept the reality. "He's been dying for a long time, but it was always going to happen someday—in the unforeseeable future." She had always clung to a tiny spark of hope that he might, against all odds, get better.

"Dr. Berman said that one of these days he will simply forget to breathe and that will be it." Biting her lip, she tried to keep the tears out of her voice. "Oh, Gus, I'm not ready. I don't think I'll ever be ready to say goodbye to him."

Gus swallowed. She saw the working of his throat, the tension in his jaw and the tendons of his neck. His hand tightened around the bottle of beer, until his knuckles were white. "You're never ready," he said, his voice low and raspy. "But at least you'll have the chance—" He clamped his mouth shut, his eyes. After a long pause, he said, sounding normal again, "How long did Dr. Berman give him?"

Sally shrugged. "It could be a week, a month." She forced her fist against her mouth, biting her knuckle until the pain overrode her need to wail her anguish. Her resentment. "It could be a year."

"Oh, God!" His words were as much a prayer as a curse.

The next thing Sally knew, she was held tightly in his arms and he was rocking back and forth, crooning into her ear. "Let it go. Face it and it won't hurt so much. There, there." Over and over, until Sally found her throat opening and the burning of her tearless eyes more bearable.

Finally she took a deep breath and let it out on a long sigh. "Gus, I'm okay. Honest."

Although grateful for his compassion, she knew the last thing she needed right now was for someone else to feel sorry for her. She was doing a good job of it all by herself.

"You sure?" His embrace loosened.

"I guess what's really bothering me is that I want him to go," she said, and waited to see the contempt steal over his face at her admission. "I want him to die."

He didn't answer immediately. Staring into the mouth of his almost-empty beer bottle, he seemed thoroughly fascinated by its contents.

"'Be careful what you wish for. You may get it.' I got that in a fortune cookie once." He drained his beer. "It's true."

Sally didn't see what he was getting at but didn't have the energy to ask. She felt as if any movement would be almost more than her exhausted body could manage, as if any thought would cost her what little mental energy remained to her.

Gus watched Sally as she sank farther and farther into silence. She was beyond despondence; she seemed almost dangerously depressed.

She needed someone to help her pull herself together, someone who could help her face and deal with this latest hurdle, but he didn't think he had the strength to lend her. So, he did the best he could to distract her.

"I really enjoyed the rodeo." He was careful to pronounce it "*ro*-dee-oh," as the locals did, with the accent on the first syllable. The first time he'd used the word, pronouncing it "ro-*day*-oh", Bernie had told him he sounded like a greenhorn Easterner. Well, he was, but he saw no reason to call attention to it.

"Ummm?" Sally's eyes opened, dull and lifeless.

"My grandfather took me to a rodeo in Madison Square Garden once, when I was nine or ten. I remember how exciting it was, especially the Brahma bull riders."

"I always hated them. I saw a clown get gored when I was pretty young, and never liked the Brahmas again." She shuddered.

"That would change how you looked at it," Gus agreed. At least she was talking, not just sitting there like a lump. "But what I liked best was the steer-roping and the cutting horse competition."

She had refused to leave her father and had insisted she didn't want him to stay in town over the Fourth just because she did. Gus had heard half a dozen arguments about whether the rodeo in Vale or the Jordan Valley event was the wildest and woolliest, so he went to both.

Sally said nothing, so he went on.

"There's a big difference between the rodeo I saw as a kid and those I saw this past weekend. And it wasn't just because they were outside. And smaller." He looked at her to see if she was listening. She seemed to be, but he couldn't be sure. "These seemed to be more or less family affairs, as if most of the contestants and the audience knew one another."

Her eyes were open but didn't appear to be seeing anything.

"There was one fellow—he must have been close to eighty—who rode one of the bucking horses backwards. When he fell off, the horse stopped bucking, grabbed him by the scruff of the neck with its teeth and carried him out of the arena."

"That's nice."

"Then there was the woman barrel racer," he continued, wanting a reaction but beginning to despair, "who wore a satin dancehall-girl outfit, complete with net stockings and high-heeled satin shoes. She won, too."

"Good for h— What did you say?"

Gus saw intelligence in her eyes once again and breathed a silent sigh of relief.

"Nothing. It wasn't important." He reached out to her and rejoiced when her hand met his. He pulled. She scooted to him and let him take her under his arm.

"I guess I wasn't listening," she said. "I seem to do that—get lost in my own thoughts—a lot these days."

"I think it's hard not to. It must be hell, waiting and knowing there's nothing you can do." He still envied her, in a way. At least she knew what was going to happen. She wouldn't be called at work to be told her life had been destroyed.

"It wouldn't be so hard if I could just convince myself it's all right to want it to be over."

Her breath caught, and he heard the agony in her voice.

"My mind tells me I'd be selfish to want him to go on living like…like he is now. My heart…" She turned her face into his neck.

Gus tightened his arms. After a few moments, he felt a tear trickling down his chest, then another. Again he stroked her back, knowing nothing he could do or say would make her feel one whit better.

Hating himself for the surge of desire that always accompanied the feel of her against his body.

He held her, forcing his own need into the oblivion it deserved. Finally, she sniffed a couple of times then raised her head.

"I'm sorry." Her voice was fogged with tears.

"It's okay. Sometimes we need to cry." He was sure of that now, for he had once needed the solace of tears, a solace that had been denied him by the strength of his guilt.

She sat back and wiped her eyes with the heel of one hand. "You must be getting really tired of my weeping all over you."

He pulled his handkerchief from his pocket and offered it to her.

Her lips trembled in a pathetic attempt at a smile and she shook her head. "No, I'll be all right now. Thanks for holding me." Her eyes were bloodshot, her nose red and her face splotchy. Her voice was tremulous, as if the tears still hovered just inside her throat.

But her chin was firm and her shoulders no longer drooped in depression.

"Sure?" he said, and wiped one last tear from her cheek.

"Sure." She tried to laugh and almost succeeded. "I've got to get home. Juana likes to get to bed about ten."

"I'll walk you home."

Always before she'd refused, telling him she enjoyed the time to herself, time to think. This time she merely nodded.

On the street, Gus reached for her hand. She let him, but did not respond to his gentle squeeze.

"Bernie called me into his office today." His voice was loud in the silence of the empty street.

"What did he want?"

"He wants to retire." He had been amazed to discover that Bernie was not in his early sixties, as he appeared, but seventy-three.

"Bernie's been wanting to retire for years." Sally stopped to look both ways before crossing a deserted Main Street. "I think he started to talk about it when I was in high school."

"He says he hasn't because he doesn't want to see the shop close." Gus could understand that. Bernie's grandfather had opened a livery stable in Whiterock almost before it was a town. He had installed the town's first gas pump, sold the town's first Ford to an early mayor. Cowles Implement had represented John Deere farm equipment for almost a century.

"It's kind of sad," Sally said, her voice a melancholy murmur in the night. "Bernie and Jim Guthrie, Wilma, Georgina and Jack, even Tom Holmes, down at the Chalk Pit. And Lyle. They're all so determined that Whiterock won't become a modern ghost town like Westfall or Harper. And it's all so futile."

"Futile?" He found he was a little irritated at her indifferent assumption that the people who were the core of the town were wasting their time and energy.

"Of course. Open your eyes, Gus. Look around." She gestured, although all either of them could see was the library and a few dark houses on the east side of Fifth Avenue. "You can't tell me this is a town with a future. When more than half the businesses are closed. When every year more of the young people move away."

"Pete and Lupe Gomez are young," he protested. "And Bill Holmes is coming back."

"The more fools they. Would you stay here, if you were young?"

A decision he had thought impossible turned out to be as simple as answering her question. "If I'd found this town twenty years ago, I might have been too dumb to see what it offers. But I'm older—and wiser, I hope—and I'm going to stay here."

"What do you mean?" With one hand on her front gate, she turned enough to look up into his face.

"I'm buying Cowles Implement. I'm investing in the future of Whiterock."

Her mouth dropped open. "You're kidding?"

"I've never been more serious." After a long, drifting time, he found his life had a purpose. "There's something special here, Sally, and I want to be part of it, to help it grow." Laughter bubbled out of him, as if it had been waiting to be set free. "Can't you feel it? The energy? If we can tap it, we can bring Whiterock back to life."

"I'm glad for you," she said, and stepped inside the gate. "Everyone should have a dream."

She turned and walked away, without so much as saying goodnight.

"AREN'T YOU GOING TO SEE GUS TONIGHT?" JUANA SAID THE NEXT evening, when Sally settled beside her to watch *Rio Lobo*. Just what she needed, a good Western. Simple. Uncomplicated.

"Not tonight." She picked up her sewing basket. This latest bundle from Tsugawa Linen contained a pair of Pendleton wool slacks that needed taking in. She wanted to baste the alterations and send the slacks back for approval before she did any cutting.

"Problems?" Juana had become a real admirer of Gus's. She practically simpered whenever he dropped by after work or on weekends. And Gus, the big flirt, treated her like a sexy girl.

Sally would be highly insulted if a man acted toward her like that.

She nipped the thread with her teeth. "I don't think you'd call it a problem. I just decided I've been leaning on him too much lately." *And weeping on him.* In retrospect, she couldn't believe how often she'd soaked his shirt with her too-ready tears. "I don't want to become dependent on him, you know."

Juana muted the TV. "Why not? Isn't that what love is all about?"

"Love? Oh, come on, Juana. I'm not in love with Gus Loring." Of course, she wasn't. She was simply using him, as he was her, to fill her sexual needs while she waited for her father to die.

And if she found any day when she didn't see him colorless and blah—well, that was because so much of her life lately was bleak and dismal.

"I'd be a fool to fall in love with him, anyway. Do you know what he told me last night?"

Juana shook her head.

"He's going to buy Cowles Implement. Can you imagine? I don't think Bernie has made a profit the past five years, and Gus is going to buy him out."

"Lupe told me today," Juana said. "She and Pete are excited. Gus promised Pete he would be in charge of the garage."

The commercial ended, and she turned the sound back on.

Sally finished basting the pants along the lines marked for the new seams. Finding that the movie wasn't holding her interest, she went in to check on Pop.

He was sleeping peacefully. She sank into the chair beside his bed and took his hand. It lay flaccid in hers.

"You'd approve, Pop," she said, even knowing he could not hear, would not understand. "You always said what Whiterock needed was a little new blood and it would come back to life."

He'd always believed that the closure of so many of Whiterock's businesses was only temporary, the signs of a weak economy. When the market improved, he'd said, and he could reopen the mine, she'd see. Whiterock would thrive again.

But she'd seen the last geologist's report. The rich vein of diatomaceous earth had narrowed until it was little more than occasional pockets intermingled with the vitric tuff that was the major geological formation underlying the town. There was a chance, the report had said, that there was a richer deposit below the layer of tuff, but verifying that would require new exploration.

The report must have arrived in the last weeks of her mother's life, because it was dated that spring. Pop wouldn't have cared then, and later he had probably forgotten, as he had so many important parts of his life.

Well, even if she had the knowledge and experience necessary to reopen the mine—which she certainly did not— she didn't have the inclination. Her career had been on hold quite long enough, thank you. It was almost time for her to think of herself again, at long last.

Only duty was keeping her here. When she had done all she could for Pop she would be free to go.

And go she would. Instead of trying to sell the house, she was going to simply walk away from it. She could deal with it later, after she'd had a time for herself again. Milly or Georgina would keep an eye on it. Lyle would come in occasionally during cold weather and make sure the roof was tight and the pipes intact.

Someday, when she had rebuilt her life, she would come back and close this chapter. Until then, there was nothing in Whiterock she needed.

Nothing.

INTERVAL

Achievement! Loring will remain.
What energy does he sense? Possible danger?
Caution!

SEVENTEEN

THE HEAT CONTINUED. EVERYONE SPOKE OF HOW THEY COULDN'T remember such a long spell of hot weather, despite several long droughts over the past fifty years. Great, towering thunderheads built in the afternoons, but all they brought were hot, dry winds and distant thunder.

Sally's visits to Gus became less frequent as Pop's condition deteriorated. She hated to leave her father, yet sometimes she had to. The only forgetfulness and peace she could find, even if only for a brief time, were with Gus.

Often she didn't feel like making love. She would have, for Gus's sake, but he insisted he wasn't so desperate he was willing to just use her. "I like being with you," he told her one night. "That's enough."

She wondered if he meant it, or was just being considerate. He was really a very nice man, for someone who said he didn't want anything more than good sex.

One night they were sitting in his front room, sweltering in heat scarcely moderated by his laboring air conditioner. Gus suggested driving in to Vale for an ice cream cone, but she didn't want to be gone that long.

"Then let's go to the concert." He stood and pulled her up with him.

"Concert? What concert?"

"In the park. You mean you didn't hear about it?" He locked the door, probably the only person in town who ever did.

"I don't think there's been a concert there in fifteen years," she said, and remembered other summer nights when life—and she—was young.

"Yeah, well, there's one tonight." Tucking her hand in the crook of his elbow, he pulled her toward the door. "I just heard about it this afternoon at the Post Office. Tom Holmes organized it, after he caught Buster and Ben letting the air out of tires of the cars parked in front of the Chalk Pit. It's his idea of giving the kids something to do."

Half a dozen cars were parked along Fifth and a few more were in the grade school lot. They strolled to join the small crowd gathered on the dry grass in front of the bandshell. Off-key squeaks and squawks and an occasional scrap of melody sounded from the room under the stage.

"Evenin', Miz Sally," Ernie Green said. "How's your pa?" He sat in an aluminum-and-webbing lawn chair beside Wilma Collotzi.

"You know Will's not gonna get any better, Ernie, so don't be botherin' Sally about him," Wilma said. "Silly old man. No more brains than a bullfrog," she muttered, and moved her chair over beside Sally and Gus. "Don't know why I carried a chair all the way over here for him, anyhow."

Since Ernie was a good five years younger than Wilma and lived closer to the park, Sally didn't know, either. She smiled and kept her mouth shut.

The band emerged, and Wilma shushed everyone around her. The kids—and a handful of adults—carried folding chairs onto the stage and set them in a ragged semicircle. Once they were seated, Angie Garcia stepped onto the overturned box before them and clapped her hands.

Sally had forgotten that Angie had been her piano teacher for one frustrating year a long time ago.

The music was loud. It was also surprisingly melodious—Angie must have worked a miracle to pull such a disparate assortment of would-be musicians together into a halfway decent ensemble.

"I would have given my right arm to have played in something like this when I was a kid," Gus said, his voice low in her ear.

"What did you play?"

"It's more like what did I try to play. I never had lessons, but I did have an old clarinet that had been my uncle's. A friend helped me learn the basics, and I used to amuse myself—and drive my mother almost to distraction—attempting to be the next Pete Fountain."

"Pop played the baritone horn." Sally remembered summer nights much like this when she and her mother would sit here on the grass and listen to music as sweet as any she'd ever heard. "One summer I even played." She had to smile at the memory.

"Just one?"

"Since they only let me beat the bass drum because they were desperate, it's not surprising they found another drummer the next year," she said. "I have a pretty good sense of rhythm, but my ear is as tin as they come."

The band began to play a medley of show tunes, and she closed her eyes. Pop had loved all the old musical comedies. He had hundreds of vinyl records, including some early Jeanette

MacDonald-Nelson Eddy performances. There were even three original Caruso disks among his collection.

How she missed the world of musical theater. She had worked in opera almost exclusively since leaving college, but her experience had included a few of the American classics like *Showboat* and *Porgy and Bess* as well. Her portfolio was stuffed with costume designs for all of her favorites.

Gus's arm stole around her waist, and she leaned back into his embrace as the band played the first notes of "Old Man River." The arrangement they were playing tonight lacked the majestic baritone horn solo that had been Pop's favorite.

"I hope they're going to make this a regular event," Gus said. "It's really great."

Sally looked around. When she and Gus had arrived, there had been only eighteen or twenty people in the park; now there were dozens. Milly Kemp stood back behind the rows of lawn chairs. Georgina and Jack were here, too. Arne Lundquist sat with his son Eric and his grandchildren. Elizabeth Alpin looked extremely pleased with herself in a shiny new powered wheelchair, with Grip wheezing and drooling at her knees. To Sally's knowledge, Mrs. Alpin hadn't been out of the house except to attend church for more than a year, not since she broke her hip.

Inexplicable tears sprang to her eyes. She loved these people. They were the flavor and texture of her life. How could she leave them, even after Pop was gone?

Yet how could she stay? Whiterock had nothing for her except its people and a house empty of everything but memories.

And Gus.

Whiterock had Gus.

SALLY SAT WITH POP MOST AFTERNOONS NOW, TALKING TO HIM, although she didn't believe he understood a word she said. It made her feel better, and maybe that was all that counted.

She told him how Mrs. Alpin's roses had gone into dormancy due to the heat, how Bill Holmes was fixing up the old Anderson place, how Georgina predicted a new life for Whiterock now that Gus had shown faith in the town by making an offer on Cowles Implement.

"I don't know where he expects to find the business," she said as she bathed Pop's face on the hottest day yet. It had hit a hundred before noon, and she had no idea what it was now—just hotter. "But I wish him luck, because the whole town is counting on him making a difference."

"I think you're mistaken about Bernie not making a profit." Juana came in, carrying a stack of fresh sheets. "Pete says Gus told him if business stays as good as it has been, he's going to institute a bonus system. Pete should get a pretty good check every December."

"I have trouble believing business is that good," Sally replied, as she gently patted Pop's cheeks with the towel. "There, now, that should feel better." She wiped the perspiration from her own forehead with her forearm. "Although I don't think anything really helps."

The two fans stirring the air in the room merely made it habitable.

"I think I'm going to bring him some ice cream," Juana said. "Cool him from the inside out. You want some?"

Sally shook her head. "But I'd take a soda, if there are any cold."

Juana stopped at the door, looking back. "You don't want to believe there's anything in Whiterock worth staying for, do you?" she said, and left Sally alone with her father—and her confusion.

She sank into the chair beside Pop's bed where she'd spent so many hours lately.

"She's right, Pop. I keep trying to convince myself I hate Whiterock when the truth is…I just don't know what the truth is." She found his hand, lying limp and lifeless on the thin sheet covering him, and enclosed it within her own.

"I don't really know what I want anymore, Pop," she said, as much to herself as to him. "I called Kate Wilson in Portland last night. You remember Kate—she was my roommate my senior year in college. She told me I was crazy when I mentioned I was thinking of coming back. Give her a chance to live somewhere like Whiterock, she said, and she'd take it so fast my head would spin."

Stroking along his flaccid fingers, she remembered when she'd thought his hands were the strongest, the safest, the gentlest.

"I've been thinking about it, too. Whether I really want to go back to the city, I mean. I hate the traffic, and the air always smells like diesel exhaust. I hate being afraid to walk at night, and having to worry about my purse being snatched and my car vandalized.

"But I can't give it up, Pop. I just can't! There's something really exciting about seeing my ideas, my dreams become real on stage. Do you remember when they used my costume designs for *Peter Pan* when I was in college? You and Mom came to Seattle for the play. And you sent me roses on opening night."

Had his hand tightened on hers? She stared at him, but he made no sign he was aware of his surroundings. He had not moved, to her knowledge, for several days, except for swallowing when food was put into his mouth. Even the slow, shallow motion of his chest was almost imperceptible.

"If there were only something here I could do. Or if I could take the house with me."

The house her great-grandfather had built would sit empty, vulnerable to weather and decay. Every room, almost every wall, held memories. The attic was full of three generations'-worth of treasures and junk; the basement was almost as bad.

Would she ever have the time to go through it all, seeking the keepsakes to give her roots as she grew further and further from where she began? Why hadn't she sorted it all out while she had the time, while Pop had still been alert enough to help her?

She knew why. If she had begun, it would have been an admission her father was mortal, and she hadn't been able to face that so soon after her mother's death.

Sally sat with Pop through most of that day, held by more than the heat. There was something about him—an elusive alertness?—that hadn't been there before. She used the heat as an excuse to avoid her daily trip to the Post Office, but the truth was, she didn't want to leave him.

She was dozing, her head against the side of his bed, late that afternoon. She woke when the floor just outside squeaked.

Juana stuck her head into the open doorway. "Telephone."

Sally released Pop's hand and stood. She was stiff from sitting so long, and her hair was damp where it had been between her head and the bed. She went to the kitchen phone because the rooms on the east side of the house were cooler than those on the west.

"Hello?"

"Are you all right?" The faint voice had that hollow, faraway sound that cell phones sometimes caused.

The abruptness of the question stopped her for a moment.

"Gus? Is that you?" The connection was so poor she could hardly hear him.

"Yeah, it's me." A loud buzz all but drowned him out. "Damn this phone!" His voice faded then grew loud again. "I had this feeling something was wrong. Is your father—", followed by something she didn't catch as the buzz returned.

"Pop's about the same." She raised her voice, spoke slowly. "A little weaker but no real change."

"I should be back in town by six. Should I come over?"

This time she heard him clearly.

"I–I don't think so, Gus. It's so hot..." Oh, God! She wanted him here more than anything, but if he came she'd want to go back to the apartment, to the sweet forgetfulness she only found with him.

"...need me...five minutes..." Again his voice came clearly, "Did you hear me?"

She nodded. "I heard you. Thanks, Gus."

The line went dead. Slowly, she replaced the receiver. Of course she needed Gus, but Pop needed *her*.

She went back to his room. Perhaps she'd bring the rollaway bed in tonight—her bedroom would be like an oven.

"Sally, I think you'd better come here," Juana said as she entered. The nurse was standing by the bed, holding Pop's hand. No, she was taking his pulse.

Sally practically ran across the room. She grabbed her father's other hand.

Did he again return the pressure, or was it her imagination?

She looked at his face that had been blank and vacant for so long. Now she had the strange feeling his eyes were closed in sleep instead of the half-consciousness of the past few days. And his lips were curved ever-so-slightly in a smile.

Sally returned the smile, even knowing he didn't see. This was her father again, as he had been. The father she'd admired, respected, loved. Once more she felt an insubstantial pressure on her hand.

She knew.

"Goodbye, Pop," she whispered. "God bless."

Even as she watched, his features seemed to sink together, to lose all character. His chest, barely moving for days, moved no more.

Juana made the sign of the cross. Her lips moved briefly, and she placed the hand she was holding carefully on his chest.

Sally wept, wondering at the eternal reservoir of tears within her. For a long time she stood by the bed, unwilling to relinquish Pop's hand, to relinquish this last touch. Finally, as Juana had done, she laid his hand atop the other one.

"I'm free," she whispered to the empty room. "I can go now."

And the cost of her freedom was unbearable. As she had known it would be.

GUS STOOD AT THE BACK OF THE CROWD ON THE HILLSIDE, LOOKING not toward the minister who spoke of all the things Will Carruthers had been to Whiterock, but gazing down on the town he'd so recently tied his future to.

He didn't want to be here. He hated funerals, had sworn never to attend another. Sally certainly didn't seem to care that he was here, no matter what Juana said. When he'd gone to the house the evening of Will's death, she'd treated him in the same impersonal way she had treated all the other people who'd come by—politely, with no hint of recognition.

She hadn't needed him. Not then. Not in the three days since then.

That's what you wanted, wasn't it? For nobody to need you?

The service ended. Sally sifted a handful of dirt onto the coffin and stepped back. She was white as a ghost, and the stark black of her dress didn't help. Even her hair seemed to have lost its sunny color, and her eyes were the same cold, empty gray as the sky.

Gus stayed where he was, ignoring the drizzle that wet his hair and sent drips down the back of his neck. He had the feeling all of Whiterock was in mourning, even the weather. At least the heat wave had ended.

The rest of the mourners lined up to speak to Sally, who was standing under the canopy with the minister and the unfamiliar woman who'd played the violin during the service. Gus overheard enough to eventually figure out the violinist was Sally's aunt from Florida. The line moved slowly, until he was concerned for Sally, greeting each person, hearing what a wonderful man her father had been.

Marilyn's funeral had exhausted him. He'd felt as if each person who shook his hand took a little of him away with them. If Sally was feeling anything like that, no wonder she looked as if a slight breeze would blow her away.

"She needs you," a soft voice said from behind him. He turned to see Georgina standing just behind him, uncharacteristically somber in a navy dress and pearls. Even her hair was tamed into a demure twist.

"No, she doesn't."

"Believe me, Gus, if a woman ever needed a man, Sally needs you right now." She slipped an arm through his. "She's had to be strong ever since she came home to nurse Elaine. That takes a lot out of a person."

He shook his head. "Any need Sally has, I can't fill."

"Seems to me you were doin' all right for a while there."

"That was a different kind of need, and you know it." He wished he could bring himself to pull free. It was time he was back at the shop.

"You know what I think, Gus Loring? I think you and Sally are two of the dumbest people I've ever seen. She's cutting off her nose to spite her face, and you're handing her the knife."

"You're not making sense." But she was, in a strange, convoluted way.

"Think about it," Georgina said, and pulled him with her to the end of the line.

He tried to free his arm.

When her grip only tightened, he said, "I've got work to do."

"Not until you pay your respects," she said, and tightened her grip. "It won't hurt a bit, I guarantee."

"That's what you think," he muttered, but when she asked him to repeat it he was silent.

Impatiently he waited, while the line inched slowly forward. He spent the time sneaking glimpses of Sally while Georgina spoke with the people around them. She looked worse, if possible, than she had when he'd first seen her. Then she'd been overweight and unkempt. Now she was too thin and too carefully groomed, and seemed to carry the weight of the world on her slim shoulders. There were lines around her mouth and dark smudges under her eyes. Her movements were abrupt and nervous; her fleeting smile was brittle.

They reached the head of the line at last. He murmured condolences to Sally's aunt, who responded with equal impersonality. Then he was before Sally, and her hand was in his before either of them quite realized it.

The electricity surged and burned up his arm, jolting him with a deep and piercing pain. He almost dropped her hand, except that he could not. It was like a true electrical shock, when muscles lock into rigidity. All he could do was hang on and hope for the best.

Sally blinked, seemed to shiver. Then she closed her eyes and shook her head, a tiny movement of denial.

"Thank you for coming." Her voice was thin and weak.

He wondered what hidden reserve she was drawing strength from. "How are you holding up?" God only knew. She didn't look strong enough to stand, let alone deal with all the stress of this difficult ritual.

"Fine," she said, in a near-whisper. Clearing her throat, she repeated, "Fine. Aunt Trudy is a real tower of strength. And Juana, too."

"Good," he said, while clinging to her hand. If her aunt was such a tower of strength, where had she been during all those months Sally was half-killing herself with the total care of her father?

"Sally, I—"

"Gus, I—"

They both stopped and looked at one another. Sally gestured for him to go ahead.

He wasn't sure what he'd meant to say, but he knew what he had to do. Releasing her hand, he took her into his arms. Holding her close, he buried his face in her hair. It smelled of honeysuckle and sunshine, but only faintly, just as everything about her was a faint ghost of the Sally he had held in his arms only a few days ago.

"Come to me," he whispered. "Tonight. Please." It was the only way he knew to comfort her.

"Oh, Gus," she breathed, so softly he could hardly hear, "I can't. Aunt Trudy—"

He released her, unwillingly but without protest. Of course. The funeral was over, but she still had obligations.

"Soon, then."

She nodded against his shoulder, but then stiffened, pulled back. "If I can." Her voice was polite and cool. She looked everywhere but at him.

"No, Sally, there's really nothing I want," Trudy said as they sat over coffee the next evening. "Remember? I took several boxes back when I was here before, after your mother's funeral."

"But what am I going to do with all this?" Sally looked around the library, at the shelves stuffed with books, the racks holding Pop's vinyl record collection, the framed needlepoint decorating the walls. "I can't just leave it here!"

"Of course, you can. You said yourself the house will be perfectly safe."

"But what if—?"

"What if nothing!" Trudy said. "I won't say that being here to take care of Will was wrong, but staying would be a crime. You deserve a life, girl!" She caught Sally's shoulder and spun her around to face her reflection in the big mirror above the fireplace. "Look at you! Gaunt, bags under your eyes and looking years older than me!"

Sally looked, and didn't like what she saw. Her aunt had just gone through her third facelift and didn't look anywhere near her age. But neither did Sally look younger...did she?

"I have lost weight the last little while. But I needed to."

"Pooh! You're so bony it's a wonder that gorgeous man didn't get bruises when he hugged you this afternoon."

Not wanting to talk about Gus, Sally turned and gestured toward Pop's desk.

"He must have gone through these before he got so bad. Everything's here—his insurance policies, the house deed, even a copy of the geologist's report on the mine."

"Oh, lordy, I hope you're not thinking of opening that old pit up again. Then you'd never get away from here."

"Oh, yes, I will. Just as soon as I can get the house closed down."

Once she'd said the words, she felt curiously adrift, as if she'd already cut her bonds to home.

"Well, then, that's all right." Trudy picked up the empty coffee cups. "Now I think I'll go on up to bed. I'm not as young as I used to be, and having to leave here at five to catch my plane means an early night."

Sally glanced at the clock as she walked with Trudy to the kitchen door.

"If you're going to bed, I think I'll go for a walk. Do you mind?"

"Mind? Whatever for? I'll be asleep. I still haven't adjusted to the time change." She started up the stairs, but stopped on the fourth step. "Sally, promise me you won't give up your dreams. Will used to send me the reviews of the productions you'd worked on, and it sounded to me like you were making a name for yourself."

Sally looked up at her. "All that seems like so long ago. Almost like it happened to someone else."

"As soon as you get back to work, it will all be real again." Trudy continued up the stairs, calling "Goodnight," as she disappeared around the landing.

"I hope so," Sally said softly, knowing there was no one to hear her doubt.

She took a sweater from the hall tree and slipped out the front door. Was Gus waiting for her, or had he given her up? She hadn't said she'd go to him.

It wasn't her abilities she doubted, she told herself as she walked down Jasper, but her pluck. In the past few days, she'd given a lot of thought to her options. Each time she'd seriously

204

considered going back to Portland or Seattle she tensed up, thinking of the stress she always felt in the city.

If there were only some way she could have the best of both worlds, she thought. She wanted to live in Whiterock and work in Portland.

How much of the uncertainty she was feeling was due to Gus and his decision to purchase Cowles Implement?

INTERVAL

Carruthers energy muted, contained. Fading.

Bonding suspended.

Loring remains suspicious.

Foreboding. Apprehension.

Fear?

EIGHTEEN

G US DIDN'T SPEAK WHEN HE OPENED THE DOOR. HE SIMPLY took her into his arms and held her. Sally clung, again sensing his great strength. After a while he lifted her and carried her to the sofa, and settled her upon his lap.

"I'm sorry," she said, relaxing for the first time since the night she'd walked away from him. "I'm sorry I stayed away."

"There's nothing to be sorry for." He buried his face in her hair, nibbled on the lobe of her ear. "I just wish I could have done something to help."

"You were here. Just knowing that helped." She shivered at the tiny pain his teeth inflicted and shifted in his embrace. "Can we talk about something else?"

"Sure. What?"

"Anything. I don't care. Tell me a joke." It would be nice to laugh at something totally dumb again.

His brows lowered, as if in thought. "Okay. Tell me: if April showers bring forth May flowers, what do May flowers bring?"

Sally had heard the rhyme many times, but she didn't think there was another line to it. "June...June something..." She was still finding coherent thought difficult. "I give up. What?"

"Pilgrims."

She groaned, and it felt almost as good as laughing.

"I'll tell you another joke. I signed the papers on Cowles Implement today."

"So, you went ahead and did it. I don't know whether to congratulate you or commiserate with you. I don't see why it's a joke, though."

"Bob Larkin says it is," he said, his mouth twisted in a plaintive grin. "He seems to think I'll lose my shirt. Offered to bet me a hundred-to-one I'll go under within a year."

"Pooh, don't listen to him. Bob's the most negative person I've ever met, and he'll bet on anything."

"Maybe I am making a mistake." He sounded almost in need of reassurance.

"I won't argue," she admitted, "but Pop always..." Her voice broke, and she took a deep breath. "Pop always said the best thing about failure is that it says you were brave enough to try in the first place." Twisting in his loose grasp, she faced him, almost nose-to-nose. "Where did you get the money, anyway?"

It was none of her business, but she had been consumed with curiosity, almost since she first met him. He certainly wasn't the itinerant man-of-all-work he'd seemed at first.

"Sold my share of a partnership." His eyes became shuttered and the lines around his mouth deepened. He buried his face in both hands, elbows on his knees. His fingers dug into his scalp, and the tendons in his neck stood out against the skin.

Quickly kneeling beside him, Sally slipped one arm around his shoulders. "Gus? What is it?"

He took a deep, shuddering breath. "Nothing," he said at the end of a violent exhalation. "Just a headache."

He raised his head and attempted a smile. It was unconvincing. If eyes were mirrors of the soul, Gus's soul was in Hell.

Sally had seen glimpses in him of great suffering more than once, back before they had become lovers, but they had been quickly concealed behind his frequent withdrawals. She honestly had forgotten, but now she saw it again, stronger than before.

She laid a hand on his arm and felt the drawn-steel strain there. "No. You're feeling something more than a headache."

His arm jerked violently, flinging her hand away. "Damn it! Let it be, will you? I told you I've got a headache, and if you can't give me credit for knowing how I feel, maybe you'd better go!"

"I don't think I should," she said, no longer angry now but worried.

"Go away, damn you!" he shouted as he leapt to his feet and strode to the window overlooking Main Street. "Go, Sally," he said again, his voice more quiet but the tension in his body no less.

She followed, to stand behind him, not quite touching.

"Do you really want me to?" she said softly, remembering the times he'd held her, soothed her, listened to her troubles.

"Yes," he said, but she heard doubt.

She waited.

"No," he said, at last. "Stay."

She could see some of the tension drain from his back, leave his shoulders.

"Please, stay."

She did, as much for herself as for him.

Gus wanted her to go because if she stayed she'd pity him, and he couldn't take that. He wanted her to stay because while she was here he wouldn't be alone with his memories.

As long as he'd been running, he'd successfully left the memories behind, but now—now that he was committed to staying in Whiterock—they were back with a vengeance.

Running had been easier—safer. It had worked, too. Until he'd come to Whiterock. He'd managed to keep the memories locked solidly away in that back corner of his mind where they couldn't hurt him. Now they were clamoring for release.

For the first time he wanted to talk about what had happened. Perhaps by talking he could erase the pain from his soul.

But not tonight.

He led her back to the sofa and pulled her down beside him. Tucking her head against his neck, he stroked his hand along her bare arm, marveling yet again how like velvet she felt. He told his body to relax. Tonight, Sally needed his comfort. Nothing else.

Especially not his confession.

"I'm such an awful person," she eventually said into the silence. He had thought she'd fallen asleep. He certainly had been close to it, himself.

"Why?"

She didn't speak for a while, but he could feel the tension in her body.

"Because I'm glad Pop is dead." A long silence, then: "Well, maybe not glad..." Her voice broke a little. "Relieved," she finally said, the word coming out on a sob.

"Shouldn't you be? I hadn't seen him for a while, but I can't imagine he'd gotten any better."

"No. He just kept deteriorating." Her voice was stronger now, but he didn't like the hysterical note in it. "Do you know what the first thing I said was, after...after I told him goodbye?"

He grunted an interrogative, but he had a good idea, given her so-obvious guilt.

"I said, 'Now I'm free.' Can you believe that? My father had just died, and all I could think of was that now, at last, I can go." She covered her face with her hands until her voice was muffled. "I can have a life again. I can do all the things… Oh, God, Gus! How can I be so selfish?"

Her words cut into a wound still unhealed. He tried to find the right words, the words that would allow her self-forgiveness. He had heard them himself. Heard and hadn't believed.

How could he offer Sally false coin?

He took the coward's way out. He said nothing, only stroked her, rocked her, murmured formless sounds he hoped were comforting. She never did weep, but he gradually felt her relax. He continued to hold her, hoping she was deriving comfort from his embrace.

After a while, when he thought she'd fallen asleep, she spoke.

"I have to go." Her voice was hoarse from tears unshed. "Trudy's leaving early tomorrow, and I want to be there to say goodbye."

"Then we'd better get you home right now." He picked her up, pulled her onto his lap. She was light in his arms, lighter by far than she had been that first day he'd carried her up the narrow stairs to this apartment.

He drove her home.

She wouldn't let him inside. "Come tomorrow night." Her kiss was more sisterly than loverly. "I'll be alone then."

Gus went back to his pickup, wondering why it hurt so much to know she was preparing to say goodbye.

Aunt Trudy was curled in a wing chair in the living room, when Sally let herself in. "We need to talk."

Talk was the last thing Sally wanted.

"I thought you were going to bed early." She wanted to bite the words back as soon as she'd spoken them. Trudy was her last close relative, and she should cherish every moment they had together. Florida was a long way from Oregon, and they probably wouldn't see each other again for years.

"I was. Until my conscience got the best of me." She gestured toward the matching chair on the opposite side of the fireplace. "I brought this to show you, and then decided not to. But when I went to put it into my suitcase tonight I realized I couldn't take it away again." She picked up a thin, shabby book that had been tucked between her thigh and the chair's curved arm. "Maybe you can make sense of it."

Sally made no move to take the book. There was something about it... Something that made her reluctant even to touch it.

"What is it?"

"Your great-grandmother Lorena's journal."

"Grandmother Lorena? The one who—" Her interest was piqued, in spite of her disinclination.

No one would ever talk about the grandmother who had abandoned her husband and son when the baby was only four months old. As far as she knew, no one knew—or cared—what had become of her.

"Does it tell why...?"

"I think so. Will disagreed. He believed, as our father did, that she'd run away because she couldn't abide living here, so far from anything remotely resembling culture. But I think she had a different reason. One that always frightened me." Aunt Trudy drew circles on the cover with her fingers, hesitated, and finally went on, almost musingly. "I found this in the attic when I was about twelve. Because no one would ever talk about her, I kept it hidden. But I read it—and had nightmares for months."

"Good grief! Now you've really got me interested. What's so scary about it?"

"I'd rather you read it for yourself. Make up your own mind whether to believe what she says. And if you do... No, I won't say any more. It's just too fantastical." She rose, tapped the spine of the book against her lips. "I left home partly because of what Grandmother Lorena says. After reading that, I could never feel comfortable here again. Even now…"

She thrust the book at Sally. "Take it. Make up your own mind. Maybe you'll think I'm crazy."

Sally took the book and held it with two fingers, still not sure she wanted to touch it but having no choice unless she wanted it to fall to the floor.

"Won't you tell me more? Why it scared you? Why you want me to read it? Why—"

"No. I've probably already said too much." Aunt Trudy's shrug spoke of confusion, indecision, puzzlement. "Just read it. And make up your own mind." She seemed about to embrace Sally, but then she pulled back, as if uncertain how her affection would be received. "I've got to get some sleep. See you in the morning."

Before Sally could object, she ran lightly up the stairs.

Sally stared down at the book, not sure whether she wanted to know what scared Aunt Trudy, who had always seemed to be one of the most self-possessed, competent women she knew. Pop had always said his sister should have gone into politics.

"With her brains and determination, she would have ended up running the country," he'd commented the day they got the news she'd been offered a partnership in a law firm.

Aware of a shivery, tingly sensation at her nape, she carried the book to Pop's office and slipped it into his desk—her desk now—where she would see it again when she started sorting through the details she must deal with before she could leave Whiterock forever.

The last thing she needed right now was a crazy family legend.

After seeing Aunt Trudy off, Sally went back to bed—five-fifteen was far too early to be up, even on a hot day in late July. She slept until after noon, and woke in a pool of sweat, with the bedclothes tangled about her feet and tears in her eyes.

Once she dragged herself out of bed, she couldn't seem to get started. She needed Gus—or someone—to give her the incentive to do something besides sit at the kitchen table drinking coffee and feeling exhausted.

Was he coming to dinner tonight? She had a faint memory of asking him to...to what? Shoving her coffee cup aside, she laid her head on the table and closed her eyes. Even thinking about fixing dinner was exhausting. Probably because of all those interrupted nights. She had hundreds of them to make up for.

The phone rang, startling her.

"Sally? Gus. Look, I got a call from Abe Zigler. Their baler is acting up, and they want to get the haying done before more weather moves in. Can I have a rain check?" He spoke hurriedly, as if he'd only remembered to call her as he was running out the door.

"Of course," she said, relieved. Now she wouldn't have to cook. "Tomorrow, maybe?"

"Can we make it Friday?"

"Sure. Anytime."

"Great. See you then."

Another yawn interfered with her answer. It didn't matter, because he'd hung up.

Well, since she was going to be alone tonight, maybe she'd just take a little nap before she scrounged up some supper.

BEING YOUR OWN BOSS MEANT YOU SOMETIMES WORKED FOR A REAL slave driver, Gus thought as he opened the door at the Bite-A-Wee Cafe on Friday. The problem with Zigler's baler had required taking a part in to Vale to be welded. *Damn, I wish Pete knew how to weld.*

This morning he'd gotten a call to go out to Westfall to look at a stubborn pump. He'd thought he'd bought an automotive repair shop. Now he was learning that one of the reasons Bernie had kept the business profitable was that he'd been an all-round handyman, willing to tackle—and fix just—about anything.

A degree in mechanical engineering hadn't trained Gus to be a mechanic, not by a long shot. Thank God for all those years tinkering with hotrods.

His usual seat was waiting, between Arne Lundquist and Roy Gilbert. He greeted both men as he sat down, accepted the sports page from Arne.

After agreeing with Georgina that he wanted the special— Hangtown Fry with garlic toast—he checked the baseball scores.

Somebody ought to teach those boys how to play ball.

Closing the paper in disgust, he asked Roy how his grandson's Little League team was doing.

"Pretty good." Roy smiled widely. "They've got a good shot at the state playoffs."

"Maybe I should follow them instead of the Red Sox," Gus grumbled. He folded the paper and set it aside as his lunch appeared. "Thanks, Georgina. Looks good, as usual."

He reached for the ketchup.

"Seen Sally the last few days?" Georgina was leaning close so that only he, Roy and Arne could hear her question.

"Yeah... Well, not since Tuesday night." A frisson of alarm went down his spine. "Hasn't she been in?"

"Nope, and Wilma hasn't seen hide nor hair of her, either."

"I'll check on her," he promised.

"You do that." Georgina poured more vitriol into his almost empty cup.

God help him, was he actually learning to like the bitter brew?

THE HOUSE LOOKED ABANDONED.

Gus paused at the front gate, noting the lowered shades, the pulled drapes. Thus had it appeared to him the first time he'd been here—a neglected old house, its paint peeling where the merciless sun scorched it all day, the yard unkempt and going to weeds. He pushed through the gate, which squealed at him like a soul in torment.

The doorbell echoed in the house, but he heard no answering footsteps. Trying the door, he found it, as usual, unlocked. Now, *that* was a habit he'd never get into.

"Sally?" He stuck his head inside. "Are you here?"

There was no answer beyond a slight echo. He entered.

The house still smelled of sickness, of old age, of dying. He'd just check, to make sure she really wasn't here.

The ground floor rooms were empty. Dust motes disturbed by his passage danced in narrow rays of a westering sun that managed to shine between the almost-closed drapes. There was no sign Sally had intended to feed a guest this evening.

Checking out in back, he saw her car parked in its usual place, so she hadn't gone to Vale or Ontario. He knew a momentary, surprisingly strong relief. She hadn't gone away.

Where the hell was she? He had walked along Main Street on his way here, so he knew she wasn't uptown.

"Sally?" he called again.

"Sally!" This time he shouted.

Silence.

He returned to the front hall. Indecisive, he put his hand on the front doorknob.

No. He had to search the entire house before giving up.

He had never been up the stairs. They squeaked. No wonder she hadn't really wanted to bring him here while Juana was in the house. He wouldn't have been comfortable, either.

The first room he poked his head into had to be the master bedroom. It still held a high, old-fashioned, brass bed and an oak dresser an antique dealer would sell her soul for. And a faint scent of lilacs, reminding him of a magic day in May.

The next room was empty, looked as if it had been for many years, with its faded posters of World War II-vintage airplanes.

The end room on the other side of the hall was Sally's. Opera and play posters, a drafting table and a tall stool looked incongruously modern and workaday in company with the canopy bed and French provincial dresser.

Then he saw her, sprawled facedown across the bed. The T-shirt she wore was hiked up, exposing pink nylon panties. Her hair, tangled and dull, hid her face.

"Sally!" He reached out, but then hesitated, almost afraid to touch her. When he saw the shallow movement of her chest, he completed the gesture, laying his hand on her shoulder. "Sally! Wake up!"

No response. He shook her and she moaned.

Her eyelids fluttered. Scrunched shut. "Go 'way," she whined. "'M sleepin'."

Laying the back of his hand against her cheek, he eliminated the possibility of fever. "Wake up, damn it! You owe me supper!"

Slowly, laboriously, she rolled to her back. Her eyes opened.

"Wh' timezit?" She lifted her arm as if to check her watch, but she wasn't wearing it.

Gus saw a digital clock on the dresser. "Six-fifteen."

"Oh, God. Too early," she said, her voice still querulous. "'M gonna sleep till noon." She turned to her side and pulled her knees up. Her arms circled the pillow and her eyes closed again.

"Six-fifteen *p.m.*" He picked her up. "Time for supper."

Ordinarily, he liked the feel of her in his arms but not now. There was a faint sour smell about her, a combination of perspiration—it must have been ninety in her room—and something else. Did despair have an odor?

He carried her downstairs. This time, before he took an unwilling Carruthers into the shower, he was damn well going to undress.

INTERVAL

Weakness.

Control over light and shadow depleted. Maintenance of glamour sporadic.

Carruthers? Contact tenuous.

Alarm!

NINETEEN

Gus had to grin. A more likely candidate for drowned cat of the year he had never seen. Sally's hair hung in dripping strands around her face. The thin towel he'd wrapped haphazardly around her covered—barely—the most interesting parts of her, but its frayed ends only added to the pathetic picture. She sat in one of the kitchen chairs, glaring at him and sipping on the tea he'd made.

"You are despicable!"

"And you're awake," he countered.

"I would have been just as awake if you'd been nicer." Her lower lip threatened to pout.

He wanted to kiss it.

"All you had to do was call me."

"Sally, my dear, I did call you. I yelled my fool head off, and you didn't even twitch. I shook you. I picked you up and carried you, undressed you, manhandled you into a warm shower. And all you could say was 'Go 'way. Lemme 'lone.'" He imitated her querulous pleas, complete to whiny voice. "You didn't come alive until I turned off the hot water."

He couldn't help smiling as he recalled how she'd yelled. One second his arms had been full of a limp body, the next she was squealing and fighting to get out from under the icy spray.

"Call it a last resort."

"Hmph." Her glare could have left scorch marks.

Gus ignored her and went to prowl the refrigerator, found nothing but condiments and an almost-empty pitcher of what looked like lemonade. He opened the top door. A tray of ice, some freezer-burned hotdog buns.

"Isn't there any food in the house?"

"In the freezer. Downstairs." She shivered, and her teeth chattered, despite the residual heat in the kitchen.

He took the cup from her shaking hands. "Can you walk?"

"Of course, I can." She stood, clinging to the back of her chair.

Gus again noticed, before he picked her up, how much slimmer she was—almost gaunt. Hadn't she eaten these last few weeks? "The hell you can," he muttered.

"You know, I get really tired of the way you just pick me up and carry me off, whether I want to go or not," she said, as he climbed the stairs to her room.

Marilyn had liked being carried, had enjoyed his—as she put it—masterful ways. He set Sally down as soon as he topped the stairs.

"Suit yourself, but get some clothes on. We're going to Vale for dinner."

"What if I don't want to?"

"Then I'll dress you myself and carry you to my truck. You need something more substantial than lemonade and potato chips."

She turned and stalked away, clothed in a meager towel and immense dignity.

Gus thought she said something about a pig's eye before she went into her bedroom. He only just managed to catch the door before she slammed it. From the gleam in her eyes, she'd planned on locking him out.

"Dress!" he ordered, and folded his arms across his chest. "Or I'll do it for you."

She stuck her tongue out at him but went to her dresser and pulled out underwear. After giving him one more scathing glare, she turned her back on him. Somehow, she managed to make the act of clothing herself seem all her idea.

Sally wouldn't admit it for the world, but she appreciated Gus's concern. She didn't know what had gotten into her, but she simply had not been able to stay awake.

Two days! She had actually slept the better part of two days, rousing only for infrequent trips to the bathroom. How much longer would she have slept if he hadn't come?

"Okay, let's go." She slipped her feet into espadrilles. "Or are you going to make me wait all night for my supper?"

His lips twitched, but he didn't respond.

Once they were on the road, he said, "When are you leaving town?" His tone was no longer half-teasing.

"Are you in a hurry to say goodbye?"

"No. But if I'm going to have to, I'd sort of like some warning."

She turned her head and looked out. The sagebrush-covered hills seemed to hide secrets in their folds, but there were no answers among them. "I don't know," she admitted

Several miles later, when they had reached the outskirts of Vale, he shook her. "Wake up!"

"I am awake." What was making her drift off this way? She couldn't seem to complete a coherent thought for the life of her.

"You couldn't prove it by me," Gus growled. He turned the pickup into the parking lot of a café. "This okay with you?"

Sally shrugged. "Anywhere. I'm not really hungry."

He slammed his door and came around to open hers. "You should be," he said as she slid from the high seat. "You don't look as if you've eaten for a week."

Sally wasn't sure she had, not really. Oh, she'd nibbled at the food her neighbors had brought over, but mostly she'd wasted more than she'd eaten.

Gus changed her order from soup and sandwich to steak, baked potato and salad. It was easier to go along with him than to argue. He said little during the meal, just watched her, made sure she kept eating. It gave her time to think.

Although she felt like a naughty little girl, Sally had to admit—to herself, never to him—that the food tasted wonderful.

"How about a piece of pie?" he said, when she'd finally cleaned up her plate to his satisfaction.

Sally refused the pie, but took a couple of bites of his. It wasn't as good as Georgina's coconut cream. None of her food had tasted as good as what she was used to, yet she knew this restaurant had a good reputation. Gus seemed to enjoy his dinner, though, so perhaps her taste buds were as numb as the rest of her.

Once they were on the highway, going home, he said, "Cat got your tongue?"

"Hmmm?" She had her cheek against the window, watching as the lights of civilization grew fewer and farther between.

"So, when do we say goodbye?" he said into the silence.

"I don't know. I haven't...I can't seem to decide anything."

"When Marilyn... A very wise friend once told me that after someone you love dies you shouldn't do anything for at least a year."

"I've already been here far too long. Right now I don't know if I have a career to go back to. In another year... Well, if I wait that long, I might as well just stay in Whiterock and forget about fame and fortune." She did her best to speak lightly, but knew he couldn't have missed the little quaver in the last few words.

"You know, you have a nasty little tendency to self-pity."

"I don't!"

"Yeah, you do. What's the matter? Can't you find anybody else to feel sorry for you? Poor, noble little Sally, sacrificing her life for her parents and never a word of thanks. So she's got to play the martyr so everyone will notice what a loving, conscientious daughter she is."

"You...you... You bastard!" She grabbed the door handle, wanting nothing so much at to get as far away from him as she could. "Stop the car!"

Only Gus's hand, jerking her away from the passenger door, pulling her to the limit of her seatbelt, kept her from trying to jump from the moving pickup.

"Suicide wish, Sally?" he said, once he'd pulled to a stop.

She'd given up struggling, but not wanting to get away from him. "Let me go. I can walk from here." She tried to free her hands, but they were both held as securely as if in manacles within the tight grip of his fingers.

"We're nearly six miles from Whiterock," he said, "and it's black as pitch out there."

"I don't care!"

"I do. Now, are you going to behave, or do we sit here until morning?" He settled back in his seat, apparently relaxed except for the hand that held hers. He looked good for all night.

As far as that went, so was she. Sally clamped her lips together and looked out the window. It was, indeed, an extremely dark night. The forecast clouds must be moving in.

The cooling engine ticked, an alien sound in the desert night. A cicada sang, and far away, a coyote called to his love. Once a car whooshed by, its headlights momentarily illuminating Gus's face. It looked carved from stone.

Another car, its tires singing on the pavement, came up on them from behind. It slowed and pulled in behind them. Footsteps crunched on gravel, and then a flashlight shone through the window. It played on Gus, on her, moved to where his hand still held hers.

Gus lowered the window. "Evenin', officer. What can we do for you?"

"You might want to move up the road to where there's a decent shoulder," the state policeman said. "It'd be a pity for somebody to come along and rear-end you."

Sally opened her mouth to ask for help, but closed it again. No sense in bringing a stranger into a private fight. She sat quietly while Gus and the cop exchanged pleasantries. When he'd left, she said, "You can let me go now."

"You given up on walking home?"

"Yes. Please, can we just go?"

She felt Gus's gaze on her for a long moment. Finally, he released her, and she folded her hands together in her lap.

Neither of them spoke the rest of the way home. When he pulled up in front of her house, she had the door open almost as soon as he stopped.

"Thank you for supper. I'm really tired. Goodnight."

He caught up with her at the foot of the front steps, catching her wrist in a light hold she could easily have escaped.

"What?"

"Will you do me a favor?"

Her nod was automatic, but she bit back the yes before it could escape. "That depends."

"Say goodbye before you run away." Without waiting for her reply, he turned around and strode rapidly to his pickup.

Sally doubted he heard her say, "Yes, of course. Of course, I will."

All evening, Gus had resisted the dull ache of desire he'd felt ever since holding her, wet and slippery, in his arms in the shower. She would probably have punched him out if he'd laid a hand on her.

"She's right," he muttered as he walked back to his pickup. "I'm a total bastard."

He could not believe he'd said those things to her. ...*nasty little tendency to self-pity...play the martyr...nobody to feel sorry for you...*

Hell! In her place, he'd have bloodied his nose, at the very least.

Tomorrow he'd apologize. If he went back tonight, he might be taking his life in his hand—or at least be risking bodily harm.

He drove slowly back to his apartment, parked in his usual spot but didn't open the door. Instead, he sat there, window down, listening to the night sounds.

The only indication there were human beings within a hundred miles was the muted hum of the refrigeration units at Lundquist's Market. A light breeze whispered among the silver maples surrounding Nagy's Cabins, and somewhere off in the distance a coyote sang to the sky.

Slowly, the silence soothed him, muting the persisting guilt, soothing the residual desire, leaving him content and at peace.

He rolled up the windows and got out, breathing deeply of the clean, sagebrush-scented air. At this moment, he was as content as he had ever been in his life.

SALLY LEANED AGAINST THE DOOR AFTER SHE'D CLOSED IT. "I HATE him," she whispered. "He's mean. Spiteful. How could he say..."

Her words echoed in her head. *...can't seem to decide...forget about fame and fortune...*

Worse, the nasal whine in her voice sounded loud and clear in her mental ear. She winced. "What a crybaby."

Somehow, the days since Pop died seemed unreal, as if she'd been trapped in thick, clinging fog, both mentally and physically. Her mind had refused to work; her body had lacked energy; and she had been so sunk in despair, in self-pity, in apathy, that she hadn't even seen how bad she'd been.

"Thank heavens for Gus." She turned out the light he'd left on in the front room, picked up the sweater she'd left on the newel post, and went upstairs. She wasn't sleepy, so maybe she'd dig out her portfolio, see what it would take to update it.

Sally woke early, plans and schemes whirling inside her head. She took her address book down with her, set it on the table while she made coffee.

She'd looked through her portfolio, decided all it needed was an updated resume. All her designs were as good as—or better than—she remembered. She'd gone to bed certain she wouldn't sleep a wink, but she had. Long and restfully.

Steaming coffee cup in one hand, address book in the other, she went to the study where Pop's desk sat, its top clear and uncluttered. *I will not cry*, she told herself as she sat in the big leather chair that still seemed to hold the warmth of his body.

Nine o'clock. Not too early to call St. Louis or Chicago. She did, and discovered the old friends she was seeking were off on vacation or had moved on to new challenges. *I've lost touch. How long has it been? Three years? At least.*

She dialed Dallas.

There was work out there, she discovered. Exciting work. Interesting work. The Dallas Opera was staging a new *Aida*, and *The Daughter of the Regiment* was on the schedule in Nashville.

Sometime during her second cup of coffee, she discovered she was losing her enthusiasm. Finding a job, going through all the rigmarole of submitting designs, changing them, working with the director, the set designer, trying to please everyone—maybe she'd be happier staying here and volunteering in the high school drama departments in Vale and Ontario. It wasn't as if she had to work. Pop's estate would keep her in comfort the rest of her life.

...a nasty little tendency to self-pity...

"Damn it, no! I've made such a big deal of going back to work. How would I ever explain...?" She reached for the phone again. Dialed a Portland number.

After the third ring, someone picked up. "...finished, email Vincent. Sorry. Distracted. This is T.J. Smithfield."

"Hi, T.J.. Sally Carruthers. Remember me?"

"Sally?" Her college roommate's shriek nearly deafened her. "Oh, God, girl! I was just thinking about you! Where have you been? How are you? Are you busy?"

"Whoa!" Sally felt herself on the edge of a laugh. T.J. always made her feel better than anybody else in the whole world. "Let me get a word in edgewise."

"Well, hurry. I can't believe this. Just when I was...So, say something!"

"I've been here, in Whiterock. My father... Pop died last week."

"Oh, Sally, I'm so sorry—"

Sally stopped her before she could say more. Sympathy still broke down her fragile defenses.

"Believe me, it was a blessing," she said. "And I'm fine. Tired, and out of touch, but fine. The reason I called..." She wondered if T.J. would be insulted if she went right to the point. After all, she hadn't called the woman who'd once been her best friend for far too long.

"This is the most wonderful coincidence," T.J. said before she could go on. "I was wondering how to get hold of you. I need you, girl. *Yesterday*."

Hope germinated, fragile, tentative.

"You were?"

"I was about to start calling around, see if anyone knew where you were. I had no idea you were still at home."

Sally heard the sound of voices in the background. They were muted, and then she heard T.J. say, "I'll be there in a minute. This is important. I've found us a costume designer."

The hope burst into full flower.

"Okay, I'm back. Now, listen. There's this new production company in Portland, they call themselves Broadway Reprise, and they want to do a modern version of *Carousel*. You know, with contemporary clothes and maybe an urban setting? And they've asked me to give them a proposal for costume and set design—all integrated—and I can't think of anyone who I'd like better to work with, so say you will. Please?"

If she hadn't been sitting down, she would have collapsed. Sally pinched her thigh, certain she was caught in a particularly cruel dream.

"Sally? Sally, are you still there?" The voice in her ear was anxious.

"Yes. Oh, yes, T.J., I'm still here. Look...I don't know...this is so sudden."

"You *have* been away too long. It's always so sudden. Now, can you be here tomorrow? You'll need to get some preliminary sketches together, so they'll see what we're doing; then we'll have a few weeks to finalize everything. But I don't want to stay in Portland for longer than I have to—Jason hates it when I'm away—so you can go back to Timbuktu, Oregon, until time for the presentation."

"Aren't you living in Portland anymore?"

"Heavens, no. I'm in Denver, and I'll be flying back day after tomorrow. So, you've got to be here tomorrow."

It took a while, but she finally got everything sorted out. T.J. was part of a group of freelancers who'd teamed up to submit a concept for the innovative production. They'd had a costume designer, but he'd been called away on a family emergency and they were desperate.

"You will come, won't you?" T.J. said, sounding uncharacteristically sober.

"Wild horses couldn't keep me away," Sally promised, while mentally cataloguing all she had to do. She hung up, her head spinning.

While she was packing and getting the house ready to be closed up for a while, she taped both of Pop's recordings of *Carousel.* After checking to make sure her credit card and gas cards were in her purse, she locked the house up. There was nothing in the refrigerator that could spoil, and the hot water heater was turned off.

She was thirty-five miles from Whiterock by noon.

She made a gas stop in Burns. That was when she realized she'd told no one she was going. Not even Gus.

Say goodbye before you run away.

And she had promised.

She finally found a pay phone at the library—*I have to get a cell phone, now that I'll be where there's decent coverage*—dug out her phone card and started dialing. Gus wasn't at the shop, so she called his apartment. An explanation would take forever, so she just left a brief message, promising to call again.

There was a lot more she'd like to say, but she felt inexplicably shy about doing so. They'd agreed that they were together for sex. Nothing else.

So I don't owe him anything.

She also called the Post Office. After asking Wilma to hold her mail and have the newspaper delivery discontinued, she said, "And would you ask Lyle to check the house occasionally? Just to make sure nobody breaks in or anything. Mrs. Alpin should still have a key."

"What about that young man of yours?"

"He's not my... I called him."

She meant to call Gus when she got to Portland. She really did. But once there she was so busy. And so happy.

Besides, she didn't know what to say to him.

WHEN GUS GOT HOME THAT NIGHT, HE SAW THE LIGHT ON HIS answering machine blinking, but he was too damn tired to care. He'd spent the day in the field, replacing the rings and bearings on the engine of Jock McEwen's baler. It had been an ugly job, and he was covered with grease and hay dust.

Every inch of his skin itched like the devil. He dropped his clothing just inside the door and strode naked to the shower. Once clean, he ate spaghetti cold, right out of the can, washed it down with a beer and fell into bed.

The next morning he was on his second cup of coffee before he saw the light and remembered it had been blinking the night before. He poked the PLAY button.

"Gus, this is Sally. I...ah...well, I'm in Burns. On my way to Portland. I don't know how long I'll be gone. I've got a job. I think. So I may not be back for a while. I'll call you."

A long silence. Then, "Well...uh...goodbye." A click and the hiss of an open line.

He felt as if he'd been punched in the gut.

Breathless. Stunned.

Numb, he replayed the message.

"…may not be back for a while. I'll call…"

That was all. She'd call him.

When she got around to it.

Read: *never.*

INTERVAL

Carruthers escapes. Astonishment!
Loring energy less obtainable.
Consequence hazardous.
Desperation…

TWENTY

Gus saw Sally when she picked up her mail the Thursday after Labor Day. He just happened to be looking out the front window, the one facing the Post Office, when she walked out.

He dropped the carton of oil filters he'd been about to set on the shelf. She hadn't taken more than four steps before he was blocking her path. He wasn't sure whether he wanted to shake her until her teeth rattled or kiss her until she melted in his embrace.

"Where the hell have you been?"

She looked up at him, her eyes lighting in unmistakable joy. "Oh, Gus, it was marvelous. And it means I can have it all."

He pulled her into his arms, ignoring the bundle of mail she held, only wanting her close and safe.

"You've been gone for three weeks. Not a word. For all anybody knew, you'd dropped off the edge of the earth. Damn it, woman, what got into you?"

Three weeks of hell, wondering what had happened to her. Wondering if he'd ever see her again.

"Let me go, Gus." Her voice was muffled, and he became aware he was holding her tight against his chest. Her arms, with the bundle of mail, were wedged between them.

He released her, but immediately captured her elbow. He wasn't going to let her get away until she explained.

"I'm glad to see you, too," she said, and her smile just a tad uncertain. "Buy me some coffee?"

"I want to talk to you, but I don't want to do it in front of the whole town," he growled.

"Then you'll have to take your turn. I promised Georgina I'd stop and tell her about my adventures on my way home."

Stifling his impatience, he said, "I'll go with you."

They took the back booth in the Bite-A-Wee Cafe, the one where he'd sat with her before. Georgina poured them both steaming coffee, and then slipped into the booth beside Sally.

Gus doctored his coffee and waited impatiently while Georgina caught Sally up on all the local news.

"Now it's your turn. You've obviously had a pretty exciting time. Tell us all about it," Georgina propped her chin on both fists.

He had to admit he'd have demanded the same, but not nearly so diplomatically.

"I have a job." Sally's smile was as wide as forever and as bright as the sun. "That's why I went to Portland." She told them of the phone call, her hurried preparation to depart. "I know I should have called someone, but I was so excited I never even thought about it."

The look she gave him asked him to forgive and forget. He wasn't sure he could, but he'd listen. Once upon a time he'd been this enthusiastic about his work. He'd be a real jerk to rain on her parade.

"I've always done my best thinking when I was driving."

She sipped her coffee, and he wondered if she even knew how she grimaced at the taste. Like everyone else, Sally drank Georgina's vitriol without complaint.

"Well, anyway, I listened to *Carousel* four or five times on the way. And I stopped to sketch—oh, at least a dozen times. So, by the time I got there it was almost midnight, but I had concepts for every scene."

Lyle Curran slid into the seat beside Gus.

"Good to see you back, Sally," he said. "Next time, let me know you're leavin' town, will you?"

She had the grace to look ashamed. "Sorry, Lyle. I was so excited I didn't even stop to think. Did Wilma tell you I called from Burns?"

"Ayup." He nodded his thanks for the coffee cup Georgina had fetched. "Guess it didn't occur to you we'd be a little worried when we didn't hear another word from you. Not even where you were staying. I was all set to put out a missing person report."

"Sure you were." Sally clearly did not believe him.

Gus had had enough of her blithe disregard for the feelings of all the people who'd worried about her. "Damn it, Sally, didn't you give even one thought to the fact we might have been concerned when you disappeared like that?"

"No, I didn't, Gus, and I'm sorry." She didn't look sorry. She looked about ten years old and in possession of her heart's desire. "Anyway, T.J. and I worked like beavers—all day and all night, it seemed like—for days and days. Finally, we had everything together, and we took it to Broadway Reprise's Board of Directors. And guess what?"

Georgina said, "Well, don't keep us in suspense. Did they like your ideas?"

"They loved them! They had planned on looking at several concepts before making a decision, but they took ours on first sight. We'll do the detail drawings, and start production in November."

"So, I guess you'll be movin' to Portland," Georgina said.

Gus echoed the thought but found he had no voice to say the words.

"Well..." Sally looked directly at him. "That depends. I don't have to, although it might be easier if I did."

He found his voice. "Depends on what?" Even to his ears, his voice was harsh and labored.

"On you," she said. "It depends on you, Gus."

Her words echoed in his ears, along with the muted conversation of the café's denizens, the rumble of a truck on the street outside and the amplified beat of his heart. He stared across the table.

"I guess you two have a little talkin' to do." Georgina picked up her carafe. "I'll see you later."

"Me, too," Lyle said. "Later."

Sally enclosed her coffee cup in her hands and looked over it at him. "I guess I shouldn't have said that, not right here in front of everybody." Her tone was thin and hesitant.

Shaking his head, as if that would put his brain back into working order, Gus took the cup from her and set it on the table. "Let's go. Georgina's right. We need to talk."

He pulled her to her feet easily, but quickly dropped her hand when she seemed inclined to follow him. They left the café amid friendly comments and farewells from everyone. For once, he didn't feel the comfortable sense of belonging that had been growing on him these past weeks.

Sally turned east. "Let's go to the park. I've been cooped up in hotel rooms and meetings for days."

He walked alongside her, not letting his shoulder touch hers. His senses were dulled, as if he were wearing a veil of some thin black fabric that shut out sound as well as light. The empty storefronts seemed shabby, with crumbling brick and peeling paint. Litter drifted along the cracked sidewalk, swept by the hot, dry wind that had been blowing for what seemed like forever.

Or was he just now seeing Whiterock for the dying town it had always been?

"Oh, no!" Sally stopped at the curb in front of the library, looking across Main Street.

"What?" He couldn't see anything different.

"The elk," she said, almost tearfully. "Someone's vandalized it again."

Sure enough, the bronze statue had lost its antlers; he tried to remember when he'd last seen them. Although he'd come past here just yesterday, he hadn't really noticed the condition of the elk—or the park, for that matter

It was time for a work party again. The rain in July had caused everything to grow faster than usual, and the whole place looked shabby and unkempt. And they were going to have to put a temporary fence around the damned bandshell before some kid climbed up into it and got hurt—the storm the other night must have been worse than he'd realized. There were shingles missing, and new holes in the stucco facade.

Sally was wringing her hands. He guided her to a bench, brushing it off and spreading his handkerchief before letting her sit on it in her white jeans. She said nothing after she'd seated herself, simply stared across the park at the willows bordering Hackberry Creek.

Finally, he could stand it no longer. "Why does whether you move to Portland or not depend on me?"

"Do you love me?" Her words were slow and almost dreamy.

"I told you—"

"So did I."

"Damn it, Sally, if I could love anybody, it would be you. But I can't."

He had made a vow three years ago, and nothing had convinced him to break it, not even the big hole Sally had left in his life when she'd disappeared.

"Why?"

God! Couldn't she just let him alone? He stood up and walked away from her, stopping a few feet from the bandshell. While he stared at the crumbling stucco, he wondered if he owed her the truth.

He decided he did.

"Remember I told you I killed my wife? You didn't believe me."

"No one who knows you would believe it."

He glanced over his shoulder and saw she was still sitting on the bench. Good. As long as she kept her distance, he could think straight.

"Then they're all wrong." He swung around but stayed where he was. "Damn it, Sally! I *killed* her!"

"If you shout a little louder, the whole town might hear you." She patted the bench. "Why don't you come here and tell me about it?"

"I don't want to talk about it," he grumbled, but he did go back and sit beside her.

"Fine. So, tell me about *her.*"

"Who?"

"Your wife. You know. The woman you claim you killed." Sally figured if she could get him talking, he would tell her. She knew he loved her—he'd shown it in countless ways—but he wouldn't admit it even to himself at this point.

And if he couldn't admit he loved her, she would be leaving Whiterock.

"Her name was Marilyn," she prompted. "Was she blond?" *Was she beautiful?* was what she really wanted to know. She almost hated Marilyn—for having had Gus's love, for having shared his life with no strings attached.

"No, her hair was sort of brown," he said, while staring off into space. "And her eyes were brown, too."

"Tall? Slim?" Sally would hate being a physical carbon copy of Marilyn.

"No. No, she was short—five-one, I think—and she fought her weight all the time." His mouth twisted in a grimace.

"And how long were you married?" This was like pulling teeth.

"Seven ye— Damn it, Sally! None of this matters."

"Gus," she said, and held him beside her with a light touch on his forearm, "everything about you matters to me."

It had taken her about three days to learn that—once she was away from Whiterock and the sorrowful memories it held for her. In clearing her mind for work, she had also cleared it of a lot of emotional baggage.

"You know, I miss Pop something awful," she said. Even virtually mindless, Pop had at least been a presence in a house that now held only ghosts. "I don't think I can stay alone in the house. It's too empty now."

"So you *are* leaving." Not a question. A statement.

"I don't want to." She had realized that within a day of her arrival in Portland. She enjoyed the excitement, the vitality, the tempo of life in the city, but she knew now she had never been comfortable there. Portland—any city, she presumed—was the proverbial nice place to visit. "I want to live here."

Mentally holding fast to her initiative, she looked him straight in the eye. "I want to live here with you."

"That's not possible."

"Then tell me why it's not. Damn it, Gus! Leave me a little pride. Tell me why you'll have sex with me but you won't live with me."

Suddenly, he was holding her, his hands gripping her upper arms like manacles, his face so close to hers she could see the tiny flecks of gold in his changeable hazel eyes.

"The road to our house was a long, curving hill." He spoke rapidly, as if the words had been lodged behind a dam in his throat and were finally breaking loose. "I had noticed that the steering on her car was loose, and I mentioned it to her. But Marilyn hated having to take her car in to the shop. She didn't understand cars. She called anything to do with them 'man stuff,' and was certain that mechanics took advantage of her."

He shook her slightly, as if making sure she caught the implication. "So it was my job to see that her car stayed in good repair. But I was busy."

She heard the guilt and agony in his voice but didn't entirely understand it. "Did you think the problem was serious?"

He released her, and she rubbed her arms, sure she would show bruises tomorrow.

"I–I don't know. Any steering problem is potentially serious, but I told myself it was simply normal wear. I was under a deadline and put a lot of things off until I'd finished the project."

He sat back and closed his eyes, his face drawn and set. Obviously, he believed he should have taken time to have his wife's car repaired.

"Gus?" she said, after a long silence. "What happened?"

He took a long time answering. When he did, his tone was thoughtful. "Marilyn wasn't incompetent. She did a lot of volunteer work—Junior League, one day a week at the Children's Hospital, reading to seriously ill kids." He looked into the distance, perhaps into the past. "She was bright and talented. Everyone liked and admired her."

If she was so competent, why couldn't she take responsibility for the car she drove? Sally bit her lip, locking the words inside.

"Gus, you said you sold your business to get the money to buy Bernie out. It must have been more than a garage…"

She'd envisioned him as an auto mechanic back in Connecticut, just as he was here in Whiterock. It was clear now she had been mistaken.

"Ayup."

"Well?"

"Well what?"

"Tell me about your business." She reached for his hand where it lay lax upon his thigh. Just to touch him gave her a sense of security. That, and hope they could resolve his lingering guilt so he would be free to link his life with hers.

She saw that she still had battles to win before it could happen. For the time being, she would be content to learn more about him—she certainly had made a number of false assumptions.

"It was just an engineering firm in Hartford. Nothing special."

"An engineering firm? You're an engineer?"

"Ayup."

He'd been drawling to the manner born for weeks now, so why was he suddenly and stereotypically a taciturn New Englander?

"Gus! Tell me." She laid her fingers on the hard muscle just above his waist, where, she had discovered, he was extremely sensitive. "Tell me."

They had been serious too long. Perhaps if she made him laugh, he would kiss her.

"Don't you do it," he growled. He caught her hand before she even saw him move. "I'm not in the mood for games, Sally."

"Okay, let me ask you something, since you insist on being so serious. How long is it going to take you to forgive yourself for Marilyn's death? What's it going to take to convince you that she was as much at fault as you were?"

He dropped her hand and seemed to retreat from her, although physically he could have been cast in stone, so immovable was he.

"Gus?"

He stared straight ahead, though she knew he wasn't seeing the decrepit bandshell. She stood, because she could not look into his eyes otherwise.

"Gus, please talk to me."

"Talk? You want talk? A while back you said all you wanted from me was good sex!"

He thrust himself upright and brushed by her, walking toward the arched bridge across Little Hackberry Creek. Sally stood where she was for a moment, wondering whether she should just give up. If she let him go, her life would be less mercurial, more predictable. Gus was not a peaceable person, but he was a lovable one. To her, at least.

I won't let him go! I can't!

She followed him, stood beside him looking down into the dry, rocky creek bed. "That was before I knew you, Gus, before I learned what a loving, caring person you are."

He swore.

"Did that make you feel better?"

He snarled.

"I think I fell in love with you the morning you took Pop into the shower and didn't worry about your uniform, not even your shoes. But I didn't realize it until the night you let me cry all over you. Everybody else saw me as strong and dependable.

You looked past that and saw how weak I really was and liked me anyway."

"Don't kid yourself. I saw the strength. If I hadn't I would have walked, no matter how great the sex was." His fingers were white where they gripped the dry, splintery bridge rail. "I told you a long time ago I didn't need anyone leaning on me."

"Because of Marilyn?"

She could understand his reluctance to get involved with a woman who might be dependent. She would never be—*could* never be—like his dead wife. Her need for him was not the leaning sort, but she needed him, nonetheless.

"Because you can't depend on me!"

"Gus, I can't think of anyone I can depend on more than you. You've been there whenever I needed you. Without you, I might not have survived those last few weeks before Pop—"

"Sally, you're still recovering from your father's death—it's only been a month, for God's sake!—and you're not thinking straight. Give it time. One of these days you'll look back and see that we had a great little affair, but I'm the last person you want to spend the rest of your life with."

He jerked away from her and stalked down the other side of the bridge. She followed, slipping into the shelter of the willow canopy to stand beside him. The water, scant now, slipped chuckling over the rocks left from the millpond dam.

She could not share its laughter. She was fighting for her future. "I think there's something you're not telling me, Gus. What is it?"

That was the only possible explanation—he was far too intelligent to carry a burden of guilt for what was really a minor bit of negligence, even if it had resulted in tragedy. He must realize that Marilyn had made choices, too, and hers had contributed to her death far more than his had.

"You just can't leave it alone, can you? What do you really want, Sally Carruthers?" He grabbed her again, surely adding to the bruises he had already inflicted. "You want a description of how Marilyn's head was all but cut off by the bed of the truck she swerved into? How about the stink of burned flesh?"

He shook her, so hard her head rattled.

"Let me tell you how it feels to get stopped on your way home from work. How I got out, thinking I could help. Black, oily smoke was still pouring out of both vehicles, but the flames had died down. They'd burned hot, though, so I didn't recognize Marilyn's car at first. It was a twisted mass of torn metal, even before the fire. But for some reason the front license plate was almost untouched, even though it was all but torn off the bumper."

His voice was firm now, almost impersonal. As if he was telling about something that happened to someone else.

"I saw that license plate and my mind went numb. I must have stood there staring at it for...oh, maybe a quarter of an hour. When I finally came to myself, all I could feel was relief. She must have died quickly. Nobody could have survived that collision."

Sally touched his arm, wanting to hold him as he had her, when her pain had been more than she could bear.

He jerked away, out of her reach.

"I stood there and watched the firemen, the rescue crew, because I had to. I couldn't turn away. They finally got the doors open and were removing the...the body. Then one of them yelled. I didn't hear what he said at first."

Great sobs shook his body, but when she again tried to reach out to him, he slapped her hand away.

"Do you know why he yelled, Sally? What was so much more frightful than a young woman's burned body? Do you?"

She shook her head, knowing whatever it was, was horrible. She had pushed him this far, though, and she owed it to him to share his pain. She had, at last, found Gus's demon.

"Tell me." She could see him holding back the awful words. "You must tell me."

"It was a child's safety seat," he whispered finally, not sobbing now, only shedding silent tears. "And my daughter was in it."

He pushed her aside as if she were no more than one of the flexible, dangling willow branches surrounding them. Shoulders hunched, almost as if he were expecting to be flogged, he strode away from her, back toward town.

INTERVAL

Frustration!

Carruthers return producing unexpected stimulus toward permanent bonding.

Loring procrastinates, laments unchangeable events.

Human emotions inexplicable and inessential.

Restore glamour?

TWENTY-ONE

GUS HAD HIS DUFFEL PACKED BEFORE THE FRENZY LEFT HIM. HE looked around his apartment, thinking that he had settled in here more than he had anywhere else. More than he should have. He unplugged the espresso machine, wrapped a T-shirt around its glass carafe. Everything went into a paper bag. He'd leave the microwave.

As he crossed the living room, he glanced out the window that overlooked Main Street. Sally was just entering the café, looking as if she hadn't a care in the world.

Damn her! Damn her to hell and back! He'd managed to wall off the pain and guilt of Emily's death almost completely until he came to Whiterock and met Sally. Since then, she had been saying and doing things that made him remember, and he would never forgive her for that.

As long as he managed to forget he'd ever had a daughter, he didn't miss the piece of his soul that had died with her.

There was a rickety outside stairway leading into the vacant lot where he parked his pickup. He had always avoided it, certain it would collapse under his weight. Today he didn't care. Going down the front stairs meant he would be in full sight of the café and anyone else on Main Street.

There wasn't anyone in Whiterock he cared enough about to tell goodbye.

He was about halfway to the highway when he remembered the shop. *Crap!* He pulled into the next side road and turned around.

Retracing his route, Gus thought about the first time he'd driven this route. Five months ago... It felt simultaneously like years and only days. He wished it had never happened.

Ernie Green was back on his bench, waving, as Gus passed the library. In the next block, Buster Holmes, Ben Kemp and Rhoda Garcia were hanging out in front of Lundquist's Market, eating Popsicles. Ben called out, and the other two smiled at him.

For a moment, he regretted his furious need to run again. He'd welcomed them when they'd dropped by occasionally to talk about college and careers. Now he was going to let them down.

Then he was passing the Bite-A-Wee, and Roy Gilbert was just coming out the door. He also waved. Gus ignored him, too.

He parked in front of the shop and cut through the parts department.

"Pete! Hey, Pete!"

"Yo?"

"C'mere." He looked around the shop. It was less cluttered than when Bernie had owned it. One of Gus's first projects had been to move the spare-parts-that-might-come-in-handy-someday into a sturdy shed behind the building. Now they had room to bring the larger trucks inside instead of having to work on them under the corrugated aluminum canopy next to the building.

"I'm taking off. I'll leave a letter on my desk authorizing you to sign checks. If you aren't sure of anything, ask Bernie." He turned, giving Pete no time to answer. Maybe it wasn't fair to leave the young mechanic in complete charge of the shop, but he didn't give a damn about fair. All he wanted was out.

Pete followed him to the office, demanding answers. Gus ignored him, quickly wrote a note to his bank and shoved it into Pete's grease-stained hands.

"You wanted to prove you're smart enough to be a manager, didn't you? Well, here's your chance." He shouldered his way past Pete. "See ya."

With a casual wave, he walked away from what had seemed, only days ago, his future.

The hell with it. He had no future. Only a past he would never come to terms with.

He had one foot in his pickup when he saw her. Even two blocks away, he recognized her—her walk, her shape, the sexy swing of her hips as she walked away from him, her arms no doubt full of mail. For just a moment, he hesitated.

Then he banished the tempting thought that he might still find peace in Whiterock. For him, there was no peace. Not here.

He didn't turn around again to go back toward the highway. Instead, he drove out Chalk Mine Road, knowing that eventually it would take him to Harper and, thence, back to US 20. Tom Holmes waved at him as he passed the Chalk Pit Tavern, one last reminder that in Whiterock he had, for a little while, felt as if he belonged.

The last time he'd come this way the pastures had been green and lush, the cattle fat and sleek. Now, late summer had dried the pasture grasses to tan, and the cattle were grazing in higher meadows. Even the scattered, shrubby willows along Hackberry Creek showed the effects of the long hot spell in their drab leaves, some already yellowed and dying.

Gus drove between the fences, his windows closed against the plume of dust that began under his front wheels. He should have seen this country at this time of year before investing in it. He'd have thought twice.

He should have anyway. Buying Bernie Cowles out hadn't been the smartest move he'd ever made. The only way out of this trap was going to cost him.

Still, he'd only used about half of what Roger had paid for his share in L/B Engineering, the loss wouldn't matter much. It was only money, and a worthless drifter didn't need much money.

The faded sign pointing to the Carruthers Chalk Mine invited him to turn aside. He drove on, despite his earlier intention to return and explore someday.

It's just a hole in the ground.

He turned right, toward Harper and US 20. The road to anywhere else.

It depends on you, Gus. As if Sally were sitting beside him, he heard the words again.

"Now she knows better," he muttered, remembering the expression of horror on her face when he told her of Emily's death. Of his responsibility for it.

Driving automatically, his mind churning with memories, he followed the winding road past the badlands. Not until the sun shone directly into his face did he realize he'd managed to take a wrong turn.

So what? There's a cutoff to the highway down here somewhere.

So, Sally would stay in Whiterock if he asked her to. Somehow or other, she'd seen something in him that made her think long-term, despite their mutual agreement to keep any mention of commitment out of their relationship.

"Changed her mind, didn't I."

The badlands were on his right when he discovered he'd missed the turnoff to the highway.

Damn! I'm really out of it today.

Not surprising, though. The roads between Whiterock and US 20 were like a maze, twisting and turning until you didn't know which way you were going. He slowed, watching for the next turnoff.

It shouldn't be too far now.

But he drove for quite a while without seeing it, until once again he was at the entrance to the Carruthers mine.

He pulled off the road and stopped. The map in his glove compartment wasn't any help. All it showed was the main roads.

Gus peered through the windshield. *Let's see. I came in from the north, so if I go north, I should come to the junction at the west end of town. And that'll take me out to the Westfall Road.*

The next thing he knew, he was driving down Main Street.

SALLY STARED AFTER GUS AS HE ALL BUT RAN AWAY FROM HER, TOO stunned to think. His daughter. Gus had had a daughter, and she had been killed in the accident he blamed himself for.

No wonder he couldn't forgive himself.

She walked slowly through the park, kicking at the tall grass, picking up litter as she found it. When she reached the trash container near the elk she emptied her hands. She only wished she could empty her mind as well.

Her love for Gus had crept upon her insidiously, unnoticed. Physically attracted to him from the first, she had been too distracted to go through the usual rituals. Getting to know Gus had been of low priority compared to her life's other complications, but she had gotten to know him better for all that. Where many people might have dated before slipping into intimacy, she and Gus had chosen sex almost as a way to avoid the emotional intimacy neither of them was ready for. In doing so, they had developed a strange relationship, one she wasn't sure she could even begin to define.

It didn't matter anyhow. He was gone.

She had started up Fifth toward home before she remembered the reason she'd come to town, other than to see if Gus was still speaking to her.

She must have left the mail in the café.

Georgina never said a word to her, nor did anyone else, but their eyes asked questions she couldn't answer, not just now. Sally tried to smile, to reassure them everything was just fine. She really did.

She didn't think she'd fooled anyone.

Ernie spoke to her as she passed his bench, and she must have replied, out of habit. Grip called her attention to his roses, coming back now after the hot spell. As if she cared about flowers at a time like this.

She had so much to do if she was going to move back to Portland. She sat at the kitchen table and started a list. First, she had to tell Frank Tsugawa to pass the word to the local dry cleaners she was no longer available for mending and alterations—if he was still speaking to her after she'd taken off without notifying him. *With three hems and a shirt to be tapered, too.*

"Let's see." She chewed on the end of her pencil. "Clean out the refrigerator. Talk to Buster about taking care of the yard. Pack Pop's stuff..."

Oh, Pop. I miss you so much.

No, she wouldn't touch his clothing and treasures, wouldn't even try to decide what to keep and what to dispose of. It was too soon and she was still too fragile. She'd simply make sure the rooms—his bedroom downstairs and the master suite upstairs—were clean, before she shut the doors on their contents.

The lists grew and multiplied. She'd have to spend a day with Max Guthrie, going over the records. Would he continue to manage everything, or would he finally, as he'd been threatening to do for years, retire and let a younger lawyer see to Carruthers Enterprises? Either way, it wouldn't make any difference to her. There was very little income these days, only what came from the leased cropland.

Then there was Pop's will. She and Trudy had met with Max about it, but she couldn't, for the life of her, remember what it had said, except that it had provided whatever was needed to bring the swimming pool fund to goal.

Gus would approve of that.

She set that list aside and began another. She'd want her drafting table and…

The pencil caught, tore the paper. It was wet.

"What in the world?"

Only then did she realize that tears were streaming down her face. Silent, burning tears. She crumpled the soaked paper in her hand and flung the pencil across the room. It hit the back door and fell to the floor, rolling back toward her with a tiny clicking sound.

"I won't…I don't want…Oh, God! I don't want to go!"

Yet not an hour ago she had told Gus she wouldn't stay if she had to live here alone. It had been a bluff, a silly, childish game played in order to get him to say he loved her.

Well, he had called her bluff, hadn't he?

Why hadn't she simply come right out and asked him?

"Gus, I want you to live with me. I'd prefer you'd marry me, but if you won't, well, I'll settle for second best."

Would that have changed his response? It might have, for he'd been fairly reasonable until she'd brought love into the conversation.

Since she knew she loved him, since she sincerely believed his feeling for her was so close to love it didn't matter, why in the dickens had she complicated matters? All she had done was give him a reason to run.

"Run! Oh, my God! What if he does?" Sally was on her feet and out the door in an instant.

Gus could have gone a long way since they'd parted.

GUS TOOK THE BACK ROAD OUT OF TOWN THIS TIME. HE DROVE BY the badlands twice more, unsure of the turns on the unfamiliar, poorly maintained gravel roads. The stark valley full of eroded columns of white chalk-like material, carved by wind and rain into fantastical shapes, were a pocket-sized version of the Badlands in the Dakotas.

At last he reached Westfall Road, just a few miles from the highway. Already his shoulders felt less burdened, his mind less clouded. Once he was on the highway again, he could forget the momentary insanity that had made him believe he could ever have a normal life again.

There was the junction, just ahead...

A few miles farther on, a familiar yellow sign showed a road off to the right.

"Wait just one damn minute!" Stopping in the middle of the road, he looked around. Yes, he was at the junction of the main road into Whiterock. "If you can't pay any more attention to your driving, you'd better get off the road."

Let's see now. If I go back to Vale, I can cut south and pick up Ninety-three, head south. I never did make it to California. He turned east. *I won't even wave as I go through town.*

He'd felt such hope the past few weeks, since making the decision to buy Bernie out. As if life—*his* life—could go on, despite the guilt and loneliness he'd carry to his grave.

As he slowed for the short drive along Main Street, he deliberately kept his eyes front.

The shabby little town looked pathetically like it had the first day he drove into it.

So much for all our hard work. Whiterock's dying, and the people here might as well get used to it.

Gus drove automatically, ignoring the pronghorns grazing beside the road, the jackrabbit that raced him for a hundred yards, the wild keen of a golden eagle hunting in wide circles overhead.

"Shit!"

He'd taken another wrong turn. Instead of heading south toward the highway, he'd taken the turn that wound through the hills south of the badlands. Sitting up straight, he leaned forward, peering through the now-dusty windshield.

Stop screwing around, Loring.

Eventually, he found himself driving the long loop to the north of Whiterock, without any clear idea of how he'd gotten there.

Now, there's *a community project worth doing. Get some signs on these back roads so people don't get lost.*

"Forget it. You won't be around to get lost, soon as you can find your way out!"

Angrily he slapped the turn indicator lever down. All he had to do was find his way to the highway, and he'd be history.

Gus slammed the brakes on so hard the pickup fishtailed all over the road before he could get it under control. How the hell had he gotten back here? *I know I went past the turnoff!*

Or had he? He couldn't remember.

Below him, Whiterock basked in the September sun, unpainted houses and shabby storefronts testifying to a loss of hope, a lack of interest. A dust devil spun paper scraps along the empty street ahead of him. Around the curve leading to Main Street, the guardrail was broken, the break marked by a faded strip of orange flagging. And as he slowly drove down Jasper Street, he couldn't avoid the potholes.

The last thing he wanted to do was drive along Main Street again. He'd left too much of himself there.

Sally.

The Bite-A-Wee Cafe, where he'd first been made to feel a part of Whiterock.

Cowles Implement. *Now I won't need to decide on a new name.*

Once more he turned onto Chalk Mine Road, intending to take the shortcut past the mine as he'd meant to do in the first place.

SALLY LEANED OUT OF HER CAR WINDOW. "ERNIE!"

"Afternoon, Miz Sally," he replied. "How you doin' today?"

"Fine. Ernie, have you seen Gus Loring?"

"Well, now, it must have been more'n an hour ago, he went whizzin' by here on his way out of town. I was—"

"Which way?"

"The first time or the second?"

Clenching her hands on the steering wheel, Sally prayed for patience.

"The last time you saw him, Ernie. Which way was he going?"

"He was comin' back into town. You see, I was down the street talking to Miz Holmes when he come by the first time, but I'd made it back here when—"

"Thanks, Ernie." She gunned the car around the corner, spraying gravel, only to brake abruptly when she saw Rhoda

Garcia and Buster Holmes leaning against the boarded-up windows next to Lundquist's Grocery.

"Have either of you seen Gus Loring?"

"He went that way." Rhoda pointed east.

"About an hour ago," Buster added.

"He was driving his pickup," Rhoda volunteered, "not the shop's truck."

Sally's next stop was the shop. Pete had his head inside the motor compartment of an old van. When she called his name, he jumped, hitting his head on the hood.

"Sorry, Pete. I didn't mean to startle you." She really resented the need for good manners when haste was so crucial. "Have you seen Gus in the last couple of hours?"

He rubbed his head.

"I sure have, Sally, and it was real strange. He came in here, wrote out a letter to the bank and told me to take care of things." He laid down his wrench. "Let me show you. I can't quite figure it out."

Sally followed him into the office. The letter Pete handed her was short and to the point. Addressed to the manager of the bank in Vale, it stated that, until further notice, Pedro Gomez had full charge of Cowles Implement, including authority to issue checks.

"I don't think he's coming back. I mean, that letter and all. Jeez, Sally, I don't know how to run a business like this."

"You aren't expected to," she said, hoping she sounded more reassuring than she felt. "He'll be in tomorrow. This was just in case he was gone longer than he planned."

Pete nodded, but he was obviously not convinced.

She was wasting time. "Did you see which way Gus went when he left?"

"Yeah. Toward Harper."

Sally was turning away when he added, "Then when he came past later, he went south. Toward the mine."

"Thanks, Pete," she called back as she ran to the door. "And don't worry. He'll be back." *If I have to hog tie him and drag him.*

Once in the car, she flipped a mental coin. East, west or south? Was he just driving around, thinking? *Oh, please, let that be it.*

She backed out, aimed the car's nose west. Without quite knowing why, she felt certain she was on Gus's trail. Then, somewhere along the road, she lost confidence until, at Harper Junction, she had no idea which way to go. He could be a hundred miles away by now, and she didn't even know in which direction.

She turned around and headed back toward Whiterock.

"He'll be back," she said, unconsciously echoing her assurance to Pete. "He has to. I love him."

She drove slowly, needing the time to come to terms with this new loss. Even if Gus returned to Whiterock, she couldn't count on his returning to her. And if he didn't, she wasn't sure she could bear it.

Inexplicably, hope grew as Sally retraced her route. By the time she reached the mine turnoff, she again felt she still could catch up with Gus.

He was not in town. She was as convinced of that as she was of her own love for him.

Just as she was convinced she would find him.

INTERVAL

Disaster!

Intolerable!

Compulsion becomes unavoidable.

TWENTY-TWO

As he approached the entrance to the Carruthers Mine, Gus slowed. He'd already wasted the entire afternoon going around in circles, and it wasn't as if he had anywhere to go. *Might as well take a look. I probably won't get back this way again.*

The log gate in the barbwire fence stood open. He drove down the incline, squinting a little at the bright September light reflected from the white rock faces. A pile of debris—crushed chalk and scrap iron, even what was left of an old wooden barrel—blocked the road where it leveled. He parked the pickup and got out.

Last fall he had pumped gas for three weeks in Butte, Montana, home of what was billed as the world's largest open pit mine. This was much smaller. He'd expected that. And it wasn't really a pit, not like the vast hole in the ground at Butte.

Columns large and small had been left, so the floor of this pit was a maze, stark-white and featureless. He imagined that the rock not removed was contaminated with—what was it Sally had said?—vitric tuff. Not worth mining, whatever it was.

He looked up and saw the sheer cliff that marked the far edge of the pit, perhaps a quarter-mile away. Because of the higher ground on that side, the wall was a good three hundred feet high, a smooth, almost dead-white surface that seemed to absorb all color except its own.

A hot wind soughed across the tops of the columns, its melancholy lament somehow suited to the barren pit. Gus picked up a piece of chalk and peered at it. Close-grained, soft enough to scratch with a fingernail, the fragment had a dirty gray-green streak running through it.

As a teenager, Gus had been responsible for the cat's litterbox. Perhaps he had used diatomaceous earth from this very mine.

He continued deeper into the pit, until he was out of sight of his pickup.

THE PADLOCK WAS HANGING FROM THE HASP, UNDAMAGED, SO whoever had gone in must have had a key. Sally parked her car in the turnaround, got out and looked at the dusty road into the pit.

I wonder who opened the gate.

Those tire tracks looked new. *But are they Gus's?* She'd be a fool to go down into the pit alone, not knowing who was there.

She looked around, trying to remember. She and Bill Holmes had come out here once, spread a blanket on a hillside where they could watch the activity in the pit. She had been so young then, and so in love.

She was no longer young, but she was in love again. And this time it was for real.

The trail was faint and overgrown. Cheatgrass seeds stuck in her socks as she scrambled through the waist-high sagebrush.

She came out onto the flat bench where a single juniper tree cast a long shadow.

There! That flash of blue at the bottom of the entrance road. She shaded her eyes to get a better view into the pit. Yes! It was Gus's pickup.

But he was nowhere in sight.

"Gus! Gus, where are you?"

Her words were carried away by the warm wind.

GUS DIDN'T KNOW HOW LONG HE HAD WANDERED ABOUT IN THE bizarre forest of chalk columns. The shadows were longer now, great patches of dimmer light at the bases of the columns, striping the dirty-white ground. He began seeing shapes in the chalk, profiles cut into the sides of columns—grotesque, inhuman figures half-seen from the corners of his eyes. Sometimes, they even seemed to move. More than once he whipped around, determined to catch whomever—whatever— was spying on him.

A curious emptiness occupied his mind, edging out the residual pain of this morning's revelation. Marilyn was all but forgotten; she might as well never have been part of his life. Emily was a poignant, long-ago memory, a grief faced and endured, but now only a bittersweet memory. Her short life had brought joy to him, given him hope in an existence that had been increasingly drear and bleak as he grew and Marilyn didn't.

Even the recent weeks with Sally were dim, as if they had occurred long ago and far away.

He wandered on, circling and meandering. Always he drew closer to the vertical white wall, higher and wider than the outdoor theater screens he remembered from his childhood.

The heat intensified, even though the sun was about to disappear over the rim of the pit. Yesterday the mercury had reached ninety; today was forecast to be hotter. Down here, heat and light collected, and were reflected again and again. Yet he went on, drawn to…something.

The hot air pulled moisture from his body, drying the trickles of sweat that coursed down his back and chest. He removed his shirt and dropped it on the ground.

The towering wall had seemed totally without tone or hue when he first glimpsed it, but as he drew closer, he saw subtle, shifting colors, shadowlike and insubstantial. The columns were broader and closer together as he approached the wall, casting wide shadows that did nothing to relieve the fierce heat. His mouth was dry.

He had to reach the wall.

The moving shadows darkened, took on faint color, and patterns developed. His mind filled in blank spaces with detail, until an image of Whiterock's Main Street formed. It looked as it had the first day he'd come to Whiterock—dingy, bleak, as gray in mood as the sky was with rain.

As it had looked today.

The shadows shifted suddenly, and their colors brightened. Now storefronts were all fresh paint and clean windows. The sidewalks were swept and busy with pedestrians. A banner extended across the street, between the Bite-A-Wee Cafe and Kemp's Drugs. Sally walked along the sidewalk, pushing a stroller. She held the hand of a boy no older than three or four. About Emily's age when…

No!

The heat was giving him hallucinations. He should go back to his pickup, get on the road. He began to turn, and an irregular piece of chalk under his foot rotated, spilling him onto the ground. White dust flew up about him, catching in his throat. He coughed. Coughed again, trying to loosen the dry, clinging dust. By the time his breathing eased, he was again seeing the moving, restless shadows.

This time he saw Sally's house, its shutters freshly painted black, its clapboards white as the chalk all around him. The roses were in bloom, and the lilac hedge was tall and green behind them. Children played in the grass beside the rose garden—two girls and a boy, plus a baby kicking on a blanket. Three had impossibly red hair, while the fourth, the larger girl, had hair as gold as a summer sun.

Gus closed his eyes, rubbing the lids until he saw nothing but red-black flares. When he opened them again, he made sure to avoid looking at the white wall as he struggled to his feet.

His right ankle protested at his weight. One hand against the scorching side of a column, he managed to take one step, then another. He hobbled away from the wall, a few inches at a time.

Damn! Could he have broken something? He sank onto a convenient chunk of chalk only fifteen or so feet away from where he had fallen. His ankle throbbed; his back and chest itched and stung. Chalk dust mixed with dried sweat made him feel like he was coated with white paint. Where the hell was his shirt? He probably looked it, too.

At least he'd found some shade. Leaning back against the column, he closed his eyes and breathed as deeply was he could. Chalk dust irritated the back of his throat and made his chest hurt.

Wouldn't it be a hoot if he were to be unable to reach his pickup? He could imagine what a surprise he would be to the next hobbyists who came to glean chalk fragments for carving. They would see his mummified carcass and think it was a carving, left behind because it was poorly executed.

Executed! That was a good one. He'd executed Marilyn and Emily. Now he was executing himself.

He let his head drop back against the column behind him. How long, he wondered, would it take him to die?

Much longer than it had taken Emily. That was all right. He deserved to suffer a little. No, he deserved to suffer a lot.

What strange hallucinations those had been. Whiterock in its rags and its Sunday clothes. It had looked prosperous in the second one, but not as he remembered it. There had been new shops where now were empty storefronts; bright, shiny, sleek automobiles where now most of the vehicles parked on Main Street were dusty pickups. And Sally had looked older. Happier.

Would Pete be able to manage the shop or would he, in his inexperience, run it into the ground? If he were half as smart as he seemed to be, he'd go to some of the older fellows in town for advice, get Bernie back in to teach him what he needed to know. Roger would help, too, as executor of Gus's estate.

He tried to swallow, but his throat was dry and coated with grit. His eyes drooped closed, shutting out the white and featureless world around him. His ankle still throbbed, but he didn't notice it so much anymore. He didn't feel much of anything, for that matter, except relieved that he didn't have to hate himself any longer.

WHERE?

Her car went around the last curve in a controlled skid, and Sally braked to a sliding stop just behind the blue pickup.

Empty.

But he was here. Somewhere.

Waiting for her.

GUS KNEW TIME HAD PASSED. HE WAS AWARE THAT THE SUN NO longer stung his chest, had stopped making his shoes feel like small steam baths. When a high-flying jet passed overhead, he felt the vibration of its engines as much as heard them, but he didn't trouble to open his eyes to see the narrow white trails it left.

Once he thought he heard a car, far away, but its sound was lost in the breeze that still swept across the tops of the columns, mourning its own passing.

The sun's retreat brought cool shade. Gus revived somewhat and took stock. His ankle seemed better. He flexed it, twisted it, and felt no unbearable pain, just a residual ache.

He looked up at the white wall, wondering what ghostly pictures it would show him now. But it was just a wall, shadowless yet shadowed. The burning whiteness had become a quiet, pale gray. He sat a while longer, wondering if the scenes had come from his tortured subconscious, or merely from thirst and incipient heatstroke.

"*Us-s-s-s-s!*"

The high, clear call echoed among the columns, pure as an eagle's keen. Far more welcome. He lifted his head and listened. Again it came.

"*Gu-s-s-s-s-! R-r-r-u-u-u-u-uuuu?*"

"Here!" he called back. He levered himself to his feet, letting his good ankle take most of his weight. Ignoring the ache, he hurried forward. "I'm here!"

Sally came around a thick column and stopped a few feet from him. Her arms were at her sides, her face was serious.

"Pete said... I thought... You didn't..." She stopped, but didn't look away from his face. A smile struggled to be born on her lips as she said, "I knew you wouldn't leave me."

As simply as that, Gus knew where his future lay.

But first...

"Have you any water?"

"I've got a six-pack of sodas in the car. They're warm—"

"They're wet. That's all that matters." He took a step and his ankle turned under him. "Damn!"

"I'll get them." She was off and running. In a few minutes, she reappeared, carrying the six-pack.

Gus drained the first can in about three swallows. "We need to talk," he said as he popped the top of the second.

Sally rolled a squared-off chunk of white rock next to him, sat on it. "I'm listening."

"I've been running," he said, "for three years."

"I know," she replied, her voice soft with understanding. "Just like I've been hiding for six."

"When I found Whiterock, it felt like a place where I could lose my past. Make a new start."

"For me it was a place to be comfortable, out of the hustle and bustle of the city."

"I didn't think I could ever forgive myself, but I thought, if I got involved enough in something demanding—building up the business—I could forget. Enough so I could live with myself, anyway."

"As long as Pop was alive, I had the perfect excuse not to go back. But then I started being afraid of what I'd have to do when he was gone."

"Maybe you can't ever... Are we having a conversation?"

Sally's eyes widened. She stared at him for a moment, and then she smiled widely.

"I think it's more like a mutual confession." Almost a giggle. "You know. Tell me your sins and I'll tell you mine?"

Gus bit back a sharp answer. Silly as it sounded, maybe she was right. And maybe he'd needed to confess. Much as he would've liked to sink into his own belly button, he wasn't going to. He'd pandered to self-indulgent guilt long enough. It was time to take back his life.

"I had the strangest experience," he said, and his gaze strayed back toward that white wall where he'd seen…

Seen what? The past? The future?

Bullshit! Hallucinations.

Whatever. But the experience had opened his eyes and his mind, as they had never been opened before.

"I was to blame for Emily's death, because I was her father and a father's job is to keep his children safe—"

"Oh, no! You can't—"

He held up his hand. "Let me finish. I can't forgive myself for not taking better care of Marilyn's car. I knew she wouldn't do it, but I was so focused on work, so wrapped up in what I was doing…"

Sally just sat there, her eyes full of sympathy. But not pity. Thank God.

"I'll carry those regrets to my grave. But I don't intend going there anytime soon. First I'm going to pick up the pieces and see if I can put my life back together." He looked at her, hoping she'd heard the implied question.

All she said was "What about the shop?"

"Tomorrow I'm going to find a sign painter. How does 'Emily's Tractor and Automotive Emporium' strike you?"

"Oh, Gus, it's perfect. And can't you just hear them, down at the café, wondering where it came from?" She stood and held out her hand. "Do you need help?"

"No. I'll make it on my own from now on." He hobbled along beside her, stopping every few steps to rest his ankle. He'd have to wrap it when he got back to town. He had a feeling, though, that it would be fine tomorrow. With the enormous burden of guilt gone, he should be about a ton lighter.

"When we get home, I'll have to tell you about my afternoon," he said, wondering if he'd really been so inattentive as to miss half a dozen turns. Or had his subconscious been keeping him in Whiterock? *Something* had kept him from making the worst mistake of his life, that was for sure.

"Home?"

"Sally, wherever you are is home. I love you."

She flowed into his arms, lifted her face for his kiss.

A long time later she smiled up at him. "Yes, Gus. Let's go home."

They didn't go home, though. Not to her house or his apartment. When they met again in her driveway, Gus suggested they go to Ontario for dinner. "Pack a bag," he said. "We'll make a night of it."

He drove his pickup into her barn and took his duffel to her car. While she was packing, he called Lyle's office and left a message they'd be back the next day.

"This is exciting," she said, once they were on US 20. "I haven't been away for an illicit weekend for ever so long."

"We need to talk," he told her, not responding to the teasing note in her voice, "and I wanted to be where we wouldn't be interrupted."

He wondered again if the impossible conclusion he'd come to would sound as crazy to her as it did, even now, to him.

He turned right at Cairo Junction, instead of left.

"Hey! I thought we were going to Ontario!"

"Not this time. I want to get farther away." He didn't know how far the influence extended, but he was going to be damn sure they got outside it.

Influence? That's as good a word as any for something so unlikely that it probably doesn't even exist.

"...when you have eliminated the impossible..."

What comes next? Think! It could be important.

They were on the outskirts of Boise before he felt safe. He pulled into a motel he'd heard had a decent restaurant attached.

Once he'd parked, he hesitated. "Do I get one room or two?"

Sally looked at him, her expression serious. "I guess that depends on whether you are willing to answer my questions. I want to know… I *need* to know more about you, Gus."

Reaching across the cab, he touched her cheek, cupped her chin. "I meant what I said, Sally. Don't ever doubt that. I love you."

"Oh, I know you do now. What I want to know is what made you the man you are. I want to hear about your childhood. What you did on your summer vacations. Whether you like to open presents on Christmas Eve or Christmas morning. All the important things you've never shared with me." She bit her lip then went on. "And whether you're planning to stay in Whiterock. Now that I've seen again what the real world is like, I can't imagine ever living anywhere else."

Once again ghostly fingers scrabbled down his spine. "You said—"

"I know what I said. But the more I think about it, the more certain I am that I wouldn't be happy away from Whiterock."

"I was afraid of that," he muttered.

"What?"

"Never mind. Let's have dinner." But he stopped at the desk on the way past. They had a suite. "I'll take it," he said.

Sally didn't argue.

An hour later, she leaned across the table, eyes searching his. "What is it, Gus?" she said in a low voice. "What's making you act so strangely?"

He cupped the snifter between his hands, swirled it gently. The restaurant was nearly empty and he'd paid the check, so they weren't likely to be interrupted for a while. But he was having second thoughts. She'd never believe him.

Hell, I'll be lucky if she doesn't call the nutcatchers.

If someone told him what he was about to tell her, he'd know they were stark, raving insane.

"Have you ever thought there was something, well, spooky about Whiterock?" he said at last.

"Spooky?" She laughed. "Gus, you really did have too much sun! Whiterock is about the most ordinary, down-to-earth town in America." Another peal of laughter. "Spooky! Oh, my. That's really funny."

He leaned forward, willed her to look him in the eye. "Who fixed the elk?"

"Why, I don't know. Bernie and Tom and some of the other fellows, I expect."

"When was the bandshell patched? The first time I saw it, there were holes in the roof and half the stucco was gone. You could see the bare lath."

She shook her head. "In April. Just in time for the May Fest."

"Uh-huh! And I suppose whoever did it painted all the storefronts on Main Street, too."

"No, those were done by the own—" Her eyes grew very wide, very round, as she thought about his questions. Her hand trembled as she set the snifter carefully on the table. "But most of them don't live in town anymore, do they?"

Gus shook his head.

"I never gave it a thought until today." He took a sip, swirled the brandy and inhaled the aromatic fumes. "Now what I'm thinking scares me."

"Tell me."

"Not here." He finished his brandy. "Drink up."

"No. I don't think I want any more."

They went to their suite in silence. Once inside, he wanted to take her into his arms. Instead, he sat in one of the wing chairs that graced either side of the gas fireplace. He toed off his sneakers and stretched his legs out in front of him.

Sally curled up in a corner of the overstuffed couch. For a moment she stared at him, evidently weighing what he'd said. "So tell me," she said finally.

"You'll think I'm crazy."

She waved his warning aside. She'd been trying to figure out Gus Loring for weeks. His sanity was the least of her worries. "I want to know why you think Whiterock is spooky."

Instead of answering, he stood and came to face her. A faint smile was on his lips as he reached out with one finger and stroked her cheek. "What did you feel?"

"Your finger. Warm. Gentle." She laid her own fingers on the place he had touched. "I like you to touch me."

"No shock? No tingle?"

"Of course not. You haven't any shoe—" She stared at him.

Always before when he touched her there had been an electrical sensation. The first time it was as if a bright spark of static electricity had leapt between them. She had come to expect it as one example of the strong attraction they had for each other.

But his touch this time had been nothing more than she'd described.

Just a touch.

Even this afternoon, kneeling in the white dust of the old quarry, she'd been ready to rip his clothes off, as she had been each and every time he'd touched her. But now she wasn't.

Why not?

Because he wouldn't commit to staying in Whiterock? Hardly. She wanted to stay there, but if the choice was between Gus and the town, there was no contest. She had realized that as soon as she'd broached the subject. But if there was a possibility...

She shook her head. *Pay attention!*

"Something's different. And you know what it is."

He seemed to be staring at something invisible. His fingers were steepled together, forefingers tapping slowly at his lips. At last he said, "No... No, I don't know, but I have a suspicion. But it's so incredible, so unbelievable..."

Closing his eyes, he sat completely still and was silent for several minutes.

"Do you ever read science fiction?" he said at last.

What's that got to do with anything? "No, not really. I've seen a few episodes of *Star Trek*, but I didn't particularly enjoy them."

"Stephen King? Dean Koontz?"

Sally chuckled. "You've seen my library—mostly videos. I'm more into Rogers and Hammerstein than King and Koontz."

"That makes it harder," he said, almost as if to himself. Suddenly he sat up straight. "I think Whiterock is alive."

Openmouthed, she stared at him for a moment. Then she burst out laughing.

He didn't.

His gravity quickly stifled her laughter.

"You're serious?"

Gus nodded.

"And sober." Leaning forward so his elbows rested on his knees, he loosely clasped his hands. He looked at them instead of her as he said, "I don't mean 'alive' as we usually think of it, but...aware... Sentient... Intelligent..."

Sally couldn't think of a thing to say. She simply waited. Watched as his hands twisted together. Listened to the crack of his knuckles. Felt his confusion.

He leapt to his feet and paced the length of the room and back. Stopping before the fireplace, he put both hands on the mantel and stared down into the cold hearth.

"Hell! I don't know what I mean."

Part of her wanted to go to him, to soothe him, to say that he'd been working too hard, that he needed a rest.

Part of her believed every word he said.

INTERVAL

Failure?

Negative. Positive outcome remains conceivable.

Patience.

TWENTY-THREE

Would it help you tell me if I promise not to interrupt and not to laugh?"

Gus looked over his shoulder. She wasn't smiling. Her tone had been calm, reasonable. *My God! She's taking me seriously.*

Suddenly, his hypothesis didn't seem as far-fetched. He sat back down and leaned back. Took a moment to organize his thoughts. "Every time I've touched you, I felt a...a spark. Like an electrical shock." He hesitated, still seeking the right words. "Sally, when Emily and Marilyn died, I thought I had, too. I ran, trying to hide from myself, I guess. For three years.

"In that whole time, I never felt the need for a woman. Never felt even the faintest hint of sexual desire." He grimaced. "Impotent at thirty-four. Probably permanently. I figured it was the least I deserved."

Her mouth opened, as if she would speak, and closed again. Her eyes were shut, but her fingers were twisting and knotting together, as he'd seen them do before.

"Then I met you. And I've been in a perpetual state of need ever since."

"Horny?"

Had she really said that? A flash of her eyes and a quick grin said she had.

"Horny," he agreed, on a chuckle. He sobered. "I hope your feelings won't be hurt if I say that while you're a lovely, desirable woman, you simply aren't that remarkable."

"I know."

"Something caused that reaction, Sally, and I can only come up with one explanation." He willed her to lift her chin, to look him in the eyes.

She did.

"Whiterock." He waited for her to respond. When she didn't, he said, "Well?"

"I'm thinking." Her fingers stilled, wove together, but the knuckles were white. "I don't think you're crazy," she said at last. "But there has to be an explanation. A town can't be alive. And even if it were, how could it possible influence how we feel about each other?"

"I don't know. But while I was down in the pit this afternoon, I remembered something I'd read a long time ago. Sherlock Holmes said it, I think. Something like '...when you have eliminated the impossible what's left,'—no, that's not right. '...whatever remains, however improbable, must be the truth.'"

"You think it's impossible that we should feel such instant... lust, for lack of a better word...for each other?"

"Sally, even when I was sixteen and completely at the mercy of my hormones, I never reacted to a woman like I do to you. That first day? It was all I could do not to take you right there in your entry." Once again he rose and paced the length of the room and back. "This is ridiculous," he said when he was facing her again. "You don't believe me. I'm wasting my breath."

"I do believe you."

"You're kidding!"

"Nope. At least as far as I know. Grandfather Sam was a peculiar fellow, even as a young man. Pop used to tell the most outlandish stories about him. According to Wilma Collotzi and Mrs. Alpin, most of them were probably true. They both remember their parents talking about him.

"Grandpa—my grandfather, Archibald Carruthers—was his only son. He was raised by his aunts, Mildred and Martha, who never married but kept house for their father and then for Grandfather Sam after—"

Her eyes widened and her face took on a...a listening expression. Gus was about to ask her what she'd heard when she said, "Of course! That's what Aunt Trudy was talking about." She rose. "I'll be right back."

While she was in the bedroom, Gus got a couple bottles of water from the small fridge under the wet bar. He'd prefer brandy, but tonight he needed his wits about him.

In a few minutes she was back, carrying a small book, thin, its blue cover faded and threadbare along the edges.

"As I came downstairs this afternoon, I remembered this. For some reason I had this—I guess you'd call it a compulsion—to bring it along." But when she sat down, she didn't immediately open it. Instead, she traced circles on the cover with her forefinger. "Aunt Trudy gave it to me the night before she left. She said I should read it before I decided whether to leave or to stay. It's... She said it's why she left and never comes back for a long visit."

"Good God!" Gus eyed the innocuous little book. "What is it? A book of spells? The revelation of some terrible family secret?"

He wondered if he'd slipped into one of those Gothic mysteries Marilyn used to read, where some mysterious force loomed threateningly over the characters.

"It's a diary. Or a journal. I don't know what it says. I've never read it." She continued to trace the circle. At last she lifted her chin and looked at him. "My aunt Trudy is a lawyer. She's like you in that if she can't taste it, touch it, measure it, it probably doesn't exist. But this book scared her enough to drive her away from home and keep her away."

"You say you've never read it? Why not?"

"I forgot about it," she admitted, looking a little sheepish. "After you...made me take a look at myself. Then I called T.J. and heard about *Carousel*, and went off to Portland, and... Well, I just never gave it a thought. But this afternoon, for some reason, I remembered it." She frowned, tapped one finger on the book's cover. "No, more than that. I had a strong feeling that if I didn't bring it, something really awful would happen."

Gus stared at her over his steepled fingers. He was beyond believing in coincidence where Whiterock was concerned. Tomorrow he might return to skepticism, but tonight...? Tonight he would suspend disbelief.

"Let's read it." He stretched out his hand.

Sally clutched the book to her chest. "You think this has something to do with what happened to you today, don't you?"

"I've never been more certain of anything in my life."

She held it out.

He took it. The book's cover felt rough under his fingertips. A faint, musty smell assailed his nose, as if it had been stored in a damp, airless place for a long time. This time he was the one tracing a circle on the cover as he hesitated, oddly reluctant to open it.

The hell with this crap! He opened the book.

The writing on the first page was spidery, elegant, with flowing, ornate capitals: LORENA MACGREGOR CARRUTHERS, HER JOURNAL, 1904. Sally came and perched on the arm of his chair, bringing her flowery scent to tease his nostrils and drive away the mustiness. Her hair tickled his cheek as she leaned close, to read over his shoulder.

"Nineteen-oh-four? I think that's the year she ran away."

"Ran away? As in abandoned her family? That's why his aunts raised your grandfather?" He turned the page.

"Uh-huh. Look, it starts on New Year's Day."

They read silently through a dozen pages of minutiae that took them to early March. Lorena Carruthers had not been a faithful diarist, and her occasional entries were mostly about how she felt. Headaches, nervous exhaustion caused by the stress of caring for a rambunctious boy-child and a colicky infant, and vaguely described aches and pains were the most common topics.

Once she complained about her husband's refusing to take her to Ontario to shop. The J.C Penney catalogue, he'd insisted, was all she needed. Often she wrote of small disagreements with her sisters-in-law, who apparently did most of the caring for her children. Lorena resented their help but accepted it, because of her nerves.

Then came an entry written in a sloppy scrawl, recognizably Lorena's but as if she was in a great hurry.

> It's happening again. IT tries to convince me to be happy here. I won't!!!!

Nothing for a week, until another scrawled entry:

> Sam wants another child. It's too soon. Yet I couldn't say no to him. IT made me submit. I hated it. Sam doesn't care how I feel.

Another, much longer than usual:

> Father Abner scolded me today. He says I should stop trying to get Sam to go away for a holiday. There's nowhere better to be than

Whiterock, he says, but that's because he hasn't been anywhere farther than Vale for years. How can he know what it's like out in the world? He's never seen a moving picture, or heard good music. He thinks that awful horse print in the dining room is great art. Millie and Martha aren't any better. I don't think either of them has read a newspaper in her life. I'd give anything for a week—just one week—away from here!!!

"How sad," Sally murmured. "She feels so trapped."

Gus turned several pages, each with only a few words about Lorena's ailments.

Then came one with a great black blot over half of it. Under the spread of ink was written, in a hand hardly recognizable as Lorena's:

I must get away, while I still can. I can feel IT taking over my mind. IT doesn't want me to go.

"The poor woman. She sounds on the edge."

"I wonder..."

He flipped to the next page. Empty. And the one after that. But then there was one last page, once again written in the smooth, ornate script that had been on the title page.

Sam refuses to withdraw. He came to me last night, and God help me, I welcomed him. His passion overwhelms me, until I have no will. And so I submit. I am not pregnant yet, but I know I will be soon. How will I bear it? Weeks of nausea, of lassitude, then months of hideousness as my body swells into grotesque parody of muliebrity.

What is worse is that the passion comes from outside me. I am not a passionate woman. All my life I have been reasonable, placid and refined, not given to emotional display.

Until I came to Whiterock.

Now whenever Sam touches me, I feel a galvanic shock. And I desire him, with an overpowering hunger.

I am convinced IT is the cause. IT needs passion. Whenever Sam makes love to me, I feel IT growing stronger, as if it feeds off our emotions.

Yet today I feel nothing from IT. Perhaps because I am melancholy. The winter has gone on so long. The world is drab and gray, just like my soul. I am trapped in this bleak little town.

I MUST escape!

There was nothing else.

He handed Sally the book. "See if I missed anything, will you?"

He walked to the window and pushed open the sheer drapes. Beyond the narrow lawn, the Boise River was a restless current sparkling in the gleam from the lamps lighting the path along its shore. The water talked to itself as it tumbled over the rocks lining its bed, and its murmur seemed to carry secrets not to be shared with mere humans.

God! I am going over the deep end! Next thing I'll be seeing fairies under toadstools.

He turned back to where Sally sat in his chair. She'd closed the book and was staring into space.

"So, what d' you think?"

"I feel very sorry for her. Somewhere I read that some women go temporarily insane after childbirth. Poor Grandmother Lorena. She certainly wasn't in her right mind when she wrote this. I don't understand why Aunt Trudy found this scary, unless she believed she'd inherited whatever it was that disturbed Lorena so."

"My God! I don't believe this! You're denying everything you've read? Everything that's happened? The evidence of your own eyes?" He snatched the book from her hands and flipped through. "This time listen to what it says. Then think about what it means. 'I feel a galvanic shock. And I desire him, with an overpowering hunger...' Does that sound familiar?"

Sally's eyes grew enormous. "The electricity..."

"Exactly." He paced the length of the room. "I didn't tell you what happened to me today before I went to the mine, did I?"

Her hair swirled silkily as she shook her head.

He told her, in great detail, retracing his route with precision, making sure she understood how he had missed turnoffs he'd taken a hundred times, how perfectly straight roads had wound into mazes.

"Something didn't want me to leave Whiterock." As he spoke the words, he realized how fantastic, how unbelievable they sounded.

"IT?"

"I don't think so. At least not the inimical IT your grandmother imagined. I didn't feel threatened." Again he paced to the end of the room and back, stopping before the chair in which she sat. "I didn't pay much attention to anything but getting out of town. I was running again, and all I could think of was getting away from your..." He cleared his throat. "Your questions."

Her eyebrow lifted.

"All right, damn it! I was trying to run away from the answers. I didn't want to think about Emily, about the mess I'd made of my life."

"I can't blame you. But are you sure the guilt hasn't become a habit? Do you feel the loss as strongly now as you did at first?"

"Of course I... No. No, I don't. Most of the time it's almost as if it all happened to someone else." Did that mean he was forgetting his daughter? God! He hoped not. She was the best thing that had ever happened to him.

"I remember feeling guilty when I stopped missing Mom so much. It seemed disloyal or something. But now I think it's healthy. We can't grieve forever." She was drawing those invisible circles on the cover of the book again. "You said you think you had a glimpse of the future. What did you see?"

Gus did his best to bring the scenes he'd viewed into focus, but they were vague, shadowy, like a quickly fading dream.

"You were there. Older, I think. And a child...children? Shit! I can't remember." Flinging himself into the chair, he bent forward and rubbed his temples. Eyes closed, he sought the elusive memory. "And the town. Renewed, busy. There was a festival. The May Fest? I don't think so. Something was going on, because there were lots of people on the streets."

"Did you hear anything? Did anything... Did anything speak to you?" Now she was twisting her hands, as he'd seen her do when she was uncertain or ill at ease.

"Just people I met. You, maybe. I tell you, I can't remember!"

Her hands went up in a gesture of self-protection. "Okay, okay, I was just trying to see if your dream was anything like the ones I was having for a while before Pop died. As if someone... something...was trying to get me to stay in Whiterock. I wrote them off to the stress I was under, but now, after reading what Grandmother Lorena wrote, I wonder."

"So you do believe there's something influencing us." Gus wasn't sure why he was so intent on her sharing his suspicions. Maybe because if she did, it would prove he wasn't crazy.

Sally sat silent for so long, he was about to demand she answer his implied question. Before he could, she said, "Pop always said that Grandfather Abner—the one who founded Whiterock—was right. That Carrutherses and Whiterock belonged together. But he'd never explain. When I was old enough to question it, I decided it was his way of saying he felt more at home here than anywhere else. But what if...?"

"What if he was influenced to feel that way? What if this IT that Lorena talks about really can compel people to stay there? That might explain her husband's refusal to go even as far as Vale."

"That's imposs—" Sally bit her lip. "What was that you said earlier. 'When you have eliminated the impossible...'?"

"'When you have eliminated the impossible, whatever remains, however improbable, must be the truth,'" he quoted, sure of himself this time. "We can't eliminate the impossible, because we have no real proof that anything impossible happened. But it's all damned improbable."

He was sick of this discussion. They weren't getting anywhere, just rehashing the same old stuff, over and over. Trouble was, he doubted they'd *ever* get anywhere, because they were trying to quantify the uncountable, describe the indescribable and pin down the insubstantial.

"What about your father? Everything I've heard indicated he was pretty ordinary."

"Oh, he was. He traveled quite a lot in his younger days, but I don't think he ever thought of living anywhere but Whiterock. When he came home after his ramblings, he stayed, except for an occasional vacation."

She started twisting her fingers together again. Her voice quavered when she finally said, "I just remembered something, Gus. I think he and my mother may have experienced the same thing we did."

In an instant he was at her knees, clasping her hands, stilling them. "What do you mean?"

"Mom came to visit a cousin. She met Pop at a church social. They were married three weeks later. Mom always said it was like lightning had struck them." She leaned back and closed her eyes. "I think that eliminates the impossible," she whispered. "Whiterock is alive."

"Bullshit!"

"But you said—"

"I was trying to get your attention." Impatiently, he slid onto the couch beside her. "Look, Sally, we've talked this thing to death. Let's get some rest. Maybe in the morning we'll think of some logical explanation."

For some reason, now that she was buying into his preposterous idea he was determined to disprove it.

He pulled her close and kissed her, gently at first, and then with increasing demand. As always, he wanted her the instant he touched her, but tonight his desire was a sweet and tender thing, not fiery, demanding passion.

She responded, just as gently. Yet the very gentleness of her answering caresses aroused him in a way he had never experienced with her. The fire was there, but it was controlled, not a raging conflagration of the senses.

Always before their clothing had been an impediment to their joining, best removed as quickly as possible. Now he found the feel of her soft cotton T-shirt erotic, the slightly rough texture of her white jeans arousing. His hands explored every inch of her, finally slipping under her shirt and cupping her nylon-covered breasts. The slick fabric was cool, until his palms warmed it. Her nipples flowered, pebbly and hot under his fingers. He covered one with his mouth, wetting the nylon, and discovered yet another new sensation.

After a while he lifted her, carried her into the larger bedroom where a king-size bed awaited them. The blankets were turned down and fancy chocolates waited on each pillow. He lowered her slowly, letting her body slide against his.

Sally slipped her hands under Gus's shirt, loving the warmth of his skin. Slowly, she peeled the shirt up and, when he lifted his arms, worked it over his head. His chest, gilded in the light from a single bedside lamp, was well-muscled, his abdomen tight and firm. *How could I ever have thought him paunchy?*

He stood, quietly tense, as she kissed her way from collarbone to belt buckle and back again. But when she laid her fingers on his buckle, he stopped her.

"Not yet," he said.

Then it was Sally's turn to endure his teasing tongue and teeth as he removed her shirt and bra, covered every inch of her upper body with slow, nibbling kisses. When her knees threatened to give way, she whispered, "No more! Oh, please, Gus!"

Once more he lifted her, this time to lay her on the bed with exquisite tenderness. He knelt above her and stroked his big, hard hands softly along her arms, down the sides of her torso, not quite touching her breasts, and along her legs. When he reached her feet, he slipped her sneakers off and tossed them on the floor. A fraction of an inch at a time, he removed her socks, kissing her ankles as they were revealed. When his teeth lightly caught a fold of skin on her instep, she shivered. And when he kissed his way back to her knees, along her thighs, she writhed in delight.

His breath was hot on her lower belly, his tongue rough in the indentation of her navel. His mouth closed over her nipple, suckling, tugging, until she felt as if her whole self was being pulled to that hot, throbbing point.

"Gus!" Her voice was high, thin.

Yet she was content to enjoy, not to demand, as she always had before. *We have all night.*

Gus kissed, licked, nibbled and laved behind her ears, in the hollows of her ankles, inner elbows and backs of knees, wherever the skin was soft, sensitive, sweet. He tasted her in ways he never had before, because this time there was none of the frantic urgency to couple of their earlier joinings.

At some point Sally worked him out of his pants. From then on, it was almost a race—a slow, sensuous, everybody-wins race—to the inevitable end. Her hands and mouth on him drove him to the edge of culmination again and again, while he took her to the peak and held her there time after time.

Her fingers closed around him at the same time her teeth nipped at his earlobe, and he knew there was no turning back. He sheathed himself in her wet heat and drove deeply. Once. Twice. And with the third lunge, he came apart, just as her high, keening cry told him she was with him every flaming, soaring measure of the way.

He turned on his side, holding her close, and kissed her once before he fell into oblivion.

The aroma of coffee lured her out of a delicious dream. It slipped away before she could catch it, but Sally knew that, this morning, reality was as good as the best of dreams.

"Good morning," she said, without opening her eyes.

The bed dipped, and Gus's mouth touched hers lightly.

"Mmmm. You taste of coffee." She opened her eyes. "Do I have to wake up?"

"Checkout time's eleven. It's ten now. Do you want to stay another night?"

She rolled to one side and glared at the clock.

"I really should get home. It's going to take some getting used to, having deadlines to meet." Sighing, she pushed herself upright. "Have I got time for a shower?"

"Sure. We can check out, have breakfast after."

THEY OPTED FOR BREAKFAST ON THE GO, PICKING UP DONUTS AND more coffee on their way out of town. Gus didn't say he was in a hurry, but somehow she got that impression. That was why she was surprised when he turned off the freeway and headed south on US 93. The detour would add an hour to their trip home. She said nothing, however, nor did he.

Last night's conversation replayed over and over in her head. If they were both crazy, then so was Pop. And his father and grandfather as well.

Hereditary insanity? She doubted it.

Gus left the highway and followed a secondary road to a high bluff overlooking the Snake River. Once parked, he turned to her, draped his left arm on the steering wheel. "Well? Any new ideas?"

She shook her head slowly, while seeking the right words.

"No. In fact, I feel more confused than I did last night when you first sprung this on me." She looked away from him, stared out across the river at the rolling, sagebrush-covered hills beyond. "It's just so fantastic."

"I think we're pretty much agreed on that. The question is, what do we do? Are we going to let some...entity push us around?"

"I think it's been pushing my family around for four generations. It hasn't hurt us yet." *And Whiterock is home. I think I've been denying that for too long. I belong there.*

He snorted. "It hasn't done you any good, either."

"How do you know?" Sally was suddenly impatient with his suspicion. "Have you seen anything that says it—whatever it is—"

"Call it Whiterock," he said, a sneer plain in his voice.

"Okay, I will. Have you seen any evidence that Whiterock means us harm?" She shook her head again, this time with emphasis. She had lost her doubts and knew, really *knew*, that whatever force affected them while they were in Whiterock, it meant them only good. "Think back. Last winter the town was dying. Now it's alive and vital and...and awake!"

"Because the people who live there worked hard to clean it up."

"Who fixed the elk's antlers? Patched the bandshell? Who?"

He opened his mouth, closed it again. His shrug wasn't exactly a capitulation, but it came close.

"I stayed awake a long time last night after you went to sleep. Thinking. Adding things up."

"And?"

"The antlers are real. Birds sit on them. The bandshell was patched. Maybe not well, and maybe not permanently..." She thought about how scruffy it had looked just yesterday. "It looked patched," she admitted, slowly, "but maybe that was an illusion."

"The inside was safe," Gus said slowly. "Lyle checked it before he okayed it for the kids to sit on."

Relief flooded her. He was going to be reasonable.

"Well, then..."

"I don't like being pushed around."

"Neither do I. But if we know... Gus, if we know it's affecting us, maybe it won't be able to push us around."

His frown told her he doubted that very much.

"The only way we'll ever know is to try." She leaned across the cab and kissed him, a light, fleeting kiss. "Let's go home, Gus. Maybe we can cut a deal."

BY UNSPOKEN AGREEMENT, GUS DROPPED SALLY AT HER HOUSE AND went to the shop to reassure Pete that all was well. They had spoken no more of the contents of Lorena's diary or of their outrageous conclusions.

Sally replaced the diary in her father's desk, tucking it into one of the pigeonholes underneath insurance papers and a copy of Pop's will. Now that she was home again and in full possession of her senses, she had to take care of all the details she'd left undone.

Or was she in full possession of her senses? How could she be, if she believed that there was even a grain of truth in her great-grandmother's diary?

The more she thought about it, the more skeptical she became. Whiterock was simply a special place. Grandmother Lorena had suffered from severe post-partum depression. Aunt Trudy had been looking for an excuse to get out of a place that held no future for her.

And Gus had experienced hallucinations caused by dehydration and heat prostration.

She went up to her room and sat at her drawing board. In a few minutes she was sketching details for the dancers in *Carousel*. Making yellow wet-weather gear and white coveralls attractive had been a challenge, but the salmon fishermen and cannery workers of this modern version of the musical would be a feast for the eyes in the costumes she'd designed.

When the phone rang an hour later, she was deep in details of Lycra inserts and reflective tape trim.

Almost before she'd said hello, Gus said, "Meet me at the park? I have an idea."

Sally glanced outside. Yesterday's hot weather had been banished by low, wet-looking clouds.

"This isn't my idea of picnic weather."

"We'll stop by the market and pick up groceries afterward. I want to check something. At the bandshell. Fifteen minutes?" His tone was abrupt, and she thought she heard both impatience and apprehension.

"I'll be there."

He hung up as soon as she spoke.

"Good grief. Tell a man you love him and he starts taking you for granted," she grumbled as she tidied her drawing board. Now that she was on the right track, the detail designs for the rest of the cast's clothing would go quickly. When she went back to Portland she'd be all ready to work with the costume shop.

There was a smell of rain in the air as she walked down the hill toward the park. A good soaking wouldn't hurt the gardens and lawns, but she hoped it would hold off until she and Gus were back inside. Like many who'd grown up in the desert, she found being outside in the rain unnatural. *One more reason not to move to Portland permanently.*

As she passed the elk, she saw that the pigeons had returned; their droppings coated its back like a ragged blanket. *Poor, pathetic thing. Maybe we ought to simply take it away, since we can't seem to protect it from vandals and birds.*

Gus sat on a picnic table waiting for her. When she approached him, he held up a hand.

"Wait," he said. "Don't touch me yet. I want to try something."

Sally stopped a few feet short of him. "Gus, I don't think—"

"Humor me, please?"

293

She thought about their earlier conversation, and nodded.

Rising, he turned to face the bandshell. "Okay, whoever… *what*ever you are. You've got our attention. What do you want from us?

"You need us. And I think the town needs you—whatever you are. The town. Not Sally, not me, not any single person. We want Whiterock to be our home. We'll stay long as you don't try any cute tricks—no coercion, no hallucinations, and no visions of the future. We'll be free to come and go, to travel whenever we want, but we'll always come back, as long as you don't try to keep us here."

Looking over his shoulder at Sally, he raised an eyebrow in query. She shrugged, not having anything to add to what he said—or wanting to feel like a fool talking to empty air.

INTERVAL

Success?

Or failure?

Awareness posits danger.

Contrariwise future energy sources probable sequent of cooperation.

Decision?

Decision!

Advantage exceeds risk.

TWENTY-FOUR

A s they waited for something to happen, Sally took a good look at the bandshell. It was shabby, with all the signs of long-term neglect. Yet she knew it had been in fair shape at the May Fest and looking good during the summer band concerts.

She opened her mouth to say something to Gus about getting together a work party to patch the stucco then closed it again. This was neither the time nor the place for housekeeping matters.

Later, she estimated they'd stood there for close to a half-hour. The slight wind that had stirred the cottonwood leaves gradually died and the birdsongs faded. Shadows long with the lowering sun stretched across the lawn, showing how badly it needed mowing.

"Look!" Gus's whisper pulled her out of idle introspection. "Good God, Sally. Look there!"

Sally blinked. And looked again. No lath was showing through the bandshell's intact plaster. Sparkling glass globes completed the shiny brass light fixtures at the sides of the great open stage.

"How?"

"I don't know. I'd swear..."

"It was falling apart," she whispered.

Slowly she turned, looked back toward the intersection of Main Street and Fifth Avenue. At an elk whose gleaming bronze back was clean, whose wide, spreading antlers caught and held glints of golden light.

"Gus?"

He came to her then, slipped his arm around her. At his first touch a charge of energy swept through her, but without the compulsion she'd felt before. She still wanted to tear off his clothes and have her wicked way with him, but not right this instant, and not without the leisure to enjoy each touch, each kiss, each caress.

"IT spoke to you?"

"No, but I think we've got our answer."

He looked around. So did she. Sunset was upon them, turning the light golden, painting the sky with pink and peach and apricot and orange, the clouds with lavender and blue and rich, deep purple. The faded brick of the schoolhouse was a bright terracotta, Nagy's Cabins looked almost new under their fresh paint, and the spire of the Community Church appeared newly gilded. Even the grass under their feet seemed greener.

"This is how I always remember Whiterock," she whispered.

"This is how it will stay." Gus pulled her into a hug. "We'll keep it this way."

Twelve Years Later

"Evenin', Miz Loring. How's your man?"

Sally smiled at Ernie Green, looking older than time, yet still able to hobble down to his bench beside the library every day the weather allowed.

"Just fine, Mr. Green. And how are you?"

"Gettin' older," he said, as he always did, "and better every day." He dug into his pocket and pulled out four cellophane-wrapped mints. "Here you go, young'uns. Mind you don't choke."

Little Will hid his face in his mother's skirt, but Merilee, Kip and Kirstin accepted their candy with polite thanks.

"You spoil them, Ernie," Sally said, "like you've been spoiling kids since before I was born." She tucked Will's mint into her pocket. "Will you be at the concert later?"

"Wouldn't miss it for the world. I was here when they first opened the bandshell, did I ever tell you that?"

"You did, indeed."

"You go on now, and meet your man. He was lookin' for you earlier."

The walk down Main Street took longer than usual because of the crowd. Ben Kemp had recently won a Grammy, so people were coming from considerable distances to hear him perform in the opening concert of the Whiterock Music Festival. That performance would dedicate the rebuilt bandshell with its perfect acoustics. At noon, Gus had told her motels were booked solid for a radius of a hundred miles.

Of course, there weren't all that many motels within a hundred miles of Whiterock. The influx of music fans was a boon to Bill Holmes's newly opened Badlands Dude Ranch and Juana's refurbished Nagy Tourist Cabins.

"There's Dad!" Kip dashed ahead. Kirsten followed, hard on his heels.

"They are such infants," Merilee said, from the superiority of her eleven years. "Sometimes I want to pretend I don't know them."

Biting her lip, Sally swallowed the reminder that Merilee had been brought home in disgrace for helping with the whitewashing of the elk during this year's May Fest. If she didn't turn Sally's hair gray before she was eighteen, her younger siblings would.

Gus joined her then, swinging Will onto his shoulder before taking her hand.

"The party's about to start. What kept you?"

"What do you think?" Sally raised one eyebrow in the direction of the redheaded twins, now with their noses pressed against the enticing window of the candy shop. She snagged their collars as she passed, and then released them so she could wave to Harriet Alpin, who stood in the door of the hardware store. Bless the woman, she'd argued with her grandmother and her father for two years before getting her chance to carry on the family business. Just the other day she'd told Sally that this year the store would make a profit.

"I'm so glad Evan decided to come home and reopen the furniture store."

It had been the last empty building on Main Street.

"I can't believe we've come so far in only twelve years."

"It's taken a lot of hard work," Gus said, "but I think it's been worth it."

"Some magic, too, I think."

By unspoken agreement, they had never spoken of the improbable notions they'd discussed that day they'd decided to marry. Sally knew what she believed, and was content to let Gus, with his greater skepticism, believe what he chose. As long as he did it in Whiterock.

"There was magic that summer we met, Gus."

"Love?" he suggested, slipping his arm around her waist. The children had all run ahead and were clustered around Jack and Georgina, who had acted as honorary grandparents ever since Merilee's birth.

"More than that. Do you remember the elk?"

"That poor, pathetic thing? Of course I do. What was it you called it? A hermaphroditic deer with something?"

"Hush! The kids will hear you."

"About the elk?" he prompted.

"Oh, yes. The antlers had been gone ever since I was a kid, and nobody bothered to replace them. Until that summer. Well, I never did find anyone who admitted doing it."

"I remember the day I told you about Emily." His mouth twisted in an old, but still painful memory. "There weren't any antlers."

Sally looked up at him, wonder in her eyes.

"So you remember, too. But they'd been there at the May Fest. And they were there the day we got married. When did they get fixed?"

"Why, I don't…They were…" Gus turned to look back toward the library, but of course, could only see a distant silhouette. "What difference does it make?"

"Just that it proves there was magic."

A peculiar expression spread over his face. "Engineers don't believe in magic."

"I do. There isn't any other explanation."

He shook his head.

"Oh, yes, there is. Like I said, it was love."

Ignoring the streams of people passing them on both sides, he took her into his arms. "Perhaps," he said, just before he kissed her.

CODA

Gratification.

Progeny satisfactory, more closely bound than prior generations.

Departure unlikely.

Dependence on limited resource misguided.

As safeguard against recurrent energy shortage, expansion of sample size indicated.

Uncertainty is...uncomfortable.

END

ABOUT THE AUTHOR

Judith B. Glad was one of those fortunate children to be raised by someone who believed in magic. A great aunt, with whom she lived until she was almost seven, filled her imagination with stories of adventure and derring-do and magic, never letting her know which was fact and which was fiction. With a childhood like that, is it any wonder she grew up wanting to create worlds in which the good guys—male and female—always win, where right always prevails, and where love is the most important force in the universe?

Sidetracked by reality, Judith started a family, followed a couple of careers, went back to school and ended up as a botanical consultant. Eventually, the kids all left the nest and she cut back on the consulting, leaving her with time to work on creating those worlds. She and her favorite hero had a long and happy life together in Portland, Oregon, where flowers bloom every month of the year and snow usually stays on the mountains where it belongs. It's a great place to write, because the rainy season lasts for eight months—a perfect excuse to stay indoors and tell stories.

Visit Judith's webpage at www.judithbglad.com to learn more about her other books. While you're there, take some side trips to view early 20th century picture postcards, read about 5,000 ways to earn a living, and see what a Mentzelia really is.

Judith B. Glad's
WESTERN HISTORICAL
"Behind the Ranges" Series
The Queen of Cherry Vale
Ice Princess
The Duchess of Ophir Creek
Noble Savage
Knight in a Black Hat
The Lost Baroness
The Imperial Engineer
Undercover Cavaliere
Squire's Quest
Lord of Misrule (a Christmas novella)

And her other books:
REGENCIES:
The Anonymous Amanuensis
A Sisterly Regard
The Portrait (novella)
CONTEMPORARY ROMANCE
Solomon's Decision
Never the Twain
Twice Victorious
A Safe and Welcome Nest
PARANORMAL ROMANCE
Improbable Solution
MAINSTREAM
A Strange Little Band